Also by Alan Balter

Different Ways of Being

Alan Balter

Printed in the United States of America
Cover Design: Linkville Graphics
Editing: Amanda Marie

Linkville Press
linkvillepress.wix.com/home
linkvillepress@gmail.com

A portion of all proceeds goes to Villalobos Rescue Center.
vrcpitbull.com

ISBN-13: 978-1519335258
ISBN-10: 1519335253

For Miriam and Max
My beloved parents

Acknowledgements

My sincere thanks to Drs. Samuel Kirk and James Gallagher, former professors at the Institute for Research on Exceptional Children at the University of Illinois in Urbana.

Their wisdom and insights were rare, as was their generosity in sharing their knowledge of children who were different. May they rest in peace.

To my wonderful students at Chicago State University: Knowing you for thirty-two years was truly my pleasure. Our interactions taught me a great deal about the reality of teaching in the Chicago Public Schools and helped me become a better professor.

My appreciation to Ms. Amanda Marie for seeing the potential in my work and for guiding my project to fruition. Her editing was precise and perceptive, and, as such, she made vital contributions to the construction and content of my manuscript. As chief executive and founder of Linkville Press, she is an important source of motivation and a staunch advocate for authors.

Finally, to my wife Barbara who makes it all possible: Thank you for letting me work, for your encouragement during the down times, for tolerating my foibles with patience and humor, and, most of all, for being my precious sidekick as we have grown older.

Part I

Willa and Robert

Prologue

"When the going gets tough, the tough get going." Knute Rockne said that. "No one knows how tough I am. I'll be out of here in a week." I said that. I'd been shot in the back, but at the time I didn't think it was all that serious. Funny how your mind works. The truth scares the hell out of you, so you deny it's true. Now, a couple of months later, I've come to know better. I'm not so tough, not that I care. Fact is, I don't care about anything these days. I'm pretty much worthless, just lying here week after week, flat on my back in bed. Are there cripples in heaven? I wonder.

Every now and then a passing car casts a shadow on the ceiling and walls. The heat comes on, and I feel a rush of warm air. I'd guess it's about three or four in the morning, not that it matters, because I'm not going anywhere for a while. Maybe never.

A nurse comes into my room, smiles way too cheerfully, and asks how "we" are doing. She enunciates each word slowly and carefully, because she thinks she's making it easier for me to read her lips. Most people who hear do that when they're speaking to a person who's deaf. They mean well; they just don't know any better. Hearing and dumb.

She gives me four pills from a paper cup and watches to make sure I swallow them. Saving up a stash and gulping them down all at once wouldn't be a bad way to go. Just pop a few dozen or so and fade to black. Forget your troubles; c'mon get dead.

Nursey moves me onto my stomach and rubs

some lotion on my back and legs so I don't get bedsores. They're like ulcers that can spread, even kill you, if you're not careful. Not such a good way to go. Then, she sponges me off with cool water, because I sweat a lot. It's strange. I've noticed that I only sweat above my waist. Everything below that stays dry; maybe because everything below that is dead.

The nurse leaves and except for a night light in the bathroom, it's dark. The darkness is soothing, and there's nothing I want to see anyway. Fact is, I wouldn't give a good goddamn if it was dark all the time. Just turn off the lights, pull the curtains, and leave me alone. Stuff your bedpans and your pills and your body lotion and your physical therapy and your phony smiles and leave me to hell alone.

I sleep for a while, maybe a couple of hours, before an orderly brings in my breakfast. Nausea on a tray. He props me up in bed but never says a word or even looks at me. I bet his mother told him it wasn't polite to stare at cripples. He's about my age and built like a football player. He probably feels sorry for me. Fullbacks have feelings too, y'know.

The sight of runny eggs and undercooked bacon sickens me, and I gag. My stomach churns and light green spit leaks out of the sides of my mouth onto my chin. I don't eat much these days, so I've lost a lot of weight, especially in my legs. They're withered, like a couple of sticks hanging out of my shorts. Same thing with my Johnson. My old buddy, once a real stand up guy, if you get my drift, just lies around like a slug.

Fact is, I can't even tell when I have to go. So, they hooked me up to a catheter, and I pee into a plastic bag. Convenient as hell; just let 'er rip, any old time I please. Don't have to jiggle, either. Not so convenient are my twice a day suppositories. I can't control my bowels, so they try to get them to move on schedule.

Have "we" have had our bowel movement this morning? Get lost.

They'll wheel me down to physical therapy this afternoon, and Mom and Dad will be visiting later on. Nothing until then on my dance card, though, so I close my eyes and sleep. It's a great way to escape. My dream, as usual, is about catching the punk who did this to me and getting even. So far, I've castrated him with a hacksaw and burned out his eyes with a hot poker. This time, with a rusted switchblade, I carve the word "Seth" onto his chest. Remember me forever, you pitiful prick.

Mom and Dad come into my room and flash the sign for "I love you." Each gives me a hug. We hug a lot; it's what Deaf people do. Willa puts a box of chocolates on my bed stand, and Robert asks if I'd like to watch the football game on TV.

They're still trying to cheer me up; I understand, but I wish they would stop. Fact is, I wish they would stop visiting me, but I don't have the guts to tell them. After all, they're hurting real bad, because I'm their only child. Or, their only half child, the one who will be rolling back and forth on round rubber legs, three feet shorter for the rest of his miserable life. However long that might be.

Chapter 1

For Willa and Robert, it's a quiet time. The sky takes on a greenish hue, and great bolts of lightning zigzag overhead. The rumble of thunder vibrates through the floor, and trees bend against the wind. Hailstones, some the size of marbles, pepper the windows and fracture on the driveway and sidewalks. Shutters flap against the siding. Soon, the street is littered with tree branches, roofing shingles, and assorted trash. A riderless tricycle blows by in odd concert with a trashcan and a soccer ball. The noise is considerable, but for Willa and Robert, it's a quiet time. It's always a quiet time.

Like many summer storms, this one passes quickly. The aftermath is the sweet smell of rain, reminiscent, to Robert, of laundered clothes, fresh off the line. To Willa, the aroma is sharper, with a hint of chlorine, but pleasing nevertheless.

Robert steps outside for the morning newspaper, now sodden with rainwater. He exchanges morning greetings with a neighbor, and, together, they gather the errant roofing shingles. Robert hauls some of the larger branches, two plastic soda bottles, and a cardboard box marked "fragile" to the curb.

Back in the house, Willa, still warm from sleep, joins him. They share breakfast, sitting at the same side of the table. When he leaves for work, she waves, places her fingers over her heart, and wiggles her thumbs up and down. Thus, in their way, she says, "Goodbye my sweetheart."

Robert works for a company that designs and sells custom cabinetry for kitchens and family rooms. People like his work, and he has a waiting list of more than a year. But, no one seems to mind; in fact, many of his customers refer their family and friends. "Robert has golden hands," they say.

Willa is at the door when he returns from work. With a sad look on her face, she pokes her index finger into the cleft of her chin. "I missed you."

In return, he crosses his arms over his chest. "I love you."

Robert showers and shaves while Willa prepares dinner. "Let's relax on the front porch a while before we eat," she says.

"Good idea. We can finish yesterday's wine."

After dinner, she washes the dishes and he dries, always standing close enough to touch. Some evenings they visit with friends or go to a captioned film at the local library. Or, they stay home to play card games or dominoes or to read.

At bedtime, Willa brushes her hair to a luster. It hangs full and loose, like a mane, to the middle of her back. Coal black, except for a silver streak on her forelock, it is her only vanity. She takes 200 strokes, now and then tossing her head and meeting his eyes in the mirror.

Willa is uncommonly lovely. Her skin is smooth and dark, the color of mahogany. Green eyes, wide on her face, hint at Asian ancestry. She has high cheekbones and a delicate nose. When she smiles, her full lips part over brilliant, white teeth. Her shape is long and slender, coltish, and she moves as gracefully as a dancer. Strangers who see her for the first time stop and stare, so rare is her beauty.

Willa flirts and tells Robert he is a handsome man. "My husband is so sexy," she says.

"What do you find most irresistible?" he asks, going along with her teasing.

"Your bright blue eyes, broad shoulders, your yellow hair, and the smile lines on your face, but it's your hands I like the most. They're strong and calloused from so many years of building things, but so soft when you touch me."

Robert loves Willa as much as a man can love a woman. She loves him in return, openly, and with equal passion. Each is, for the other, the center of all things. So it has been since they were children.

Chapter 2

When Robert was a child, he lived with his parents in an older section of town. Some of the buildings were rundown; a few stood vacant, windows boarded with plywood. Litter lined the curbs much of the time, and storm sewers backed up after heavy rains. But, the area was safe enough, and families stayed, either because they couldn't afford to move or because they had roots in the neighborhood and didn't care to leave.

Their apartment was one of 12 in a U-shaped building. The rooms were neat, spacious, and filled with furniture his father built. With only one bedroom, Robert slept on a sofa in the living room. He didn't mind; he thought all children did.

Every spring, the janitor turned the soil in the front yard and planted grass seed. Every summer, the result was an expanse of dandelion and crab grass. "At least it's green," Dad said.

In the rear, rickety wooden porches overlooked a yard rimmed by a dirty blue fence. The neighbor kids learned enough signs to communicate with Robert, and, together, they played in the yard except on days it was muddy from recent rains. Mrs. Lintz, an ill-tempered old hag who lived on the second floor with four Siamese cats and an anxious goldfish, threw hot water on them when they got too noisy. They didn't treat her with kindness on Halloween.

"Can we go sledding or ice skating?" Robert asked. "It's a perfect day for it."

"As soon as your father finishes the Sunday paper," Mother said. Such outings weren't unusual. The family enjoyed winter sports, bowling, and picnics.

On Sunday evenings, they went out for chicken dinner. In the fall, they picked apples and carved pumpkins. As a special treat, Father got tickets for a football game or the circus. Every summer, they vacationed at a lake house where Robert learned to swim and fish.

The first time Robert saw Willa was at school. She and her parents were walking toward the administration building, and they stopped to watch his soccer game. He kicked the ball out of bounds, in Willa's direction, to get a closer look at his new classmate. He had never seen a girl so beautiful.

"You're new here, aren't you?" he asked. "I'm Robert; what's your name?"

"I'm Willa," she said, "and I'd like you to meet my mother and father." Every morning, he hurried to the dining hall to see her. When Willa saw him, she smiled and waved. He felt a tightness in his stomach, a new feeling, strange, but not unpleasant.

"Come and have breakfast with me," he said. "We can sit here at the same side of the table."

"There's Robert with his new girlfriend," one of the older boys teased. Robert didn't respond, because he knew, for sure, that this boy, and every other boy at school, was jealous.

On rainy days, Willa taught him how to play card games and dominoes. During bus rides to town, they took turns at a window seat. When they played pinball, he worked one flipper and she worked the other. At lunch, they split the french fries. Both of them like gobs of ketchup.

On sunny days, they played hide and seek and climbed trees. He taught Willa how to spin a top and fly a kite. They swam in the lake and ran races. They went on hikes and chased butterflies.

"You are my best friend," he said.

"As you are mine," she answered.

Chapter 3

One rainy afternoon, after Willa had thrashed him at dominoes, they talked about her growing up. "Where did you live and what did you do before you came to school?" Robert asked.

"It's an old bungalow, and my parents still live there," Willa said. "All the houses on the block look just about the same—dark brick with seven or eight steps leading to the front porch and entrance."

"What's it like around your house?"

"The neighborhood is like most others, nothing special. Fathers go to work, and most of the mothers stay home to care for the children and take care of their houses. Sometimes, the neighbor kids go to a city park, a few blocks away. But, most of the time, we play in the alley behind our houses. We have to be careful to dodge the garbage cans and a rusty old Pontiac. Stray cats eat most of the rats, and once a week, a grubby old man limps by. 'Rags and old iron', he yells. It took me a couple years to figure out what he was saying."

"What's your favorite thing to do at home?"

"I like going grocery shopping with my mother every week. I put on clean clothes, and we walk, hand in hand, to the store. Mother shops at Ostenkowski's Food Pantry, because the prices are fair and the owners know some sign language. On our way home, we always stop for an ice cream cone or a hot chocolate."

"Do you ever go away for a vacation?"

"Father drives a beat up Chevrolet station wagon that only runs because he's so good at fixing it. Once in a while, he drives us to the outskirts of town for a picnic or swimming, but we never had a real vacation at a resort or other fancy place. His dream is to take us to see the Grand Canyon and the big trees and the Pacific Ocean, but there is never enough money for that."

"When we get older, I'll take you," Robert said.

"Cross your heart," Willa said. After school one day, they went for a walk.

"I'll bet you a nickel I can climb to the top of that oak tree before you can count to a hundred," he said.

"Make it a dime," she answered. He made it to the top with time to spare, and when he came down, he sat against the trunk to rest. Willa took his hand and leaned forward to kiss him on the lips.

"Mushy stuff," he said, pulling away, but it wasn't long before climbing trees became less important to him. Instead, he liked to sit under them and do mushy stuff with Willa. She smelled so good to him, even better than the sweet smell of rain.

Some might scorn at the notion of children falling in love, but Willa and Robert surely did. They felt lucky to have those feelings as children, and now, as adults, they felt blessed.

Chapter 4

Willa and Robert were born deaf, the only children of deaf parents. They were, as it is said, "Deaf of Deaf." Their progress through early childhood was excellent. They crawled and walked when they were supposed to and showed equal facility with dressing and feeding themselves. Because their parents were fluent in sign language, their communication skills developed precisely on time. They socialized easily with other children, and they were ready for school at the same age as the others were. In fact, the only difference between them and so-called "normal" kids is that they used a different language.

Robert was four years old when his father introduced him to tools, and, with an admirable display of paternal patience, he taught him how to use them. "No matter what we learn in school, a man must always know how to build things," he said. Robert had a natural aptitude, and his father was pleased.

When it was time for formal education, there was no question that his parents would enroll him at a residential school. "Our son will attend the same school we did," Father said. "He will go to school with other children who are deaf, and he and his classmates will be taught by deaf teachers who are fluent in sign language."

Another choice would have been a public school program for deaf children where Robert would go during the day while continuing to live at home. One might have thought that his mother, pleased with the prospect of having him remain home rather than moving several hundred miles away, might have been willing to consider such an option.

"Not a chance," Mother said with staunch resolve. "At public school programs for deaf children, teachers aren't deaf. Sign language and the finger-spelling alphabet are forbidden.

Children caught using them are punished, because their teachers believe deaf children must learn to speak. Without speech, they believe our children will be set apart and isolated. What they apparently don't know is that without sign language, our children will be illiterate."

At the residential school, children weren't forced to speak. No one pulled stockings over their hands. No one slapped their hands with rulers or tied their hands behind their backs. Instead, they were free to communicate in what, for them, was the most natural way. Sign language and the manual alphabet were encouraged and took the place of voice.

It was a good school, a community of Deaf people where Willa and Robert thrived. They learned their academics, they learned to relate to their classmates, and they learned about their culture—the social beliefs, behaviors, art, literary traditions, history, values and shared institutions of deaf people who rely upon signed language as their primary means of communication.

Willa and Robert were excellent students. More often than not, both made the honor roll. In high school, Robert competed on the wrestling and soccer teams and was vice-president of the senior class. Willa was on the student council and a member of the dance club and community service club.

Like students everywhere, they were rebellious enough to question authority on occasion. The student council invited the headmaster to meetings during the spring semester of each year in order to hear, and most often ignore, student grievances. "What is at the top of your list this year?" he asked, stifling a yawn.

"Actually, there are several things at the top," Willa said. "Our council, representing the entire student body, urges you to address all of them before the year ends."

"I'm ready as I'm ever going to be," the headmaster said, only slightly more gracious in his demeanor.

"First, the food has gone from bad to worse," Willa said. "There are some nights when dinner is inedible, or at least unidentifiable, and lunch and breakfast aren't any better. Furthermore, our mattresses are lumpy and our desks are old, pockmarked, and too small. Finally, the student code of conduct, which hasn't been revised since our school opened, needs to be brought up to date, particularly with respect to curfew and the need for chaperones."

"Is there anything else, young lady?" the headmaster asked, looking over his half moon spectacles.

"I could go on," Willa said, "but improvements in these areas will suffice for the time being."

In the end, they got new mattresses and desks, which, given the degree of prior administrative cooperation, constituted a rather massive victory.

As valedictorian, Robert was chosen to address his classmates and their parents at the graduation ceremony. He rehearsed diligently, most often in front of Willa. "Slow down," she said. "It looks like you're in a hurry to finish, and some of your signs are hard to understand, even for me."

His slower speech was well received, and when he finished, the audience "clapped" by waving their hands above their heads and rotating their wrists back and forth. Such is the Deaf way of applauding.

After graduation, Robert rented a room in the attic of a boarding house and applied for a job with a company that built custom cabinetry. He completed the paperwork and waited for his interview with the boss. A sign language interpreter was present, as well.

The boss was a big guy, friendly, and quick to smile. "Hey, I'm Bill Constantine," he said, "but everyone calls me Connie. Good to meet you."

"Good to meet you, too," Robert said. "Thanks for the interview."

"Actually, I've hired a few guys, five I think, from your school before, and all but one worked out really well. C'mon, let's see what you can do."

"What do you have in mind?" Robert asked.

"Follow me." In a workroom next door, Robert found a pile of wood and some tools. "I'll be back in 45 minutes," Connie said. "Make me anything you like."

Robert had seen a picture of a little girl on the boss's desk who looked about four or five years old. When he returned 45 minutes later, Robert showed him a dollhouse he'd made for her, complete with a few windows and a door that swung open and shut.

"Show up Monday morning at seven, and we'll put you to work," Connie said.

With no one to wake him, Robert needed a "loud" alarm. A special clock attached to a vibrator he kept under his pillow did the trick. He set it for six and woke up shaking.

Willa continued to live at the school working as a teachers' assistant in classes for the little ones. She enjoyed being with the children in a familiar place. She liked the art projects and socialization activities, but, most of all, she enjoyed helping the children expand their knowledge of sign language. Despite being exhausted at the end of the day, there wasn't an evening she didn't see Robert.

When he asked Willa to marry him, her parents were delighted. "Marriages of Deaf and hearing people are 'mixed marriages,' and such marriages are destined to fail," they said. So strong is this belief among the Deaf that 90 percent marry other Deaf. It's not a mortal sin if one doesn't, but it's close.

Their wedding was muted and beautiful. The chaplain conducted the ceremony in sign. The bride and groom signed love poems to each other, and the choir sang hymns in sign. Overwhelmed by the excitement of it all, the maiden of honor, a classmate of Willa's, fainted.

Their families and a group of friends rejoiced at a boisterous reception that evening. Before dinner, a friend of Willa's parents proposed a toast: "May the bride and groom prosper, enjoy good health, and produce many deaf children."

Their honeymoon spanned a long weekend at a nearby inn. They checked in, and a bellman hefted their luggage and led them to the honeymoon suite, all the while smiling, as he must have done for every other set of newlyweds. He ushered them in, and the source of his good cheer became obvious.

"Look, Willa," Robert said, "the bed is shaped like a heart." He pulled back the spread and saw red silken sheets.

"Yes, I've already noticed," Willa said, pointing toward the ceiling.

Neither of them had ever seen a heart shaped mirror affixed to a ceiling before, but they made the necessary adjustments quickly.

"Sort of helps you see things from a different angle," Robert said that night. Several times.

Back home, they moved into a small apartment. He carried her over the threshold, set her down on their bed, and gave her a yellow rose. He made several large circles in the air with his index finger before crossing his arms over his heart. In their way, he said, "I will love you forever."

Chapter 5

Robert and Willa had a close circle of friends, all of whom were Deaf. They felt isolated when they were with hearing people. "Hearies," they called them, and any time spent with them was boring at best and often exasperating. So many hearing people considered them less than whole; they were inclined to view their inability to hear as a handicap. Such an attitude hardly forms a solid foundation for a friendship.

So, they socialized with former classmates from the residential school and other Deaf. They went to theater and out to dinner together. They worshipped, traveled, shopped, and gossiped together. They belonged to the same social clubs and read the same newspapers and magazines. For those who had children, they baby-sat and otherwise watched over their kids.

They shared a common folklore as well—stories, poetry, anecdotes, legends, and myths—all relating to deafness. They even had their own jokes. "Hey, Willa, did you hear the one about the three hard of hearing guys?"

"No, but I'm sure you're going to tell me, so get it over with."

"Three hard of hearing guys are at a street corner. The first one says, 'Brrrr, it's windy!' The second one says, 'No, it's Thursday.' The third one says, 'Me too, let's get a drink.'"

Not to be outdone, Willa came back with one of her own. "A friend of mine, obviously happy and excited, came up to me at the mall. 'I just got a new hearing aid, and it works beautifully,' he said.

"'Oh, how nice,' I said. 'What kind is it?' 'Two-thirty,' my friend replied."

They and their friends were scornful of deaf people who attempted to speak or otherwise cross the line into hearing society. In fact, their "separatist" position was so strong that were it possible to know in advance, many would have chosen to abort a pregnancy rather than have a hearing child.

"Did you ever notice how stiff and formal hearing people are?" Willa asked.

"Yes, they shake hands a lot, but they hardly ever hug, at least in public."

"I like our way better." she said. "We are informal, much more physical and affectionate, ready to exchange hugs for any reason at all. I'm not sure why it is."

"I'm not sure either," Robert said, "but sometimes I think the friendships we have are better, somehow deeper, than hearing people have. Look how long it takes us to say goodbye. It's as if we want to prolong the contact, so we hug."

"As long as we're talking about people who hear," Robert said, "has anyone ever asked you if you'd like to hear?"

"More than a few times," Willa said.

"How do you answer?"

"I tell them I like being deaf, and I'm proud of my deafness. I tell them I'm happy with myself just the way I am. What really surprises them is when I tell them that the thought of losing my deafness is just as frightening to me as the thought of their losing their hearing."

"I 'hear' you," Robert said. "Hearing people think their way is normal. 'It's a hearing world, a world where people speak,' they say. That's why they think we're deficient, and they call us 'hearing impaired.'"

"They're entitled to their opinions," Willa said, "but, to us, our way is normal, too. Our world is a Deaf world, a world where people sign. So, perhaps it's the hearing people who are deficient, and maybe we should call them 'sign impaired.'"

"Or, it might be that there are no deficiencies," Robert said. "Just different ways of being."

Chapter 6

Robert had been on the job about a month when the sign language interpreter who had been present at his initial interview approached him. "The boss would like to see you for a while before you leave tonight," he said. Robert thought he'd been doing a good job but was still a little apprehensive.

Together, they entered Connie's office. "Sit down and relax," he said. "My foreman tells me you're a fine, able worker, and if you have some time, I'd like to talk."

"Sure thing, boss. My wife won't have dinner ready for a while, so what can I do for you?"

"Actually, over the years, the only contact I've had with folks who can't hear has come from the guys I've hired to work for me. Tell you the truth, I've always been interested in deafness, and I'd like to learn more about it. So, if you could spend a couple hours a week with me and my wife giving us information, we'd appreciate it. I'd like to learn some sign language too, at least enough so I won't need an interpreter, and of course, I'll see to it that you get paid for your time."

"I'll be happy to do it, boss; a couple of hours a week is nothing, and you don't have to pay me."

"Nope, that's part of the deal; either you accept the extra pay, or the deal is off." The following week they started. Robert hadn't prepared anything like a formal lesson plan. Connie, his wife Marilyn, the sign language interpreter, and a pot of coffee awaited him at the conference table.

"I think I'll start by giving you some basic

information about sign language," Robert said. "Fact is, there are a lot of things about our language that are going to surprise you. Stop me any time you have questions. If I don't know the answer, I'll make something up."

"Go for it," Connie said.

"American Sign Language, ASL, we call it, is one of about 6,000 languages in the world. Some, like Mandarin Chinese, are alive and well, used by almost a billion people. Others, like Ter Sami, once spoken in northern Russia, are comatose, right on the edge of extinction. Only two speakers remain, both elderly gentlemen, and when they die, so will their language."

Connie and Marilyn seemed very interested. "Wow. I had no idea there were so many languages," she said. "How many deaf people use ASL?"

"Over a million people in our country and Canada," Robert said. "My wife and I, her name is Willa, by the way, learned it naturally from our Deaf parents, just as you learned to speak English from your hearing parents."

"Isn't it like the 'Indian talk' we've seen in 'shoot-em-up' movies of the old West?" Marilyn asked. "Y'know, like 'me find horse, Kimo Sabe.'"

Connie nodded in agreement.

"A lot of people think that," Robert said. "They think signs are simple gestures used to convey simple ideas. Next, they assume that those of us who sign are simple people with limited potential for abstract thinking. It's why we've been called 'deaf and dumb' for so long."

"I'm so sorry," Marilyn said. "Please forgive me; I meant no offense."

"None taken," Robert said. "I know your husband only hires smart guys, and, fact is, ASL is anything but simple. It's a visual and manual language with a complicated, fully developed grammar. It has its own sentence structure, idioms, style, and regional variations."

"Do you mean like accents?" Connie asked. "That's incredible."

"Unlike all other languages," Robert continued, "which are received through the ears and expressed vocally, sign language is received through the eyes and expressed with movements of the hands, arms, body, and face. Like true languages everywhere, it is handed down from one generation to the next. Those of us who are fluent, and even some who aren't, consider it a very beautiful form of expression."

"Does everyone who signs do it exactly the same way?" Connie asked.

"Signers sign differently just as speakers speak differently," Robert said. "Willa, for example, is a graceful signer. Her signs are large and clear, carefully 'enunciated,' you might say, and easy to read. My signs, though, are choppy, fast and harder to read, as if I'm mumbling or slurring. 'Slow down' are the most common words in our house."

"They're 'take out the garbage,' at our place," Connie said. Marilyn only smirked.

"You should know, too, that ASL, being a visual language, can be seen from a long distance," Robert said. "So, while you, as hearing people, are able to overhear conversations from only a short distance in an environment where it's quiet, deaf people can 'overeye' conversations a long distance away, even across a crowded room where it's noisy. That means when you get good enough to communicate in ASL, you'll have to be careful to protect your secrets."

"The last deaf guy who worked here didn't communicate much, but he did tell me that most deaf people have nicknames," the boss said.

"Yes," Robert said. "They're called 'name signs,' and we think of them as gifts from one Deaf person to another. We value our name signs, because they mean we're accepted members of the Deaf community."

"What's yours?" Marilyn asked.

"House Builder," Robert said.

"Do we get name signs if we get fluent at ASL?" she continued.

"Hearing people can have name signs," Robert said, "but only if given to them by a Deaf person. Maybe, if I get good raises...."

"OK, let's say we study and practice hard," Connie said. "Would we be able to talk to deaf people in other countries, wherever we travel?"

"A lot of people think that, too," Robert said. "They assume that ASL is the universal language of the deaf, a language that can be used to communicate all over the world. Fact is, most countries have their own sign language. So, if you and Marilyn learn ASL and make it to France or Spain, you won't be able to converse with deaf natives. Of course, that's no different than the problem you would have conversing with hearing natives if you traveled to France or Spain and didn't speak French or Spanish."

"OK, we already have a better understanding of ASL, but tell us more," Marilyn said. "Surely there must be a system underlying all those random movements."

"There is, of course, and don't call me Shirley. Oops; sorry, I couldn't help myself."

"It's OK; we like your style," Connie said.

"Fact is," Robert said, "it's not random at all. What you need to remember is that signs consist of three basic elements: hand shape, hand location, and hand movement. Watch as I make the sign for 'happy': I open my right hand (hand shape) with my palm facing my body at chest level (hand location) and strike my heart several times. I lift my hand up and off my chest after each strike (hand movement). Are you happy now?"

"Yes, and I see that as you sign, you're moving your body a lot and making faces," Connie said.

"Body language and facial expressions are important parts of ASL," Robert said. "Both add meaning to what is signed in the same way that vocal tones and inflections add meaning to spoken words. English speakers, for example, signal questions by raising their tone of voice at the end of a sentence. For the same purpose, users of ASL raise their eyebrows and widen their eyes. Depending on the type of question, they may also lean slightly forward and furrow their brows."

"Let's freshen the coffee," Marilyn said. While she was pouring, she asked, "Is it going to be harder for my husband and me to learn ASL because we're older?"

"Unfortunately, it probably will be," Robert said. "The same rules that apply to learning any language apply to American Sign Language. It's best learned early in life, certainly before the age of three, and most effectively from infancy, but it's never too late to learn, especially if your goal is realistic, like learning enough to communicate on a basic level.

"People like Willa and me, who had the benefit of early exposure, become the most fluent and are able to communicate as rapidly as speakers who communicate vocally. Fluent as we are, we can express joy, grief, jealousy, anger, and all other emotions. We can tell jokes and tell fibs, make speeches and make love, recite poetry or curse, convey abstract ideas, transmit folklore, and sing songs. Fact is, the scope of our communication is just as broad as it is in people who speak."

"Wow, the hour is almost up," Connie said. "Before we quit, how about leaving us with a few signs to practice?"

"Some signs are very easy to learn and remember," Robert said, "because the position of the hands and the required movements relate logically to the object or idea they represent. To express 'sadness,' for example, the fingers of both hands are spread, placed at eye level, and moved down the face as if tears were flowing. To express 'brush teeth,' the index finger of the right hand moves across the teeth in a side-to-side, horizontal movement. To sign 'baby,' the arms, one resting atop the other, are moved from side to side to suggest cradling."

"Those are easy enough," Connie agreed.

"Remember them," Robert said, "and we'll start there next time. I brought you some books, too, that will introduce you to more signs. Go through them and practice with each other. Me find horse now, Kimo Sabe."

Chapter 7

Robert worked hard at his job, and it wasn't long before he was promoted. Willa stayed on as a teachers' assistant at the residential school. Sticking to a conservative budget, they saved enough to buy a plot of land. Friends helped them build a house with three bedrooms, a family room, and a playroom with space for toys and games.

Soon Willa was pregnant. Of course, they were elated, as were their parents. The same friends offered a crib and other baby furniture. When she wasn't feeling sick, Willa craved pistachio ice cream and fried green tomatoes. She flourished as their child grew within her.

"I have a vision of our child in my mind," Robert said. "He will be a strong, handsome boy, well-liked by others and motivated to do well in school. I will teach him to wrestle, play soccer, and build things with his hands. I will be a good father."

"I'm sure you will," Willa said, "but my vision is slightly different. She will be an intelligent, beautiful girl with innate talent in dance and painting. She will be kind to others and generous, and I will teach her how to sew and bake chocolate chip cookies."

While their dreams were different, both Willa and Robert wished for a child who would grow up to be like they were—a Deaf person who communicated with signed language. Like most parents, they hoped their apple wouldn't fall far from the tree.

Willa's pregnancy proceeded without complication. She endured more than the typical amount of morning sickness, and later, they marveled at the stretch marks on her abdomen. She grew very large and uncomfortable toward the end, especially when she passed her due date by a week. Finally, to their relief and delight, she delivered a perfect baby.

They named him Seth. Robert shared cigars at work, and his boss was delighted, too. At their lesson a few days later, he and Marilyn had a gift. "It's his first tool box," Connie said. "It'll be some time before he can use it, but you can never get started early enough."

They also had some questions: "How could the doctors tell Seth was deaf so early in his life? How often do parents who are deaf have deaf children? How do hearing parents communicate with their deaf children? Do you want Seth to learn to speak?" Robert answered them the best he could.

"Not long ago doctors only had rough measures to detect deafness in newborns," he began. "They would stand outside of the infant's line of sight and make a noise with a rattle or bell to see if the baby responded. While easy to administer, these tests weren't reliable enough to be acceptable. Sometimes an infant wouldn't respond simply because he was sleepy or bored."

"So testing children that way might have resulted in a lot of children being called deaf who really weren't," Marilyn said.

"That's right, but now a better test is being used," Robert said, "a test that measures an infant's ability to hear without requiring any response from the baby; in fact, it can be done in about ten minutes even when the baby is sleeping. During the test, the baby wears small earphones and electrodes are attached to his head. Sounds are transmitted through the ear canal to the brain. If the child is hearing, the electrodes show a response in the temporal lobe of the brain. If no response is detected, the doctor will order a more comprehensive evaluation of hearing. It's an important test that is being given to all newborns, because the earlier deaf children are identified, the better their future is likely to be. Let's see, what was the next question?"

"How often do deaf parents have deaf children?" Marilyn said.

"You may be surprised," Robert said, "but about 90 percent of all deaf children are born to parents who hear, parents who are shocked and saddened when they learn their child is different. It's likely that their knowledge of deafness is limited; in fact, they've probably never known a deaf person. So, deafness is foreign to them, alien, a pathological condition in need of a cure."

"What kinds of cures have people tried?" Connie asked.

"You'll be surprised at that, too," Robert said. "Some of them were peculiar, to say the least, particularly those that folks tried in earlier times, say a couple hundred years ago."

"Can you give us some examples."

"Sure. Parents collected their kids' urine, mixed it with garlic and olive oil, stirred gently, and had them drink the brew three times a day. They fried peach kernels in hog lard and put drops of the hot liquid in their children's ears. They gave their children opium and had them eat nothing but tomatoes over a period of four consecutive days."

"Yeah, I'd say those things were peculiar, actually closer to bizarre," Connie said.

"There are others that were even worse," Robert said. "Parents took their children to high places and forced them to jump. They went so far as to strap their children to chairs and deprive them of food and water for a few days."

"I wonder what would motivate parents to try

such things?" Connie asked.

"Actually, I'm not all that surprised," Marilyn said. "I think most parents would be willing to try just about anything when it comes to the well-being of their children, but are there any newer cures for deafness that are being tried today? There must be approaches that are more scientific than the ones you've told us about, cures that are advocated by medical doctors."

"There certainly is one new approach, a surgical procedure that is very controversial," Robert said.

"Is it the cochlear implant I've read about?" Marilyn asked.

"Exactly," Robert said. "More and more are being done every year. Usually, the first people that hearing parents turn to for advice after discovering their infant is deaf are ear doctors, 'otologists,' they're called, and neurologists. These medical specialists, all with the ability to hear, know a tremendous amount about tympanic membranes, auditory nerves, cochleae, and temporal lobes of the brain, but they may know very little about what it is like to be Deaf. Still, many of them are advising parents to submit their deaf children to major surgery as a way of curing their deafness."

"I understand parents who choose the implant surgery for their kids," Marilyn said. "Let's say Connie and I had a deaf child. While we're adjusting to the shock and disappointment, we hear about cochlear implants. We talk to doctors, who are, after all, the most respected people in our community, and they recommend the surgery for our child. Like most parents, we want our children to grow up to be just like we are—people who hear and speak. So, I think we would go along with the doctors' advice."

"And I understand your feelings," Robert said. "You should know, though, that there is another side to the story. Before you submitted your deaf child to implant surgery, it would be wise to consider some of the negatives."

"Tell us," Connie said.

"First of all, this is indeed invasive surgery. In the process, any residual hearing your child happened to have would be destroyed, and a hole is cut in his skull. Of course, general anesthesia is required, and the risks associated with any surgery are present."

"What else?"

"OK, let's say your child has the surgery between two and three years of age. Up to that time, he can't hear his parents' words, and his parents don't know how to sign. That means he's spent his early years, the most critical years for learning to communicate, without being exposed to any language at all. So, his language development is delayed for a couple of years, which is very likely to slow his progress when he gets to school.

"Is there more?"

"You bet. Parents who have their deaf children implanted should know that their children's hearing and speech would never be normal. Sure, they're likely to hear music and environmental sounds better, which is important, but insofar as hearing the speech of others and making their own speech understandable, follow up studies indicate that the improvement is quite limited."

"You present some strong negatives," Connie said. "But wouldn't you want to give your child a chance to be normal, despite the risks and other problems?"

"Bear with me a minute," Robert said, "while we talk about what's 'normal' and what isn't. You've said that hearing parents want their children to grow up just like they are; that is, hearing and speaking."

"Yes, I believe that," Connie said.

"Then, do you also believe that Deaf parents want their children to grow up just like they are; that is, deaf and signing?" Robert asked.

"I understand that, too," Connie said. "So, if Willa and I had a hearing baby, you would understand if we submitted her to major surgery to make her deaf; after all, we would just be trying to make our child like we are."

"Whoa. Wait a minute," Connie said. "I couldn't go along with that, because in our case, the surgery makes our child normal, but it your case, it makes your child...well, not normal."

"With all respect, boss, aren't you being a little self centered?" Robert asked.

"I don't follow," Connie said.

"You're saying hearing people get to determine what is normal but Deaf people don't.

Isn't it possible that for us, deafness is just as normal as hearing is for you? What you've said is that you and Marilyn can do whatever you want, including surgery, to assure your children grow up to be just like you, but Willa and I can't.

"I know it's hard for a lot of hearing people to grasp, but we celebrate our difference; we like the way we are; we are proud of our deafness, and we don't want to hear."

"I see your logic," Connie said, "but for hearing people like Marilyn and me, and I bet millions of others like us, this is all brand new. It wasn't until very recently that we even knew that a Deaf Culture existed, and honestly, the idea that you don't want to hear is still very hard for us to understand. We've always thought that, given the opportunity, deaf people would like to hear as much as paraplegics would like to walk and blind people would like to see."

"Your position is indeed foreign to us," Marilyn said. "To help us understand, if you would counsel hearing parents not to pursue the cochlear implant for their deaf babies, then what type of advise would you give them?"

"I'd begin by telling them they must expose their children to language from infancy, and the only way to do that is with American Sign Language I'd tell them they must take whatever steps are necessary to learn ASL themselves, at the same time as their babies are. I'd tell them to arrange for their children to interact, inside of school and out, with as many other deaf children and adults as they could. Finally, I'd advise the parents to have as much contact with Deaf adults and learn about our culture, because it is the Deaf world in which their children are ultimately going to live."

"It will take us a while to digest all you've told us, and it's possible that we may never agree," Marilyn said. "I've got to ask you something, though. If you and Willa ever have a hearing child, would you really go ahead with surgery to deafen him?"

"Not at all," Robert said. "Willa and I would be disappointed, for sure, but we would love our hearing child; we would teach him to sign at the same time as he learned to speak, and because he would ultimately live in a hearing world, we would see to it that he had plenty of time with hearing children and adults. We would do all that for our hearing child without ever allowing anyone to cut holes in his head, and we would like to think you would do the same for your deaf child."

Chapter 8

Willa and Robert knew that non-deaf children learned to speak effortlessly, without formal lessons, by hearing and imitating the spoken words of their hearing parents, and from their own language development, they had learned that deaf children can progress equally well, with the same natural ease, by seeing and imitating the manual language of their deaf parents. They understood, of course, that the product would be different—signs rather than voice—but they were certain that the process of learning to communicate was the same.

"We must surround our son with signs," Willa said. "We will do this when we feed him, when we change him, and when we bathe him. We will do it at home, at the grocery store, in our car, at the doctor's office, and at the homes of friends. We will do this constantly, whether Seth is close or far, interested or not."

As conscientious as Willa, Robert agreed. He truly bombarded his son with sign language, starting even before they brought him home from the hospital.

Willa was in the midst of changing Seth one morning before Robert left for work. "Wow, a real whopper this time," she said.

"Yes, I'm glad it was your turn."

"You get your share."

"Y' know, I've noticed that you sign differently when you're talking with Seth than when you talk with me or to our friends," Robert said.

"How's that?" Willa asked.

"You're more repetitive, and your delivery is slower and more exaggerated."

"You do it too," Willa said. Neither had realized it but Willa and Robert were actually engaging in "Motherese," the same kind of rhythmic, singsong talk that hearing parents use when speaking to their hearing infants. It's clear that an inability to hear doesn't change parental instinct.

Willa and Robert routinely looked in on Seth while he slept. "Look, he's moving his hands," Robert said one night.

"He's dreaming," Willa said. "It's like the eye movements hearing people do when they dream."

Seth played with his fingers and hands while he was awake, too. He was babbling, just as hearing babies do, except manually instead of vocally.

Robert and Willa didn't miss a chance to reward Seth for his attempts to communicate. They picked him up, smiled, cuddled, fed, and otherwise spoiled him mightily any time he reached out to them. Their behavior was no different from that of any set of parents interested in accelerating their child's speech development.

"Wow, it's only his first birthday, and look what he can do," Willa said. "He already knows dozens of signs and he uses them correctly."

"Yes, it seems to me that his language development has been very fast," Robert said, "maybe even faster than it is in children who hear."

By age three, Seth had a vocabulary of hundreds of signs. He used singulars and plurals, and he was beginning to understand tense. He could name his body parts, favorite toys, and common household objects. He related his daily experiences in chronological order and logically enough to be easily followed.

Only signing enabled Willa and Robert to expose Seth to the complexity and richness of language during the best time, the first three years of his life. These first three years, the so-called "window of opportunity" or "critical period" is when the brain is most receptive to learning communication skills. It's why hearing babies, fortunate enough to have more than one language spoken at home, become bilingual with ease, but hearing adults, long past the critical period, must really struggle to acquire a second language. The window of opportunity closes quickly.

Seth was due for a routine physical examination, and afterwards, through an interpreter, Willa and Robert spoke with his pediatrician. "He's fine," she said, "healthy in every way, very alert and bright. What's your secret?"

"His mother and I feel that Seth has had a tremendous advantage over deaf babies born to parents who hear, people who don't know, and, in most cases, don't want to learn sign language in order to communicate with their babies."

"They want their babies to speak, don't they," the doctor said.

"Yes, most often they do. They try to refashion their deaf babies into little people who speak and therefore more closely resemble their own self-centered views of normalcy."

"You can understand that, I'm sure," the doctor said.

"I'm not sure I do, " Robert said. "Hearing parents of deaf children are asking their kids to accomplish a near impossible task—learning to speak without every hearing the sounds of the language."

"Is it really impossible?" the doctor asked.

"Think of a child born blind," Robert said. "Would you expect him to understand the difference between blue, red, yellow, and green? Fact is, learning to speak without being able to hear is so difficult that the vast majority of children born deaf never develop speech that others can understand. Yet hearing parents act as if any amount of spoken English, comprehensible or not, is better for their children than the most eloquent sign language. Indeed, they prefer that their deaf children speak just a *few* words, poorly articulated in an unnatural voice, over full and fluid communication with beautifully articulated signs." Robert suspected that he didn't change the pediatrician's mind, but, at least, he'd given her something to think about.

On the ride home, Willa said, "You left out a few things, you know."

"What's that?"

"You might have pointed out to the good doctor that hearing parents of deaf children who insist their kids learn to speak are the same parents who are so despondent when their deaf adolescents are still illiterate, fifteen years later, at high school graduation. You might have pointed out, too, that these are the same parents who are so dismayed when they discover their adolescents will always be dependent upon them, unable, because of their very limited language and academic skills, to find jobs beyond the unskilled level."

"I didn't want to hit her with too much at once," Robert said. "When we see her again, I'll remind her that deaf children like Seth who are exposed to sign language early and continuously are the ones who go to college, the ones who become lawyers, physicians, teachers, and business people."

"I'm not sure you'll make a dent," Willa said.

"You may be right," Robert said. "It's very hard to change anyone's mind, even though the implications are so clear."

"Yes," Willa said. "All that hearing parents must

do is learn sign language with their deaf infants and make it their child's primary language at home. They must see to it that their children meet and associate with other deaf children and adults, because it is the Deaf world in which they will ultimately live."

"If they would just do that," Robert added, "joy would replace despondency when they watch their children express themselves with natural fluency using *thousands* of signs that convey the full range of human experience and emotion. Joy would replace despondency when they attend their child's college graduation ceremony, and joy will remain when their children assume productive employment, move into their own homes, and begin functioning as fully independent adults."

Chapter 9

Working as a teacher's assistant in the preschool taught Willa a lot about how children learn to read. "The kids who read first," she said, "and the ones who go on to become the best readers are the ones whose parents begin reading to them very early."

So, she and Robert started looking through picture books with Seth when he was two years old and began reading to him before he was three. He followed the words in children's books as they moved their fingers and hands. His eyes focused directly on the printed words, but, at the same time, he saw their movements on the edges of his vision. In fact, Seth attended to two streams of visual information at the same time.

Those deaf people who are good at signing have the same kind of "split vision" that Seth demonstrated. They are able to maintain eye contact while conversing with other deaf people instead of having to look directly at their hands. Indeed, to break eye contact while signing with another person is considered inattentive and rude.

"Your turn to put Seth to bed tonight," Willa said.

"I don't mind; sometimes we men need a little down time together. Our bedtime ritual is up to two or three stories, a trip to the bathroom, a glass of water, and checking under the bed for monsters," Robert said. "It's taking about an hour."

"Which one of you is more afraid of the monsters?" Willa asked.

"I'd say it's Seth, at least two out of three times." In fact, both Willa and Robert were happy to spend time with Seth at bedtime. Apart from the fun of being with him, they were certain that any time they invested in reading to him would pay off handsomely when he was older and it was time for him to learn to read on his own.

At the same time that Seth's language skills were developing so nicely, so too were his movement skills. He rolled over, sat up, and crawled very early. He was walking by ten months and racing through the house and backyard by his first birthday. Neighbors were impressed that he could balance on a beam, jump over obstacles, catch and throw a softball, and kick a soccer ball when he was barely out of his diapers.

"Y'know, Seth actually sat still for thirty minutes today," Willa said.

"What did you have him doing?" Robert asked.

"I just put some stuff on the floor, and he did puzzles, tied knots, and tried to put a model airplane together. He didn't even realize I was watching him even though I was only a couple of feet away."

"Maybe, the fact that he can't hear is actually an asset," Robert said. "He can concentrate fully on whatever he's doing without being distracted by irrelevant noises."

Robert and Willa were pleased with Seth's physical development. They began an early morning routine of calisthenics and jogging. Robert taught him some wrestling moves, and they grappled on a makeshift mat in the garage. He picked up some boxing gloves, too, and they went at each other a couple of nights a week.

In his attempt to harden Seth's edges, Robert went so far as to teach him the signs for some curse words. Willa wasn't happy when she saw the men in her life swapping profanities in the back yard. After wagging her finger and scowling in anger, she showed her remarkable sense of humor: "I will wash your hands with soap and water if I ever see you using those words again."

When it was time for Seth to go to begin his formal education, they enrolled him in the same residential school they had attended. He was an excellent student from the first. Words fascinated him; learning to read came easily, and he spent a lot of time in the library. Spelling, writing, and math were easy for him, as well. At home, he was an active participant in their after dinner discussions. Willa and Robert always encouraged him to present his own point of view, and he did, almost every night.

"So what do you think of our guy?" Willa asked, one evening after dinner.

"To me, he's all we could have hoped for," Robert said.

"Yes, he's deaf and smart, isn't he?"

"Not to mention, extremely good looking, like his mom."

Chapter 10

Jacob was Seth's best friend. Like Seth, he was born to deaf parents and proficient in sign language. On a snowy Saturday in February, Jacob's father was killed when a truck ran him down. Jacob was three years old at the time. Mother, tough and resolute as she was, raised Jacob by herself. Often, she sat with him to look at family pictures. "You must never forget your Papa," she said.

"I never will, Mama; I will look at his pictures every day."

When Jacob approached school age, Mama marched over to the local public school, written note in hand. "How can I help you?" a secretary asked.

"As you can see," her note read, "I'm deaf. I'd like an appointment with the principal to talk with him about my son Jacob who is also deaf. Of course, you will have to arrange for a sign language interpreter to be present at our meeting."

A week later, Mama had her meeting. She wasn't pleased with the services available for Jacob at the neighborhood school. Nor, was she pleased with the principal.

"We have no other deaf children at our school," he said. "In fact, the only special education program we have is a program for children who are slow learners."

Mama's displeasure increased when the principal, commenting on Jacob's "handicap," said, "Your son, 'deaf and dumb' as he is, ought to do very nicely in that program."

"Thank you for your time, but I'm not interested in what you have to offer," Mama said, standing to indicate that the meeting was over.

The interpreter caught up with her in the hallway. "Have a cup of coffee with me," she said. "You have every right to be angry."

"Yes, I do," Mama said. "Here is a principal, the leader of an elementary school, the guy who's supposed to stop the buck, who still thinks deaf children are dumb. What a jerk."

"Yes," the interpreter said, "and, he acted with an incredible lack of tact, in front of a woman who is deaf herself. Who is dumb, we must wonder?"

Jacob's mother didn't like the idea of sending her son hundreds of miles away to a residential school. In her wisdom, however, she recognized that his best, indeed, perhaps his only opportunity for a good education, depended upon his going to a school with other deaf children. He needed to be taught by teachers with enough experience and insight to recognize that Jacob, although profoundly deaf, was also quite intelligent.

Jacob and Seth hit it off immediately. They sat together in the dining hall, used the same locker for their books and other belongings, borrowed each other's school supplies, chose each other to play on the same teams, and shared each other's clothing and secrets. Indeed, they grew up together.

"Where did you learn to draw like that?" Seth asked.

"Never had a lesson," Jacob said. "When I want to draw or sculpt, I just do it. I'm not sure how, but I know I can do it when I want to."

"Y'know, you're a better artist than anyone I've ever known," Seth said. "You're better than anyone here, for sure, even the art teachers."

Jacob's works were indeed skillful and creative; however, his talent didn't always result in products that were wholly appreciated by the school administrators. One of his sculptures, in fact, created quite a stir.

A bronze statue of Thomas Hopkins Gallaudet was prominently displayed at the residential school. Every student learned that in 1817, he established the first school for the deaf in the United States. He called it the "American Asylum for the Education of the Deaf and Dumb." Gallaudet University in Washington, D.C., the only liberal arts university for the deaf in the world, is named for him.

"Gallaudet is the man," Seth said. "He's a hero to Deaf people."

"Yeah, I know it," Jacob replied, "but I wish the person who founded the first American Asylum for the *Hearing* and Dumb would be remembered too, with at least equal veneration."

A second statue stood, very briefly, in the shadow of Gallaudet's. It was Jacob's testimonial to Alexander Graham Bell. Although the world honors Bell as the inventor of the telephone, his primary interest was in bringing speech to the deaf. This interest was surely motivated by the fact that his mother and wife were deaf.

"Bell was a colossal jerk, a pompous, egotistical ass," Jacob said.

"Why do you think so?" Seth asked.

"To begin with, he lobbied for legislation that would have made it illegal for deaf men and women to marry each other, and if he had his way, he would have banned the use of sign language and finger spelling in schools for deaf children."

"Was he one of those so-called 'oralists' who thought all deaf children must learn to speak?" Seth asked.

"You bet," Jacob said. "His idea was that our language set us apart by making our 'disabilities' immediately visible to others. I guess he didn't realize that deaf people, speaking in an unnatural, unintelligible voice, were immediately visible, too."

"How did he feel about residential schools for the deaf?" Seth asked.

"He would have banned them if he had his druthers," Jacob said. "He thought they segregated us from the rest of the population and limited our opportunity to mix with people who could hear. He believed, too, that deaf adults should not be allowed to work as teachers of deaf children."

Jacob's sculpture was fashioned from supplies he smuggled out of art class over a two-week period. When he was done, he and Seth slithered outside in the predawn hours and exhibited a nude, three-quarter length, frontal portrayal of Alexander, in clay elegance no less, for all to admire.

Jacob had taken considerable artistic license by fashioning a bloated, indeed heroic, caricature of Bell's genitalia. Seth propped a crudely lettered invitation against the statue, a sign that invited their classmates to "Step Right Up and Ring Alexander Grahams's Bells."

Only a few hours passed before the ever-vigilant headmaster had the sculpture removed, so despite rave reviews from the students, Jacob's one-man show enjoyed a very short run. Every student at school was interrogated, but the perpetrators were never caught.

Diversions such as these occupied only a small amount of Seth's time. He studied hard, practiced his sports, and was recognized for academic and athletic achievements. Only a brief giggling fit marred his behavior during an academic awards ceremony. It was held out of doors, in the shadow of Gallaudet's statue. He covered a few small remnants of clay elegance with his shoes.

Chapter 11

"C'mon, wake up," Seth said. "It's Saturday and the bus will be leaving for town soon. We both need some things at the drug store, and we can play some pinball and eat lunch at the mall."

"Why don't you go by yourself," Jacob said. "I'm going to sleep in for a while."

"Not a chance. There's a captioned film playing at the movie, and the chaperones got us tickets."

Seth and a still sleepy Jacob entered the pharmacy. They signed back and forth while pretending they weren't looking at "girlie" magazines. After a pleasant interlude, they bought some toothpaste and deodorant. A young, heavyset girl, stood at the cash register picking at her pimples. The boys gathered their selections, brought them to the front, and she took their money.

"Thank you very much and please come again," she said, speaking very slowly and enunciating each word very carefully. By speaking in such an unnatural manner, she assumed she was helping the boys read her lips. In fact, all she needed to do was speak as she normally did. That, plus the context of the situation, would have been enough for the boys to understand what she was saying.

Outside, the boys discussed their encounter with the cashier. "Y'know," Jacob said, "one of the myths that hearing people still believe is that we deaf people all rely a lot on reading lips when we communicate. They honestly think our vision is so acute that we can read lips perfectly from the opposite end of a football field at dusk with 25,000 bearded fans jumping up and down and waving their arms."

"And it's foggy, too." Seth added.

"You've got to wonder who starts these myths." Jacob said.

"It's always someone's third cousin, twice removed, who happens to be out of town when you ask to see a demonstration," Seth said.

In reality, lip reading, or "speech reading" as most deaf people prefer, is a very difficult thing to do. Like any other skill, it's possible to improve a little with practice; nevertheless, in the most favorable environment, with good lighting where the speaker is close and at a good angle, the best speech reader in the world will only be able to understand about 40 percent of what is being said.

One of the problems is that words like "kick" and "king" and dozens of others are spoken without much movement around the lips. These words are simply not visible, thus no more useful to communication than written words that have been erased or blackened out from a line of print. What cannot be seen cannot be read.

Another problem is that some sounds which are different, like the "P," "B," and "M" sounds, look exactly the same on a speaker's lips. On silent lips, the result is that words very different in meaning look exactly alike. So, misunderstanding abounds when "bride" is confused with "prize," "mama" cannot be distinguished from "papa," "no new taxes," looks exactly like "go to Texas," and "vacuum" looks precisely the same as "fuck you."

Add these problems to the fact that many speakers wave their hands in front of their mouths when they speak, have facial hair that partially covers their lips, do not directly face the person they are speaking with, or, like Cary Grant, are just naturally tightlipped, and the difficulty with speech reading becomes even more apparent.

"There are other myths, too," Seth said.

"You mean the one that assumes we're all dumb?"

"That, for sure," Seth said, "but also the idea that we all work as tradespeople, specifically in the printing trade. None of us are physicians, lawyers, accountants, engineers, architects, or teachers; instead, if we work at all, we're printers."

"Yes, I've come across that too," Jacob said. "Maybe it has something to do with the idea that printing presses make such a constant racket, they're so loud, that only deaf people can stand being around them all day."

"Did you ever notice, too, how many hearing people think all they have to do is speak louder and we'll understand them?" Seth asked.

"Yeah, I've had some folks scream at me. So many people who hear just don't get the idea that no matter how loud they yell, the sound will still be distorted and unintelligible to us. If only more of them would learn to sign, it would be so much easier."

"Maybe it will happen," Seth said.

"What's that?" Jacob asked.

"I've heard that some colleges and universities are thinking about offering American Sign Language to students in order to fulfill their foreign language requirement. If the trend takes off, maybe more hearing people will be able to speak with us without screaming."

Chapter 12

Seth came home during summer breaks from school. Jacob usually returned to his family as well, but between their junior and senior years, Robert got both of them jobs as carpenter's helpers at a company that built garages. So, Jacob packed his bags and moved in with Seth and his parents. The guest bedroom never had a more talented occupant.

The three of them left for work each morning well fortified by another of Willa's delicious breakfasts. Indeed, each day began with a large heap of heaven. It might have been hot cakes and sausage, home made cinnamon buns, ham and cheese omelets, thick slices of bacon and sunny side up eggs on English muffins— whatever the treat, Willa sent them off to work sufficiently fortified.

At the beginning of the summer, most of what the boys did, shoveling and spreading sand and gravel, for example, involved more muscle than skill. Seth filled out nicely. The muscles in his stomach rippled, his biceps bulged, his legs thickened, and his shoulders and back broadened. Some of the young women in town were less than subtle with their flirtation, and he did nothing to discourage them.

After work, they waited for Robert to pick them up. Sometimes, they lagged pennies on the sidewalk; more often they just sat at the curb talking about their work. One afternoon, a couple of would-be bullies approached them. "Hey look at the dummies," one shouted. Such words, especially "dummies" are relatively easy to speech read.

"I think we've just been insulted," Jacob said.

"No doubt about it," Seth said, motioning for the tough guys to keep coming. Seth bloodied a nose and blackened an eye, and Jacob kicked the other one square on his baby making equipment. They took off, as bullies tend to do when they're stood up to.

The boys were about a month into the summer when the foreman called them aside. Without an interpreter, they made do with speech reading, gestures and written notes as best they could.

"You boys are good workers. You do whatever I ask you to do, so I want you to do more challenging things," the foreman said.

"Tell us what you need," Jacob said, "and we'll do it. We're ready."

So, Seth and Jacob learned how to build forms and pour and level concrete. They measured and cut two by fours, nailed frames together, and even learned some of the basics of masonry.

Jacob's eye for detail and his experience with how structures fit together made him quite an asset. By the middle of the summer, he worked up enough nerve to suggest some minor architectural modifications to the chief carpenter. These were forwarded to the owners of the company who liked what they saw.

"We're giving your suggestions serious consideration," they wrote. "Please interview for a job with us when you complete your schooling."

Jacob and Seth ate lunch every day at Round Rosie's Cafe, and Robert joined them whenever he could. Rosie's cooking was second only to Willa's. "Everything is so delicious here," one of her customers said. "How do you do it day after day?"

"Everything has to pass my personal taste test," Rosie said. "That's why the name of my restaurant is what it is."

Ellie was a waitress who worked at Round Rosie's. She had bleached hair, a nice figure, and a sad, tired look in her eyes, especially for someone only twenty years old. Word was that her husband had recently left her and had taken up with a student at a nursing school in the next county.

Seth had little contact with Ellie for most of the summer. She brought their food promptly and was pleasant enough. Only occasionally did she stop working for a moment to watch their signing. Then, on a Monday afternoon in early August, after scarfing down meat loaf and mashed potatoes smothered in brown gravy that was just greasy enough, it was Seth's turn to pay the check.

Ellie handed him his change and winked. She ran her tongue over her upper lip and brushed her fingertips across his palm. Neither Jacob nor Robert had witnessed the encounter, and Seth didn't share any details.

On Tuesday, Seth and Jacob sat at a booth near the windows. "What'll it be?" Ellie asked. Seth pointed to chicken fried steak, baked beans, coleslaw, corn bread, and iced tea. "And how about you?" Ellie asked, looking at Jacob. He held up two fingers, and she understood he'd be having the same.

Seth looked in Ellie's direction several times during lunch, but she avoided eye contact and went about her business in a detached, professional manner. He began to think she had just been kidding with him the day before, but when they finished lunch and headed for the door, she pressed a piece of paper into Seth's hand. She had written her address and the time she got home from work. The paper smelled of perfume, and his mouth went dry.

Seth went to Ellie's house that night. The first time he saw her body, he gasped. He hadn't known that a woman could be so beautiful. He went to her house the next night and as many nights as he could. He taught her some signs, and she taught him how to make love.

She was a patient, generous teacher, and she taught him well. "I know I'm the first woman you've been with," she said. "Don't worry, you can see me as long as you like, and whenever you need to stop, it will be OK." When that happened, he dreamed about her for a long time.

Chapter 13

Sex was important to Willa and Robert, a precious thing, something they savored. They flirted, kissed, and caressed freely, as a matter of course. Indeed, they had a hard time keeping their hands off each other. Their open, liberal attitude served as a model for Seth. Never seeing anything to the contrary, he assumed that the open affection they displayed was the way it was in all marriages.

When they felt it was time to discuss sexual matters with Seth, they did so, without awkwardness or delay. He was barely twelve years old at their first family conference. Willa made certain to be present; she wanted her son to benefit from a woman's perspective and insight.

Robert began the meeting with typical confidence and directness. "Your mother and I have decided it's time for the three of us to have a discussion about sex," he said.

With equal confidence and directness, Seth responded, "Sure, Dad, what do you need to know?" They had a good laugh, but, to himself, Robert wondered if Seth were really joking.

"You don't have to show me any pictures or diagrams," Seth said. "I've already learned about the various anatomical parts and their functions in sex education class."

"And more informally, I'm sure, from your buddies in the dormitory," Willa said.

"Yes," Seth said, "and once in a while, although

not often, we even use the biologically correct terms,"

"We're glad you know those things already," Robert said, "because there are more important things we need to talk about."

"What's that?" Seth asked.

"You must always respect and care about the needs of your partner," Willa said. "Sex is so much better when both of you feel some affection for each each other."

When Willa and Robert learned of Seth's affair with Ellie, they called another family conference. They thought he was a little young, but they didn't discourage him from seeing her. Their main concern was that he behave in a responsible and gentlemanly manner. Seth had the feeling, although his dad didn't say so, that Robert was thinking "chip off the old block" or "way to go, Son," almost as if his boy had beaten the state champion in a wrestling match or been accepted at Harvard.

"Do you care for each other?" Willa asked.

"We really do, Mom. She's having a great time learning to sign, and she's already very good at finger spelling, and she's taught me how to play gin rummy and honeymoon bridge. Believe it or not, we're vertical a lot of the time."

"And, you're using condoms, I hope," Dad said.

"What are condoms?" Seth asked, raising an eyebrow.

"You better be kidding," Robert said.

"Just playing around with you a little, Dad; you don't have to worry." During this conference, Seth felt a new kind of relationship with Willa and Robert. His time of dependency upon them was coming to an end. Now, instead, it would be, "Thanks for getting me here; sit back and watch me make it on my own."

Chapter 14

Senior year in high school was "big fish" time, and the boys took full advantage of their status. Jacob won several awards for his art projects, and Seth was appointed editor-in-chief of the annual yearbook. Both served on a joint faculty-student committee that promoted their school to younger deaf children and their parents. This work required some traveling throughout the state, a diversion they both welcomed and enjoyed.

On one of their trips, Jacob said, "We need to make some decisions, soon."

"You talking about college?" Seth asked.

"That, for sure," Jacob said, "but we also have to decide who to take to the senior prom."

"About college," Seth said, "I'm not sure where I want to go yet, but wherever it is, I'd like it if we went as a 'package deal.'"

"What's that?"

"That means we'll both go to the same school and be roommates."

"Sounds great to me," Jacob said, "but who are we going to take to the prom?"

Willa, Robert, and Jacob's mother hoped the boys would go to Gallaudet University in Washington, D.C. Along with demonstrating proficiency in sign language, the admissions criteria were rigorous and similar to those at other selective universities—letters of recommendation, grade point average, performance on college entrance exams, a personal essay—all were considered.

"These are a pretty hefty set of admission requirements," Seth said.

"Not so bad; I'm sure we can handle them," Jacob replied.

"Probably the easiest one is demonstrating that we're skilled in sign language." Seth said.

"Yeah, I'll bet we're at least as good as the professors." Seth and Jacob discussed their options and decided to take their best shot at Gallaudet.

The idea of studying with other college students who were Deaf was very appealing to them, and the prospect of living in the nation's capital was exciting, as well.

Seth and Jacob picked up their tuxedos and formal shoes, outfits for the senior prom. They barely got home before dark clouds gathered followed shortly by a torrential rainstorm.

"I can't remember a rain like this," Seth said.

Four hours later, Jacob agreed. "This is what we call a 'toad strangler,'" he said. The storm flooded the gymnasium with a foot of dirty, brown water. Blue and yellow balloons and pieces of crepe paper floated by, bobbing in random patterns. Electric power went out killing the lights and fans. The sewers backed up, and the gym reeked of unpleasant odors. The ambiance was hardly conducive to waltzing or otherwise tripping the light fantastic, so the dance was canceled. Jacob "consoled" his date on the sofa in the lobby of her dorm.

The Rotary Club sponsored a brunch to honor the graduates the next morning. Later in the day, dozens of students became violently ill with food poisoning from some bad Hollandaise. Jacob, who had skipped the Eggs Benedict, asked, "If you're paying homage to the 'porcelain goddess,' but no one hears you wretch, are you really sick?"

Between projectile vomits, Seth managed a smile

and a very shaky affirmative.

Two weeks later, both boys received their acceptance letters from Gallaudet. Their classmates would be two thousand others, six percent of whom were international students. About five percent were non-deaf, most preparing for work as sign language interpreters. Their packets included undergraduate course catalogs and information about housing options.

"Look here," Seth said, "we have six undergraduate residence halls to choose from."

"Let's find out which one is closest to a women's dorm," Jacob said, ever obsessed with the need for female company. "It's called social adjustment," he said.

"Have you given any thought to what you're going to study?" Seth asked.

"I'm not sure yet, but according to this book, we've got 29 majors to choose from."

The graduation ceremony proceeded without inclement weather or food poisoning, although one mother, apparently overcome with excitement, leaned a little too far over the mezzanine guard rail and had to be pulled back to safety.

Proud parents came from all over. Some signed, some spoke, some laughed, and some cried. Some had never completed high school and a few had advanced degrees. Everyone was happy.

Jacob spent the summer with his mother, and Seth went back to building garages. At the beginning of August, he began sifting through his things and packing. The night before he left for college, he went to Ellie's to say goodbye. It was a memorable farewell.

Chapter 15

Seth and Jacob lived in a corner room, on the third floor of a freshman and sophomore residence hall. Campus buildings and the football stadium were nearby. So were a couple of restaurants and bars, a few laundromats, and Clyde's Clippers, the local barbershop.

"I'll be darned," Seth said. "There's another dorm right across the driveway, no more than fifty feet away."

"I already checked it out," Jacob said. "It's for guys, and I'll bet they're just as disappointed as we are. Bad luck for us, but I'm sure our binoculars will still be useful at football games."

Their room was generic, much like dorm rooms at all universities. A bunk bed took up most of the space along one wall. Each of them had a dresser, desk, study lamp, and closet. One green leather chair, with a slit in the cushion and yellow stuffing sticking out, backed up to a corner. The walls were pocked with dozens of thumbtack holes.

"I wonder what became of Kathleen and Mary Ann?" Jacob asked.

"Who are they?"

"No idea, but their names and phone numbers are carved on my desk, and they're known for providing good times."

"They're probably old hags by now," Seth said. "There's no way their phones are lighting up these days." Their room was equipped with a telecommunication system for the deaf, a device for sending and receiving phone calls. It had a keyboard, display screen, and a modem. Messages typed into the machine were transmitted electronically over regular telephone lines. When the signals reached their destination, another telecommunicator, they were printed back into letters that appeared on the display screen or were printed out on paper. Instead of a ring, a light flashed to indicate an incoming call.

"I'm going to try it out," Jacob said.

"Who are you going to call?"

"Why don't I try Mary Ann, one of the hotties whose number is carved into the top of my desk?" Jacob made the call and got a Chinese restaurant. "Y'know, this telecommunication device is cool, certainly better than no phone at all," Jacob said. "But it's clumsy and completing a call is slow. I've got a better idea," he said.

"I'm all eyes," Seth said.

"Almost everyone has a television set today," Jacob said. "Why not equip them with small cameras that could be mounted on top? A deaf person makes a call to another deaf person who detects the incoming call by a flashing light. The person receiving the call turns on his TV, also equipped with a camera, and both parties see each other on their TV screens."

"You're a dreamer," Seth said.

"Maybe, but think about it. We could talk with other deaf people as if we were in the same room, without delay. We could communicate naturally, even interrupt each other during the conversation. Even hearing people could use it, maybe grandparents who live across the country and want to see their grandkids at the same time they're talking with them."

"It's science fiction," Seth said. "It'll never happen, not in our lifetimes."

"I'll flip you for the lower bunk," Jacob said.

"It doesn't matter; I don't mind the upper." In

fact, both mattresses were lumpy and uncomfortable; they squeaked, too, but who would know?

Each floor had a lounge with bean bag chairs, couches, vending machines, and a television set. Students used the lounge when they weren't studying, felt like some company, or just needed to get out of their rooms for a while. The resident counselor, a senior who accepted free room and board in exchange for doing his best to avoid underclassmen with problems, had a single room just off the lounge. He more or less enforced mandatory study hours from seven to ten each school night.

The cafeteria and dining hall were on the top floor. Seth and Jacob had been spoiled by Willa's and Round Rosie's cooking, so meals at the dorm were more like punishment than reward. "Dinners are mystery meat with gravy," Seth said.

"Yes, but at least there's plenty of it," Jacob replied.

Freshman orientation week was devoted to tours of the campus, meetings with academic advisors, and registering for classes. After his tour, Seth waited in line outside his advisor's office for the better part of an hour. A young assistant professor with neat, shoulder length hair and a well-trimmed mustache and goatee spent more time with a few pretty coeds than anyone else. Finally, Seth enrolled in college algebra, history, rhetoric, psychology, and physical education. Jacob took the same courses, but he substituted an art class for history.

They spent the rest of the week meeting their dorm mates and checking out the locations of the women's residence halls. At a freshmen mixer, they were pleased to meet many new people including some who were quite attractive. Jacob practiced his new word. "Pulchritudinous," he said. Over and over.

They played some touch football with other "newbies" and had beers together afterwards, and they sat through a welcoming address by the university president.

Seth got to thinking: *How come he isn't Deaf? I mean, here we are at the only college for the Deaf in the world, and the guy calling the shots isn't Deaf. I wonder when his term is up.*

One of the good things about Gallaudet was small classes. Usually class size was between fifteen and twenty, so students got to know each other quickly. With little opportunity and few places for students to hide, their professors got to know them, too.

Their classmates were an impressive group. "Aren't they all so smart, and don't they seem to know an awful lot?" Seth asked.

"You're not intimidated, are you?" Jacob replied.

"No, fact is, I'm happy that we're going to college with the brightest and most accomplished Deaf students in the country. Things are turning out exactly as I hoped they would."

Chapter 16

At the residential school, there were regular neatness checks. Should Jacob's room be messy, the consequence was no dinner until everything was put in order. Repeated untidiness meant cancellation of special privileges including Saturday trips to town.

When he stayed with Seth for the summer, Jacob was on his best behavior, because Robert and Willa were around. But now, at college, without parents nearby and no one in authority doing room checks, his true personality emerged. In fact, Jacob had an amazing tolerance for disarray, which is to say, he was a slob.

His desk was disorganized and his closet was worse. Each night, he threw his dirty clothes on the green leather chair, and when he ran out of underwear, he picked some from the bottom of the heap and wore them again. He had an industrial sized wastebasket next to his desk that served as a depository for crumpled wads of paper, half eaten apples, pencil shavings, and all manner of unidentifiable organic and inorganic matter.

The first and last time Jacob made his bed was never. A book of Monet's masterpieces, a pair of 10-pound dumbbells, and a round of Gouda cheese kept his blankets and sheets on the bed.

"I don't mind, but how come you never make your bed in the morning?" Seth asked.

"You mean so I can unmake it at night," Jacob replied. It was hard to argue with the logic. Seth believed that Jacob's style was because of the artist in him. He was so incredibly imaginative and creative that the more mundane aspects of daily living never had a chance. But, with so many other things going for him, Seth was happy to take his roommate as he was. They grew close as brothers.

They studied hard for their midterm exams and proved they could compete with their classmates. The college sent a list of grades, mostly A's and a few B's, to their parents. A few days later, the boys got congratulatory notes and "care packages" from home.

"What did Willa send you?" Jacob asked.

"A tin of her chocolate chip cookies; her note says half are for you, and what did your mom send you?"

"A hard salami; I love it," Jacob said. "Have some whenever you like."

Jacob whacked off a hunk just about every day, and he used what remained as a paperweight for unfinished term papers. "I really believe that garlic scented term papers get better grades," he said.

The boys, flush from their academic successes, rewarded themselves by making reservations for Sunday brunch at a nice restaurant. On the way out of the dormitory, Seth noticed that Jacob was wearing one brown loafer and one black one.

"Hey, you clown," Seth said. "You're wearing two different colored shoes."

When he looked down and saw the mismatch, Jacob shrugged and said, "There's got to be a pair just like them in my closet."

They took a taxi to the restaurant and sat at a table near the kitchen. The place was uncomfortably noisy for everyone but them. With practiced nonchalance, Seth ordered a Bloody Mary, and Jacob opted for a screwdriver. Unconvinced, the waiter asked for identification, so they provided the phonies they had managed to obtain through the campus source.

64

They stuffed themselves for the better part of two hours topping things off with chocolate cake and bread pudding.

"It's not that far back to the dorm," Seth said. "Why don't we walk back and burn a few calories?"

"Yeah, I'm in no hurry to start studying, so lead the way," Jacob replied.

Seth and Jacob strolled along, signing back and forth, enjoying the afternoon sun. A silver Buick, without hubcaps and pitted with rust, pulled up to the curb and kept pace for a few yards. A young man, with a six-pointed star tattooed on his forearm, a Z-shaped birthmark on his cheek, and an Oakland Raiders cap turned to one side, leaned out of the driver's side window. Certain that Seth and Jacob had been flashing disrespectful gang signs; he fired a pistol and changed Seth's life forever.

Chapter 17

What am I doing down here with my face on the sidewalk? Whose blood is that? Where's Jacob?

Strangely, Seth felt little pain. Neither did he realize that two bullets had ripped through his lower spine. Jacob cradled Seth's head in his hands and screamed until a police car arrived.

"What happened here?" one of the officers asked. Jacob, in a panic, pointed to his ear and shook his head in the negative. "Are you deaf?" the policeman asked.

"We both are," Jacob said, pointing back and forth. Finally, he saw cars pulling over to the curb and an ambulance arrive. Jacob continued cradling Seth's head in his hands.

"I'm cold," Seth said, "and I can't feel my legs." Then he passed out.

The next morning Seth woke up in the hospital with an intravenous tube in his arm and a catheter in his penis. He craved ice water for his parched throat and to wash away the vile taste in his mouth. Though they were out of focus, Seth recognized Willa and Robert standing at his bedside.

I've never been this tired. I know I keep phasing in and out, but I just can't keep my eyes open. Willa and Robert are here, and I should talk with them. I don't think I'm dead, but maybe I am. Where's Ellie? There's Jesus.

A statuette of Christ hung on one wall, and a picture of the United States flag hung on another. A silver bedpan sat atop the nightstand next to his bed along with a box of urine collection bags. A nurse flitted about. As if directing her question to more than one person, she asked, "How are we doing?"

In a waiting room down the hall, a sign language interpreter and two policemen sat with Jacob. "Tell us everything you can remember," a policeman said. "Anything at all, no detail is too small."

"I think it was a gray or maybe a silver car that was old and rusty," Jacob said. "I know there were two guys in the front seat. It all happened so fast, and it was such a surprise that I didn't see much. I wish I could tell you more, but I just can't."

"It's OK. Let us know if you remember anything else. We'll talk with Seth just as soon as he's feeling up to it, and we'll keep you and the family informed of any new developments."

"Maybe someone on the street saw what happened." Jacob said.

"It's quite possible; we've got two teams of detectives canvassing the area, talking to people and checking things out."

The policemen interviewed Seth a couple of days later. "I remember walking home with my roommate, and I remember being face down on the concrete wondering where all the blood was coming from. Jacob was holding my head, and then I woke up here in the hospital. I wish I could give you more, but that's all I know."

"Other things may come to you as you get better," an officer said. "If that should happen, your parents know how to get in touch with us."

It was a while, maybe ten days or so, before Seth remembered a tattoo and a birth mark that looked like a Z.

Chapter 18

Seth was paralyzed from the waist down, a paraplegic. To his doctors, he had a "complete spinal cord injury between the third and fourth thoracic vertebrae." To his fellow patients, neither interested nor versed in neurological diagnoses, he was a "new crip."

Seth cooperated with his doctor, grudgingly, at best. "Why do I need steroids?" he asked.

"You need them because they reduce the risk of your spinal cord swelling even more and because they improve the flow of blood through your injured area," the doctor said. "Poor circulation often leads to blood clots, a complication you certainly don't need. I'll get you off the steroids as soon as it's safe."

"Am I going to need more surgery?" Seth asked.

"You've got some pieces of bone that are pressing on your spinal cord that I've got to remove, and, at the same time, depending on what I see when I get in there, I may have to insert metal rods and screws to give your spine more support."

Seth made a few signs with which clergymen, either hearing or deaf, wouldn't be all that familiar.

At first, like many others with new spinal cord injuries, Seth went through a period of denial. He understood that his back had been broken and his spinal nerves had been severed. Nevertheless, he stubbornly insisted that his injuries were merely a temporary setback. "I'll be up and around soon, hustling to make up what I'm missing at school. No one knows how tough I am; I'll be out of here in a week," he said.

A couple of weeks passed, as did the requisite surgery. Then, a couple more weeks passed. Seth, still paraplegic but no longer quite so stubborn, came to accept the truth. With Willa and Robert at his bed, he said, "I guess there's a real good chance I may never walk again."

Once past denial, Seth settled into a deep depression. He didn't care to see anyone, do anything, or make any decisions. He had no appetite, and he lost weight. He was humorless, sometimes nasty, and always unpleasant to be with. He sat for long periods of time, as if catatonic, choosing neither to move nor communicate. Had the nurses at the rehabilitation center allowed it, he would have been content to turn off the lights, pull his blanket over his head, and hide from the walking world.

"I don 't know how much longer I can stand this," Robert said.

"I know what you mean," Willa said. "His injury is bad enough, but his depression is heartbreaking. It's as if he's left us and what's left isn't our boy anymore."

"We need to talk with a professional," Robert said. "There must be someone who can help us with this."

A counselor helped them understand that, in fact, Seth's sadness was a good thing. "Your son is depressed," he said, "because he's no longer denying the truth. It's hard, I know, but this means he cares enough about himself to worry about his future, and he needs some time to mourn his past. This is real progress, so stop trying to cheer him up every time you see him."

Seth had good reason to be depressed. Rubber wheels had suddenly replaced his legs. Forever bound to a chair, he would be a couple of feet shorter, looking up to just about everyone from now on. Absent feeling below his waist, he was unable to detect the urge to eliminate, necessitating intimate relationships with

69

catheters and suppositories. If he didn't empty his bladder promptly, serious infection was likely, so he had to strap a urine collection bag to his thigh.

Bone loss from his legs led to excessive calcium in his bloodstream and the agony of kidney stones, and his penis, his "Johnson," as he called it, which heretofore had been quick to rise to many occasions, hung limp as a strand of overcooked fettuccini. Sometimes, when a nurse bumped his bed or he felt a draft from an open window, his legs would jerk. At first, he was excited; he thought his legs were coming back to life. But, these movements were nothing more than spasms—uncontrollable, worthless, twitches.

At times, he felt a burning sensation in his legs, and they would lock until a nurse or therapist moved them. When he was warm or anxious, he perspired profusely, but only above his waist. Everything below stayed dry. Like something dead.

Robert tried to foresee the future. "When he comes out of his depression, Seth is going to have to learn a lot of basic things all over again."

"I know," Willa said. "Right now, even sitting up in bed or in his chair without passing out is hard for him. The doctor told me it's because the muscles below his injury can't pump enough blood back to his heart."

"Not only that," Robert added. "Transferring from his chair to the toilet, shaving, showering, getting in and out of bed—all these things, and others we haven't even thought of yet, are going to require a lot of training and practice."

"And what about driving a car?" Willa asked.

"Yes, he's going to have to learn how to drive using hand controls. I wonder where we find one of those and how much they cost?"

Seth had a hard time believing he was lucky, but, in fact, had the bullets sliced through his spinal cord a little higher, he would have been quadriplegic, unable to move any of his limbs. Such an injury might have made it impossible for him to breathe on his own, as well. "In the world of the blind, the one-eyed man is king." To Seth, the analogy was somewhat appropriate but not at all comforting.

Willa and Robert came to the rehabilitation center as often as they could, almost every day. Seth would usually be asleep when they got there. It was his escape, and sometimes he slept as much as 18 hours a day. In this dreams, he was whole again. He ran like a stallion, at least for a while.

Seth awoke with a start, heart pounding and pajama tops moist with perspiration. "What is it, Son?" Willa asked.

"I had my first crip dream," Seth said. "It was incredibly real, but I'm OK."

"Do you want to tell us about it?"

"I suppose it can't hurt. I was hiking through a forest with Ellie. She ran ahead of me and hid behind a tree, on top of a hill. I hurried to find her, but when I looked behind the tree, she was gone. A sculpture of Alexander Graham Bell, with gigantic privates stood in her place."

"Oh my goodness," Willa said, between gasps.

"You wanted to hear it," Seth said. "Should I stop?"

"No, go ahead and finish; I hope it doesn't get any worse."

"The headmaster chased me. He was wearing a pair of shoes that didn't match and threatening to clobber me with a hard salami. He was catching up, but my legs were so heavy, I could barely move. I fell and rolled the rest of the way to the bottom of the hill where Dad was waiting for me with a wheelchair, a bottle of suppositories, and a rusty chain saw."

"Well, this certainly isn't a musical comedy," Robert said.

"And the ending isn't a happy one either," Seth said. "I pulled myself onto the chair and took the chain saw. Then, I wheeled toward a guy who was face up on a sidewalk next to the dented fender of a silver car. His Johnson was fully exposed, hanging out of his fly. He flashed a gang sign with his left hand, and with his right hand, flat over his heart, he made the sign for 'Please.' I fired up the chain saw and cut off his hands. His blood oozed onto the sidewalk and formed the shape of a six-pointed star. Then, I lowered the saw toward his Johnson. It was fully erect and pulsating."

"Good thing for him you woke up when you did," Robert said.

After his parents left, Seth analyzed his dream. He came to understand the enormity of his rage, to realize how much he sought revenge, and to admit, at first reluctantly, then with increasing willingness, that he was quite capable of maiming, maybe even murdering, another human being.

It was the first time in his life that Seth had felt this degree of hatred. It was palpable, as if a dark monster were seething inside of him, seeking a vent, always seeking a vent, from which to spew its toxin.

Seth decided, too, that he would withhold information from the police. He alone knew of the birthmark and tattoo, and he alone would find the person who crippled him. Then, he alone, would exact swift and sweet revenge.

Chapter 19

For people with spinal cord injuries, the rehabilitation process is seldom smooth. More often, there are highs and lows, and such was the case for Seth. Leaving the rehabilitation center and returning home was good. Having to use ramps to get in and out of the house wasn't. The familiarity of his own bathroom was good. A leaky catheter and bowel accidents weren't. Looking out the living room window was good. The thought of going outside wasn't.

For Seth, the lows were more frequent and lasted longer than the highs. Months passed, and his depression worsened. He contemplated suicide, even to the extent of hoarding his pills. But for the need to satisfy his rage, he might have acted.

"Dad and I have found a psychiatrist we'd like you to meet with. We think talking with him will make you feel better," Willa said.

"I'll go if you really want me to, but I'm not sure that he or anyone else can get me out of this. Honestly, Mom, I don't know if I want to get out of this."

With unremarkable insight, the shrink told Seth he was depressed and prescribed antidepressant medication. A boy from the pharmacy delivered his pills every two weeks. Once in a while, Seth swallowed one when he was supposed to. More often, he added them to his stash.

He stayed in all day, seldom changing from his pajamas. He didn't bother to cut his fingernails, now ragged and dirty. He shaved and showered only sporadically, and he had a slovenly look about him. He had meals with Willa and Robert, but, for the most part, he picked at his food or just moved it around on his plate.

He skipped sessions with his physical therapist and left circular tracks on the living room carpet in the middle of the night. Sometimes he turned the pages of a magazine or stared at the television, but more often, he just sat and looked out the window, alternating between entertaining his revenge fantasies with thoughts of ending his life. Once well groomed and cheerful, Seth had become foul smelling, hateful, and melancholy.

Finally, Robert would have no more of it. "Your psychiatrist, neurologist and physical therapist have all tried to help you Son, but you're not getting better."

"What do you want from me, Dad? I'm a goddamn cripple. How would you like it?"

"I wouldn't," Robert said, "not for a second. We're sorry this has happened to you. But, if you aren't willing to help yourself, there's no medical specialist in the world that can do it for you."

"That's crap, Dad. Just words with no action. How, exactly, do I help myself? What do you have in mind?"

Robert brought out the boxing gloves. He sat on an old bar stool in the garage and challenged Seth to a bout. Seth circled his father warily before launching a series of wallops. For five minutes, they punched each other silly. Finally, completely arm weary and spent, each slumped over, gasped for air, and hugged each other. Seth took a long, hot shower, shaved, and began the slow process of getting better.

"What do you say we go swimming?" Robert suggested the following week.

"I don't have a lot going on," Seth relied, "so let's do it." Seth's upper body was strong, so pulling himself through the water was easy. Being in the pool was very effective physical therapy, too. The water was buoyant, and there were a few minutes when he almost forgot about his legs dragging along behind him and the urine collection bag strapped to his thigh.

"How about a race," Robert suggested. "One lap and the loser buys lunch."

"Sure, but if you win, I'll want a rematch when I'm in better shape." Robert won, but only by a little.

With continued exercise and better compliance with his medication, Seth's mood finally began to lift. Gradually, he resolved to get on with things and try to bring a semblance of normalcy back to his life. He went the library and read about spinal cord injuries. He joined the National Spinal Cord Injury Association. He sent for information about wheel chair athletics, and he continued working out at the gym. He flushed his stash down the toilet.

"Hey, I hear you're coming back to school in September," Jacob said.

"Yeah, on one condition though."

"Anything man. What is it?"

"You start now cleaning up the room."

Jacob was happy. His best friend, although permanently altered, would be with him again. Willa and Robert were elated with Seth's improvement. Their son, clean once again, smiled more often and even laughed on occasion. They had no way of knowing, however, that his revenge fantasies remained, vivid as ever, always festering.

 # Chapter 20

"You've got grass in your hair and dirt on your nose," Jacob said.

"Yeah. I was cutting across the field by the math building, and I did a face plant. The guy I was with, another crip, made the sign for a first down. I called it a 'dirt bath.'"

Indeed, getting around campus presented some problems at first, and Seth fell from his chair a few times. The first time it happened, he was rolling down a hill. His momentum tipped him forward, and he landed in the grass. Curbs were difficult as well, and once he got mired in some soft dirt and sat there until he got a push.

Doing "wheelies," a technique requiring that he balance on his back wheels while negotiating hills and curbs, made things easier. Seth mastered it after a few trials and had no further problems with mobility.

Like all colleges, Gallaudet accommodated the special needs of students with disabilities. Busses with lifts transported non-ambulatory students across campus. Classrooms were accessible with ramps and elevators, and restrooms were modified for people in wheelchairs.

Jacob had stopped to pick up their mail and burst into the room with a wide smile on his face, pumping his arms.

"What's up? Seth asked.

"I got a letter from my mom. As a reward for my grades, she's buying me a used car."

"Fabulous! What kind is it?"

"She says it's a seven year old beater that belches a lot of exhaust fumes but starts every time, even when it's cold. Really, I don't care what it is, 'cause from now on, no more taxi cabs or busses for us. Don't worry, I'll help you in and out."

"I'm not worried, but you've got to let me split the cost of gas with you."

"It's a deal."

The evening before classes began, Seth and Jacob went to see a French film at the campus art theater. They drove by the restaurant where they had eaten the day of the shooting. The building had been gutted, and a sign advertised the impending arrival of "Luxury Living in Two Story Lofts." Further along, they paused for a stoplight only feet from where Seth had been shot.

"At least someone scrubbed my blood from the sidewalk," he said.

Seth's school-week ended on Friday, after a two o'clock history class. He dropped his books at the dormitory, rolled over to a beer hall a couple of blocks away, and lifted himself into a booth by the windows. Soon, Jacob joined him, armed with a sketchpad and some drawing pencils.

"Why the art stuff?" Seth asked.

"Just sit back and relax my friend." Jacob said. "I'm about to embark upon my 'Coed of the Week' campaign."

"And just what the hell is that?" Seth asked.

"I begin by looking for the prettiest girl in the place," Jacob said. "Then I stare at her until she feels my eyes on her and looks back."

"What if she doesn't look?"

"I promise you; it never fails. When she looks at me, I flash my most boyish, innocent smile and begin sketching her portrait."

"Then what?"

"Overcome by curiosity and ego, she'll saunter over, usually accompanied by a girlfriend or two."

It was the most effective technique for meeting girls Seth had ever seen. Except, Seth had no interest in meeting girls. Denying the severity of his injury, climbing out of his depression, learning how to manage his bodily functions, and getting used to his physique and how he looked had required so much energy that little was left for other pursuits.

Even had sufficient energy remained, Seth wasn't emotionally ready to pursue a sexual relationship. Like many new paraplegics, his injury had a very negative effect on his self-esteem. He questioned his masculinity. *What kind of man have I become now that I can't have sex in the normal way, the way I used to before I got shot?*

His rage remained to effectively suppress his libido. In place of reveries about intimate acts with attractive, willing coeds, he fantasized about what he would do to him when he found him.

Chapter 21

Without the ability to move below his waist, Seth's upper body strength developed far beyond what it had been. That level of superior strength, plus agility in his wheelchair, helped him become proficient in a number of sports.

He competed for the wheelchair track and field team and specialized in middle distances and the shot put. He played wheelchair basketball and tennis regularly and enjoyed an occasional game of softball and billiards. He continued swimming once or twice a week. These activities kept him in decent shape and cleared his mind, at least for a time.

"How about we do some bowling?" Jacob asked one Friday night. "There's a place I know where the manager isn't particularly concerned about the age requirement for drinking beer, and they serve decent sausage pizza and burgers, too."

"I'm ready," Seth said. "We can play for a buck a game."

Seth converted a difficult spare to win the first game. He waited, savoring his victory, while Jacob left to purchase some refreshments. A young man with active acne and a ponytail began bowling one lane over. He rolled a ball into the gutter on his first attempt and knocked down only three pins on his second. His friend, medium height and unkempt, rose to take his turn. He stood in profile, just a few feet away, a red, Z-shaped mark clearly visible on his sallow cheek.

"Why aren't you eating?" Jacob asked. "I've had

most of the pizza myself, and you've barely sipped at your beer."

"I will; I've just had a temporary loss of appetite."

Jacob finished stuffing himself and motioned for Seth to begin another game. Seth sat expressionless for a few seconds, then rolled up to the line and delivered his ball smoothly. He scattered nine pins and glanced toward the next lane. There was the tattoo, a six-pointed star on the young man's arm, exactly how he remembered it.

Jacob won the second game easily. "Let's bowl one more and see who's champ," he said. "A tie is like kissing your sister."

Seth begged off. "I'm tired," he said, when in truth, he felt energized, unusually strong, and clear-headed.

Jacob changed to his street shoes, and they headed for the exit. A silver Buick, rusted and without hubcaps, occupied a space reserved for drivers with disabilities. Jacob saw it and stopped in his tracks. He widened his eyes and leaned toward Seth.

"I know; I saw him." Seth said, at the same time memorizing the numbers on the license plate.

Chapter 22

The next week Seth and Jacob didn't bowl; instead, they waited in the lounge, whiling away the time playing pinball or simulated car racing games. They had a pizza and nursed their beers. Every few minutes Seth checked the front door. They showed up about nine.

"There they are," Seth said, nudging Jacob.

"Yeah, dirty as they were last week."

"Let's just watch them from here for a while to see what they do."

They were clumsy, no more skilled at bowling than rank beginners. Each tried several balls, as if the equipment were deficient rather than their skills. At once unkempt and ill-mannered, their demeanor was rude and offensive to people nearby.

They finished their game and, after changing their shoes, they walked toward the restroom.

"They're coming our way," Jacob said.

"Just be cool. Just sit here and be cool." They passed Seth closely enough to brush against his chair. Time seemed to slow, and a flow of adrenaline sharpened his senses. They had blackheads on their faces, bad teeth, and grime under their fingernails. The smell of sweat and marijuana clung to their clothes. Their jeans were slung low on their hips, and they had rolled up their shirts to show their biceps.

Seth's saliva flowed, he tasted bile, and his pulse pounded in his ears.

Done in the restroom, they sat at a booth in the

lounge and gestured toward two nice-looking girls. Their approach was no less clumsy than their bowling, and the girls turned away in obvious disgust. Seth couldn't be sure, but he thought he read "Losers" on one of the girl's lips.

They finished their drinks, and the losers settled their tab and walked toward the exit. The Buick, with a parking ticket under the windshield wiper, occupied the same space reserved for drivers with disabilities. This driver, able-bodied and flippant as he was, sauntered right up, tore the ticket to shreds, and deposited his litter on the ground.

After three weeks, Seth said, "Their pattern is clear. Friday night is bowling night. They show up every week, at about nine. They bowl three games and go to the men's room. They have some beers in the lounge and insult some young women. Except for the parking space, nothing varies."

Jacob and Seth followed them to a run down neighborhood. One of them got out of the Buick and pulled his ponytail over the collar of his jacket. He lit a cigarette, checked the mailbox, and walked into a house. The other parked in front of a fire hydrant and joined his mate inside. A few minutes later, the lights went out.

Part II

Rachel and Angelo

Prologue

Check it out. I was out late tonight, chillin' with the crew. Some of 'em was providin' curb service, sellin' bombs on the street; them are joints laced with heroin, if you don't know the talk. The rest of us home boys was juss kickin', layin' back lookin' for frogs, y'know chicks who lay down easy.

For sure, none of us was lookin' for no demonstration, but sometimes trouble juss finds you when you leas' expect it. I mean, one minute you're juss suckin' on a cold one an' shootin' some pool, an' before you know it, some punks from a different hood, an alien crew, you could say, are dissin' you. Honest, none of us was lookin' to bang, but what was we s'posed to do when six of 'em, flyin' their flag, blocked our bucket, iron that Raphael just stole.

Anyways, we took 'em on, an' they wasn't much. Raphael blasted one of 'em acrost the kneecaps with a tire iron, an' I did a Rambo on another one with a bat. While he was layin' there out cold, I shanked off his thumb. I strung a shoelace through it, and I wear it 'round my neck. I polish it, too. A used thumb should always be polished. When them other punks figured who they was messin' with, they booked it, real quick.

I jumped into the crew a coupla years ago. Yeah, everyone raps 'bout how bad we are, an' I ain't sayin' they're wrong. None of us is like, whatdya call 'em, altar boys, or like that. Ain't too many old ladies we help acrost the street is what I'm sayin. We bang an' we steal an' we sell drugs, but I'll tell ya what. I got nice threads, a bitchin' stereo, an' I got heavy bread in my pocket. I mean, why should I work at McDonald's for a few crummy bucks an hour, when I can hold heavy an' live the good life like I'm doin? An' ain't nobody tells me what to do, neither. Nobody.

Tell you the truth, sometimes, particular late at night juss before I conk out, I think about Rachel an' Angelo, my mom and dad. Both of 'em grew up in, whadya call it, one of them homes for kids whose parents maybe died or juss up an' left 'em alone. I think "abandoned" is the word for it when parents leave their kids behind. I s'pose you could say I miss 'em once in a while, my parents I'm talkin' about, but I don't see myself goin' back there. I mean, we wasn't gettin' along for a long time, arguin' with each other all the time, an' them always tellin' me what to do.

You prolly noticed I ain't too good with the English language. Angelo ain't neither, not that I'm blamin' it on him. If you want to know the truth, I gotta give him some credit. He goes to classes a lot at night, after work, trying his best to get better at talkin' the right way. Rachel helps him a lot, too, 'cause she's pretty good at it. Talkin' English, I'm talkin' about.

It's not juss English that I'm bad at, neither. Far back as I can remember, there wasn't a single subject I was good at in school. I mean, I don't think I'm dumb or nothin', 'cause I sure learn stuff fast in the hood. Onliest thing is, at school, I never learned good, even from the first, an' I didn't have such good behavior, neither. An' if you don't behave good an' you don't learn too quick, they usually don't let you stay with the regular kids.

So, all them big shots at school had their meetin' an' they decided to put me in Special. Us kids an' everyone else called it "Horror Hall," 'cause everyone thought we was horrible, I guess. Our teachers did for sure; seemed like every year we got us a new one. I actual liked a few of 'em, my teachers I'm talkin' 'bout, but I guess me an' the other guys, 'specially the ones that did bad behaviors too, made 'em nervous, which is why they left.

After a while in Special, Jeez, maybe seven or eight years, they said I could dress up in my good clothes an' graduate. So, I went to high school for a while, but I couldn't read none of the books they passed out. None of 'em even had pitchers, for Chrissakes. So after a while, a coupla semesters when I flunked juss about everythin', I juss stopped goin'. I mean, think about it. How can anyone keep on goin' to the same place, day after day, when all you do is flunk?

That's when I jumped into the crew. They're my close buddies, my home boys. I got branded with the six-pointed star, an' they respect me. We have good times, an' nobody cares if I can read or not. Yeah, I miss Rachel an' Angelo once in a while, but when I'm with the crew, I feel, whadya call it, comfortable. Like I finally found a place for myself.

Chapter 23

Her mother was an 18-year-old prostitute with scoliosis, psoriasis, and irritable bowel syndrome. Her father was a neighborhood pimp with holes in his arms from a hundred dollar a day habit. She never knew them.

Four days after contributing to her conception, Father died from a combined overdose of heroin and peppermint schnapps. Seven months later, Mother squatted in a restroom at McDonald's, grunted a few times, and gave birth.

Mom was back on the street by the time a maintenance woman entered the stall and found a dirty, woolen coat wrapped around a three and a half pound newborn and her bloody umbilicus. Much of the baby's skin was covered with a white, cheesy looking substance, and what wasn't had a distinct yellow tinge. Her eyes were puffy, and her head was misshapen. Her tiny lips and fingertips were blue from lack of oxygen, and she was mewing like a hungry kitten.

"What is your emergency?" the 911 dispatcher asked.

"We've got an abandoned infant here; send someone quick."

"They're on their way. Hold him to your body and wrap him in whatever you've got, towels or something, to keep him warm."

"Will do, except him is a her." The ambulance rushed her to Providence Hospital where doctors hooked her to a respirator, feeding tube, and heart monitor. Her sucking reflex kicked in, her lungs matured, and she gained weight.

"It looks like she's going to make it," a nurse said. "What shall we name her?"

"I've always liked Rachel," another said. "Whadya think?"

A few months passed, and Rachel was transferred to the Holy Family Children's Home, a county orphanage that received a substantial endowment from the estate of a deceased thoracic surgeon who grew up there. Certainly, her life at the orphanage, while not ideal, was better than it would have been had "Old Mother Hooker" decided to take her home.

Caretakers, some of them volunteers from the community, fed, changed, and bathed baby Rachel. They gave her all she needed to grow and survive, and never once did they mishandle or abuse her in any way. But, with so many others to provide for, time for bestowing real love and affection was limited.

During the first five years of her life, Rachel had less than her fair share of cookies and milk, bedtime stories, and hugs and kisses. Even during those nights when she had bad dreams, most of the time, no one was available to comfort her. She and her mates were punished if they broke the rules, rigid as they were, and they didn't get out much.

"Rachel, you know it's against the rules to sleep late. You've got to be up and dressed by 7:00 each day."

"How about 7:30?" she asked. "Breakfast isn't 'til 8:00."

"The rule is 7:00, Rachel, and it applies to everyone."

She knew the rule, of course, but, like a lot of kids, she ignored it, at least some of the time. She knew, too, that she was supposed to brush her teeth and shower each morning with the same group of seven girls. They shared tubes of Ipana toothpaste, bars of Ivory soap, and bottles of Prell shampoo, and they dressed in clothing donated by charitable organizations and wore their hair cropped short.

Rachel ate bland cafeteria food at Table 4B, seat number three. She went to the orphanage school, did her homework as best she could, and completed her chores. If she had any spare time, she read or watched television for an hour. Finally, at 9:00 every night, she knelt at her bed for prayers and went to sleep. Each day, weekend or not, was essentially the same. What little contact Rachel had with children who lived in neighborhood homes with their parents and siblings was hurtful.

"Hey girlie. How come you don't live in a 'real' house? Did your parents toss you out with the trash? You look like a mouse with that hair and crummy clothes."

No one ever asked her to visit at their homes or invited her to join them in any sort of activity. In fact, Rachel and her mates at the orphanage were essentially outcasts, a surplus population never summoned in.

So sheltered was she that Rachel didn't chew a piece of bubble gum until she was twelve years old. She never rode a bicycle, played Monopoly, skipped rope, or spun a bottle. She learned about birthday parties, sleepovers, hanging out at shopping malls, menstruating, talking on the telephone, going out on dates, kissing boys, eating at restaurants, or having any sort of privacy by reading or watching television.

Rachel matured into a responsible, literate, and lonely young woman. No one took her into their home; indeed, during her childhood and adolescence, she didn't have a single visitor. She had no parents, so, when she reached her teens, she made some up.

Rachel sat at her table in the cafeteria deep in

thought, ignoring her chipped beef on toast. "What are you thinking about?" a handsome young man named Angelo asked.

"A pretend story about my parents."

"Wanna tell it to me? I listen good."

"Sure, if you promise not to laugh."

"Cross my heart; hope to die."

"All right, then. In my fantasy, I'm the love child of a beautiful high school cheerleader and the football player and honor roll guy who lives next door. While doing their solid geometry homework in her family room one night, they get turned on by each others' cylinders and cones, so to speak. A rush of passion overcomes them and they do the deed. In a few months, the cheerleader puts away her pompom, and the football player's poor play gets him demoted to the second string."

"Hey, Rachel, your story is a little sexy, so keep on keepin' on," Angelo said.

"Well, they're young and scared, and there's no way they can take care of a baby, so they confess everything to their parents. The cheerleader moves to the next county to live with her aunt for six months. The football player quits the team and takes a job after school working at a hospital. Right after I'm born, they hand me over to a nurse in the back of a black car. Dad's varsity letter sweater warms me in my cradle."

"Is that it?" Angelo asks.

"No way, the best is coming. Mom and Dad finish high school and go to college. They earn their degrees and decide, with the blessings of their parents, to get married. Mom goes on to earn a Ph.D. at a fine university and pursues a career as a clinical psychologist. She practices group and individual psychotherapy with pregnant teenagers and their families. Dad completes medical school and decides to specialize in reconstructive surgery. Along with maintaining a lucrative private practice, he takes regular trips, at his own expense, to impoverished, third world countries, where he performs cranio-facial surgery upon disfigured orphans."

"Hey, you make pretend real good, an' you made up a fine set of parents," Angelo said.

"Why not, when I make up stuff, they can be whatever I want them to be, and there's more," Rachel said.

"I wanna hear the rest of it, an' I'm hopin' for a happy endin' to it."

"My parents get a lot of awards for their contributions to the field of child welfare. They're appointed co-chairs of a blue ribbon committee to study the quality of medical and psychological services provided for children and adolescents living in orphanages. As part of their research, they happen to visit here at Holy Family Children's Home. They meet a lonely young woman wearing an old and tattered varsity letter sweater."

"Jeez, it's you, ain't it?" Angelo asks.

"Yes," Rachel says, "of course it's me. My parents and I have a good cry and a joyous reunion while a trio of violin, flute, and harpsichord play a particularly poignant rendition of the Ave Maria in the background."

"That's the end, ain't it?"

"Yes, what do you think of my story, Angelo?"

"It's a real winner, Rachel, but I got a coupla questions."

"Go ahead, ask me anything."

"Well, where did you learn all them fancy words? I mean, I'm not even sure I know what a blue ribbon committee is, an' what's 'lucrative' an' a 'third world country?'"

"I guess I've learned a lot of words, because I read a lot. What else, Angelo?"

"Will you let me into your dream, if I let you into mine?"

Chapter 24

Angelo's parents, grandparents, pet terrier, and goldfish died in a fire right after his father flung him out of their third story window. He flipped twice and fell safely into the arms and ample belly of a fireman named Seamus O'Houlihan, It was Angelo's third birthday.

That evening, Seamus said to his wife: "Dearheart, the poor little fella's got no one left; let's adopt him so's he can have a good upbringin'. The good Lord will take a likin' to us for it."

Dearheart was clearly less than enthused with the idea. "Are you crazy? We've already got eight livin' here, plus your mother with the irritable bowel symptom or whatever they call it, and the good Lord hasn't seen fit to like us for it yet, at least that I can see. See this thing attached to my leg? Well, it's my foot, and I'm putting it down."

So it was that Angelo and Rachel came to grow up together at Holy Family Children's Home.

Angelo was bright enough, but he had a difficult time learning to read. Proficiency with phonics eluded him, so when he saw letters of the alphabet, it was hard for him to associate them with sounds. His pace was painfully slow; he lost his place routinely, and, on occasion, he read words in reverse. The mechanics of reading were so difficult for him that by the time he got to the end of a line of print, he had forgotten its meaning.

Angelo's frustration with his failure at reading grew. He avoided situations where he might be required to read, particularly in front of classmates who were quick to criticize. "Dumb dago," they said. He heard it all the time.

When he couldn't escape reading out loud, he struggled through a line or two before slamming the book closed. Sometimes, he threw the book to the floor. Other times, he threw himself to the floor.

Indeed, more than a few times, Angelo's frustration spilled over in the form of temper tantrums, some of them violent. Once, in a rage, the muscles around his eyes twitched and unintelligible sounds gurgled in his throat.

"Don't you dare tear pages from your book," his teacher said.

Between sobs and curse words Angelo said, "I'm gonna do whatever I wanna do. Juss leave me alone."

"Calm down, Angelo; I'm here to help you, if you'll let me."

He did calm down. "I promise not to lose my temper again," he said, and Angelo made good on his promise, until the next time he was asked to read aloud.

In contrast to his poor reading, Angelo's manual dexterity was excellent. From an early age, he was adept at taking things apart and putting them back together. Given his strengths and weaknesses, he barely passed literature and history courses but truly excelled in woodworking, metalworking, and every other shop course offered at school.

On the night that Rachel and Angelo graduated from high school, they had sex in the orphanage chapel. Each was tentative, so inexperienced and insecure at love making that they might just as well have been in separate pews.

"I love you more than anything," Rachel said, words of endearment she remembered reading in a romance novel.

Never terribly loquacious and similarly deficient at outwardly displaying affection, Angelo left it at, "Yeah, me too."

"We're gonna have to leave here soon," Angelo said.

"Yes, I know," Rachel replied. "According to the law, we've got to move out when we're eighteen."

"Do you feel like you're ready for livin' on the outside?" Angelo asked.

"Don't worry. They're not going to make us leave without getting us prepared. There's a place we go first, a 'transition school' they call it, where we'll learn all we need to know about living by ourselves."

"Like what are they gonna teach us?" Angelo asked.

"Things like how to prepare a budget, write checks and balance an account, shop for groceries and clothes, fill out job application forms, pay our taxes, open a savings account, and anything else we need to know."

"It's a good thing," Angelo said. "Fact is, I don't know a lot of that stuff."

"Yes, me too, and I forgot to tell you that while we're there, we get free room and board and a couple hundred dollars a month for spending money."

Rachel ultimately found a job as a receptionist at a health clinic, and Angelo was hired to do auto repairs and pump gas at a service station. He saved enough to buy her an engagement ring. "The rough spot on the top is the diamond," he joked.

The parish priest married them. Rachel wore a plain white dress with shoes to match, and, for the first time in her life, she had her hair done at a beauty salon. Angelo, uncomfortable though he was, looked dashing in his navy blue suit, striped tie, and shiny new shoes. That evening, some old friends from the orphanage and a few new friends from work joined them for a reception and pizza party in a private room at the rear of an Italian restaurant.

After antipasto, Angelo proposed a toast. "We grew up together, an' now Rachel an' me are husband an' wife. She's so beautiful, my bride, an' we love each other a ton. So, here's a toast to us an' all the children we're gonna have. May our family grow an' be healthy."

They moved into a one-bedroom apartment above the beauty salon. It was furnished with a double bed, a kitchen set, and a sofa in the living room. They bought bed sheets and a set of dishes for six, and Rachel bargained for a used television set and toaster oven at the thrift shop on the corner. A new mattress would have been nice, but it would have to wait.

Angelo began classes at a community college three evenings a week. He earned an Associate of Arts Degree in Heating and Air Conditioning and took a job with a company that doubled the salary he was earning at the service station.

His company provided full health care benefits as well, a most welcome perquisite, because Rachel was "with child."

"That means pregnant," Angelo said. "Mamma Mia, get me some overtime."

Chapter 25

"You gotta eat right," Angelo said, "an' no drinkin,' either booze or coffee, neither."

"And how do you know all these things?" Rachel asked.

"I been readin' up; I still ain't that great at it, but I'm gettin' better. I learned some new words, too, fancy ones like you know."

"What might those be?" Rachel asked.

"Wantcha try 'neonate' an' 'postpartum' on for size?"

At a routine prenatal care visit, Rachel had an ultrasound. Before the doctor showed them the picture and talked about the results, he said, "Do you want to know if you've got a boy or girl in there?"

"We've been wondering if you'd ask," Rachel said. "Angelo and I have discussed it and decided we'd like to know in advance."

"OK, from the ultrasound, I can tell that everything is developing normally. Here are his ten little fingers, and this eleventh one isn't a finger."

While Angelo calmed down, Rachel's doctor reemphasized the importance of moderate exercise, and she did her best to comply. She walked around the block every day the weather wasn't too cold or rainy. She enjoyed the exercise, only occasionally being bothered by the neighborhood gangbangers. She came to know them by their colors, red and black, their low slung trousers, their bandanas, and their threatening manner.

"If anyone bothers you, lemme know," Angelo

said.

"They haven't yet," Rachel said. "When I see them coming, I usually cross the street to avoid them."

During her pregnancy, Rachel and Angelo went to birthing classes. What occurred during each stage of fetal development and how to tell when labor began were discussed. So were the stages of delivery and what would be involved should a cesarean delivery be required.

Rachel learned about epidurals and deep breathing exercises for pain management. Also, she was coached regarding the proper techniques for breast-feeding. Angelo learned his role, as well—to encourage and provide emotional support for Rachel. He practiced infant care skills, too, holding, feeding, burping, and changing diapers.

"Hey, Rachel," he said one night on the way home from class, "hows about I do the holdin' and you do the changin'?"

"Not a chance, Angelo. When it's your turn, you clean his bottom, top, and any other part that needs it."

Toward the end of her pregnancy, when she was too uncomfortable to sleep, Rachel imagined what her son would be 25 years in the future. "I see a brilliant scientist doing research or a lawyer defending the rights of poor people," she said.

"Wow, you sure don't aim low," Angelo said.

"I can settle," she went on. "A neurosurgeon removing a child's brain tumor or a legislator on the floor of the senate will be fine, too."

"Y'know, I got my dreams, too," Angelo said. "They ain't as high fallutin' as yours, but still, they're my dreams."

"Tell me."

I see our boy learnin' to catch and throw a ball and swing a bat. I'll teach him to use a hammer an' screwdriver an' power tools. We'll build things together, maybe a tree house or a fort. I'll take him to work with me an' to baseball games an' hikes an' picnics. We'll learn how to swim an' fish together. I'll be a good father."

The baby's birth was difficult, because, unlike his mother, he didn't follow the rules. He presented himself sideways instead of head down, and it took some time before the doctor was able to manipulate him into the correct position. At last, after a long, exhausting delivery, the doctor assured Rachel and Angelo that everything was fine. They had a healthy and robust son whose only blemish was a red, Z-shaped birthmark on his cheek.

Angelo, brimming with pride and a little giddy with relief, suggested naming him "Zorro" for the Z. Rachel, still sore from the delivery, suggested "Mario." She won.

Rachel wanted to breast feed, but Mario wouldn't stay still long enough to complete the task. "He gets real stiff," she said. "Sometimes, he arches his back and spits, like a cat."

She worried that Mario wasn't getting sufficient nourishment, but the doctor reassured her.

"He's gained weight, and he's within the expected range for babies his age," he said. Still, after struggling a few more weeks, Rachel switched to formula feeding.

As an infant, Mario startled very easily, too. He seemed overly responsive to everything around him— the sound of a door closing, the flushing of a toilet, the mobile hanging above his crib, even his parents' faces.

"He's real jittery," Angelo said, "an' he never seems to stop movin'. Rachel says he'll grow out of it, though, an' I hope he does, like real soon."

But, Mario didn't grow out of it. He was irritable

much of the time. Seldom did he relax, and he cried a lot, often for hours. On one of those bad nights, Rachel was nauseous and vomiting from a nasty stomach virus. Weak from fever and dehydration, she couldn't get out of bed.

Angelo was left alone to soothe his son, now crying inconsolably. "I can handle this," Angelo said aloud. "Now's the time to use what I learned."

He sat with Mario and rocked him. He cradled him in his arms and paced around the living room. He changed him, tried to feed him, stroked him, and sang lullabies, but nothing worked; it was five in the morning, and still Mario cried—a piercing, never ending, aggravating wail.

Frustrated and exhausted, Angelo didn't know what to do. His anger swelled and turned to rage. The muscles around his eyes twitched. Some unintelligible sounds gurgled in his throat, and he shook his son. He shook him violently for 30 or 40 seconds. At first, probably out of fear, Mario's crying worsened. Finally, he quieted down and fell asleep.

The next day, Mario told Rachel what had happened. "I'm sorry, Rachel," he said, "but I lost it; I lost my temper an' I shook our baby. He quieted down, so it's prolly all right. Maybe it's all right."

What Angelo had done, in fact, was damage his son's brain. Like all infants, Mario's neck muscles were not yet strong enough to support his head, so shaking him caused it to rotate uncontrollably. The movements, violent as they were, tossed his brain back and forth within his little skull, rupturing blood vessels and nerves and tearing brain tissue. Daddy shook him and when his brain struck the inside of his skull, it bruised and bled.

As Mario grew older, his impulsiveness, his need to move and touch everything he saw, and his inability to focus his attention became even more pronounced. It was difficult to take him out, particularly into the homes of friends, because he was so destructive. He broke ashtrays, scratched tables, and scribbled on walls, and if there were other children present, there was bound to be a conflict.

Chapter 26

Rachel spoke to Mario every time she changed and fed him, and she encouraged Angelo to do the same. "Your speech is so much better now, Angelo," she said. "Just speak slowly and in complete sentences, and it will be good."

"Let's read to him, too," Angelo said. "I know I can handle those baby books. For sure I can handle 'em."

But, Mario didn't relax when they read to him, nor was he able to focus his attention. "It seems like the story an' the pitchers don't interest him any more than the tickin' of the clock or the noise a truck makes when it passes by," Angelo said.

"I've noticed the same thing," Rachel said. "I finally took my earrings off, and it helped for a while, but now he plays with the buttons on my blouse. Everything seems to distract him the same, so he doesn't really pay attention to anything."

In the end, Mario was slow to develop speech and language. He understood what Rachel and Angelo said to him, but he didn't speak himself. In fact, on the occasion of his third birthday, Mario remained effectively mute and relied primarily on pointing, gesturing, and grunting to make his needs known.

At the doctor's, Rachel asked, "Should we ignore him when he points and gestures? Maybe if we do, it will encourage him to speak."

"No, keep responding as you have been. I know he hears you, so maintain the same routine and be patient. Sometimes it takes boys a little longer to mature and get going," the doctor said.

At last, Mario did get going. He began by imitating some of the words he heard around him. First, he repeated them much like a parrot, mindlessly, over and over, not yet aware that words were used to convey a message. Finally, well after his fourth birthday, he began using spoken language meaningfully, first one word at a time and then in simple two and three word sentences.

Mario's movement skills and coordination didn't lag as much as his language development. He crawled and walked a little late, and he was somewhat clumsy, at least with respect to gross motor skills. He fell a lot; he knocked things over, and throwing and catching a ball were difficult. Buttoning his shirts and tying his shoestrings, things than required fine motor skills were easier. So were hammering nails, putting puzzles together, and building things with an erector set. Like everyone else, Mario had his strengths and weaknesses.

On a Sunday afternoon, Angelo took Mario to the local supermarket. So many boxes, cans, and jars, in so many colors, textures, and sizes, along with so many people making so much noise, overwhelmed Mario. Unable to escape what, for him, had to be no less than an assault on his senses, his strategy was to respond to everything indiscriminately.

Like a dervish, he ran up and down the aisles shrieking and, at the same time, strewing cans of soup, Jell-O, and Hamburger Helper in his wake. He moved so fast that Angelo lost him for a minute. In a loud voice, he asked, "Anyone seen a little boy alone?"

"Yeah, there's one in produce," a gray haired lady said. "Last I saw he was squeezing the tomatoes, sticking asparagus in his ears, and licking apples."

Angelo finally found him in the dairy department

just as Mario had picked up a carton of eggs. "Put that down," he said.

Mario said, "Me bad boy." Over and over.

Back home, Angelo related what had happened at the grocery store. Rachel's eyes narrowed and she said, "Try not to be angry with him. I don't think he can help it."

She was correct, of course. Mario couldn't help it; he couldn't control his behavior, because his brain was damaged.

Chapter 27

Mario's impulsivity, hyperactivity, and inattentiveness exhausted Rachel and Angelo.

They had no respite, no escape, for just as their son was hard to manage during the day, so too was he when it was time for bed. He didn't fall asleep easily, and when he did, he slept fitfully. "If I get up in the middle of the night to go to the bathroom, I'm afraid to flush," Angelo said, "because I sure don't wanna wake him."

"I've noticed," Rachel said.

They never got used to Mario's night terrors, even after dozens of episodes. "Jeez," Angelo said, the first time it happened. "I ain't never seen nothin' like this. What are we s'posed to do?"

"Not much we can do, I don't think. I'll call the doctor and see what he suggests," Rachel said.

They usually happened in the evening, shortly after Mario had finally fallen asleep. He would sit straight up in his bed, erect and rigid, with an expression of fear and panic on his face. Although his eyes were wide open, he wasn't awake. His breathing was rapid and shallow, and he perspired profusely. Then, he would let loose with a series of frightful screams that lasted anywhere from five to twenty minutes.

"There is no use in trying to wake him," the doctor said. "Just comfort him as best you can and wait until he quiets down."

Those few times that Mario woke up on his own, he was confused, impossible to console, and he didn't even recognize his parents. Neither could he remember the content of his dreams. But, as difficult and disturbing as these behaviors were, Mario did things that were even worse—things that were truly pathological.

A neighbor girl's pet hamster was doing typical hamster stuff. Harvey, as the little girl called him, ran, more or less vigorously, on his wheel for a time. Then, he rummaged among some seeds and nuts to sate his appetite. Finally, he had a drink of water and rested, licking his paws.

"I want see close," Mario said.

"You can open the cage, if you want."

"I open cage and touch tail," Mario said.

"Be careful with him," the little girl said.

"Him look like rat, and him smell bad, too."

"He's a hamster, silly. Don't you know what a hamster is?"

"Yeah, him a dirty rat." Mario held him in his left hand, by the tail, and swung him back and forth. Then, with his right hand, he wrung Harvey's neck. The little girl screamed in horror as Mario dropped her dead pet, kicked it across the floor, and laughed hysterically. A predator had slain its prey.

Mario saw no connection between his acts and their consequences. It seemed as if he had no capacity to feel shame, guilt, or remorse. He had no conscience and no sense of compassion; thus, he was unable to empathize. When others felt pain, he felt nothing, or, even worse, he was amused.

A damaged brain increases the likelihood of damaged behavior, and it doesn't seem to matter whether the damage results from a high fever, a traumatic blow to the head, swallowing poison, or Daddy shaking you when you are an infant.

Chapter 28

Teachers, principals, guidance counselors, and other professionals who work at schools call it "special education." To cynics, however, it is the "school dump," a garbage heap where very little is special and hardly anyone gets an education.

Students who wind up in special education are actually called "exceptional children," a glaring euphemism for "bad kids." They are so bad, their behavior so deviant, so intolerable, that they are banished from the educational mainstream so they may coexist with other children who are similarly exceptional.

Rachel dreaded answering the phone on weekdays between nine and four. The assistant principal called several times a week, certainly not to inform her that Mario had been nominated for the "Student of the Month Award," but instead to deliver a litany of her son's most recent transgressions, both academic and behavioral. The phone rang a little after nine.

"We need you and your husband to join us at a multidisciplinary staff conference," Madame assistant principal said.

"Could you please tell me what it is, this multidiscipline thing?" Rachel asked.

"It's a meeting; we would like to sit down with you and your husband and discuss how we can help Mario at school."

She didn't tell Rachel, but the real reason for the meeting was to chronicle and document Mario's manifold deficiencies and initiate banishment proceedings.

Rachel arrived ten minutes early. *Why do people who work at schools, principals and teachers and the rest, always use such fancy words. If it's a meeting they want to have, why not just call it that instead of making up big words that regular people don't understand anyway?*

There were nine chairs in the conference room. Seven were filled with the principal, assistant principal, guidance counselor, school psychologist, social worker, Mario's first grade teacher, and a special education teacher. Clearly outnumbered, and without an advocate, Rachel sat in the eighth chair.

"Is Mario's father coming?" the assistant principal asked.

"He's my husband, and he couldn't take another day off work."

"OK then, let us call the meeting to order." For the better part of an hour, the learned professionals took turns describing Mario.

With phony erudition and authentic rudeness, they spouted terms like "socially maladjusted," "antisocial personality disorder," "attention deficit hyperactivity disorder," and "specific developmental dyslexia."

Rachel sat quietly, occasionally smoothing her hair. *Most of this is like a foreign language, not English.*

The school psychologist actually said, in stentorian tones no less, "Mario's cumulative and combined academic and social deficiencies are manifest primarily as a result of organic factors with secondary contributions resulting from concomitant emotional overlay."

Say what, you pompous prick?

Seldom did the learned professionals bother to look at Rachel while they puked their jargon, not that it mattered, since her eyes were averted toward the floor anyway. She never stopped thinking, though. *I am the most important person in this room. I know my son better than anyone here, and yet nobody bothers to talk with me in a way I can understand. I might as well not even be here, because I am no more important to them than Angelo's empty chair. They have bad manners.*

Finally, the last person finished her speech. No one had the courtesy to ask Rachel if she had any questions or needed anything explained. Clearly, they were in a hurry, because another mother was already waiting in the hall, soon to be served her own helping of gobbledegook.

"Let us vote," the assistant principal said.

The learned professionals voted to remove Mario from his first grade room and place him in a special education classroom for children with learning and behavior disorders. None of those present bothered to tell Rachel that no child could be placed in a special education program without the informed consent of a parent. They simply slapped the papers in front of her and pointed to where she should sign.

"It's just perfect for Mario," the assistant principal said, a little too cheerfully. "Only seven other children are in the class, and Ms. Conroy here is a specialist who knows precisely how to help him, and just as soon as Mario improves, he'll go right back to his regular class."

Such a triumphant return never happened, because much like a prison, it is a lot easier to get into special education than it is to get out. Life sentences without parole seems to be the rule.

So it was that Mario languished in his special education class. Parents were allowed to visit their children in special education, and one year Rachel went.

"What's it like?" Angelo asked that evening.

"I'm not sure you want to know," Rachel said.

"How bad can it be? There's only seven kids in there, you said."

"Yes, but two of them don't speak at all," Rachel said. "One goes back and forth between rubbing saliva on his face and belching. One sat quietly at his desk and rocked, once in a while saying 'Ah ooh gah' like an old time car horn. Another pretended he was a chicken; another crapped in his pants, and the last one, the only one who seemed OK, sat next to Mario. Both of them just sat there, looking around in amazement at their classmates, because, just like me, they've never seen anyone like them."

"Jeez, was anyone doin' any schoolwork?" Angelo asked.

"Mario did some coloring," Rachel said. "I hung it on the fridge."

Mario's special place of learning was a windowless room that had originally been used to store teaching supplies, outdated textbooks, and scrap wood. It was in the basement of the school, between the boiler room and the wood shop; thus, a steady stream of high decibel noise prevailed. Indeed, a rather constant din bombarded Mario and his classmates, the same children who the learned professionals had labeled "attention deficit disorder," and who might, therefore, have benefitted from a little peace and quiet.

So effectively were Mario and his band of deviates shunned that they had their own gym class, their own time for recess, and their own lunch period. They were allowed to watch the Christmas and Spring assemblies but only from the back of the auditorium with both school security guards hovering nearby.

The same security guards marched the boys back to their special classroom or "Horror Hall," as it came to be known by the teachers and staff. Their march began five minutes before the assemblies ended in order to eliminate any chance that the boys might rub shoulders with the rest of the kids. One might have assumed they were carriers of virulent and deadly communicable diseases.

Year after year, Mario and his classmates, isolated as they were from children whose behavior was acceptable, had only each other's deviance to imitate. All that Mario heard was other kids calling him a freak, dummy, or weirdo and all he saw was deviant behavior. Even Angelo, certainly not an educational psychologist, noticed it.

"How is our boy gonna learn to behave right, when all he sees is kids who don't ?" he asked.

"I'm not sure anyone at his school really cares," Rachel said. "Or, if they do, they surely don't know what to do for him."

"Tell me what you mean."

"Just take a good, hard look at Mario," she said. "He still can't pay attention; he still can't read; he's still as hyper as ever; and he still doesn't care about other people. Can we honestly say he's any better now than when they put him in special years ago?"

The reality was that year after year Mario's dislike for school and everything associated with it increased, and given the glut of negative reinforcement, he grew to dislike himself, too.

Once a year, as the school year drew to a close, the assistant principal convened another meeting. An "annual review," she called this one. "We must meet to discuss Mario's progress this year, and make recommendations for next year," she said.

By the third such meeting, Rachel was quite able to anticipate exactly what she would hear: "You must get Mario private tutoring, three times a week, outside of school," the special education teacher would say.

"I recommend that you find a physician to write a prescription for medication that will help Mario relax and focus his attention," the school psychologist would say.

"You need family therapy to help everyone develop 'coping mechanisms,'" the social worker would say.

While everyone spoke in turn, the assistant principal would sneak peeks at her watch.

When Rachel asked who would pay to implement such recommendations, she got silence and paper shuffling in return. In fact, these dedicated professionals in charge of educating children with special needs inside the walls of Mario's school, could only recommend the services of other professionals, at considerable parental expense, outside the walls of Mario's school.

On the walk home, Rachel was alone with her thoughts. *For our son Mario, his school has been a failure. He doesn't have any friends there. They keep him away from the other kids and pass him along until he's old enough to leave. Then, they won't have to be bothered with him anymore, because he'll be someone else's problem.*

However futile it was, Mario's special education did accomplish something. It made him a willing recruit for the neighborhood gangs. They offered him prestige, recognition, and acceptance—powerful enticements he had never before encountered. At last, here was his chance to get some respect from his peers, or, at least a chance to get even.

Chapter 29

Three boys were spray-painting graffiti on the rear wall of a neighborhood business, in this instance, a dry cleaning establishment. They wore gang colors—red baseball caps skewed to the left, Raider jackets with the team logo prominently displayed, and red and black bandanas tied loosely around their biceps. Low slung, baggy jeans with the right pant leg rolled to mid calf, and necklaces made of black and red beads rounded out their ensembles.

Graffiti is not always the work of gangsters. If the message is easy to read and consists of rounded, "bubble" shaped letters, applied with more than one color of paint, chances are the work is simply that of a neighborhood artist looking for a place to display his work. This type of uncommissioned artistic expression qualifies as vandalism, but it is not gang related.

If, however, the letters are angular, reminiscent of stick figures, and only one color is used, the graffiti was probably produced by gangsters. This probability increases when the work reflects religious or satanic references and is difficult to interpret without knowing the code.

For gangsters, graffiti is the "newspaper of the street," an oversized tabloid used to transmit cryptic messages. The message may be a statement marking the gang's home territory, their turf, as it were. A "No Trespassing" sign would be equivalent. Other messages represent threats to rival gangs: "Death to the Uptown Warlords," for example.

Mario approached the three boys, but they weren't concerned. "He's just a little neighborhood punk lookin' to suck up," one said.

"Yeah, be easy, Dawg," another said. "He's lame."

They stopped their art project only when Mario flashed a sign, a signal he made with his fingers and hands. Like graffiiti, gangsters use these signals to advertise their affiliation with a particular gang or to challenge members of rival gangs they happen to encounter.

Mario had been way out of line. Eleven-year-old gangster "wannabes" don't flash gang signs until they prove their mettle. Even the privilege of doing scut work for the gang, menial tasks like serving as lookouts, running errands, or hiding guns and drugs, would not be granted until he demonstrated his worthiness. A show of toughness and ruthlessness was the prerequisite.

"You wanna jump in with us, you show up right here tomorrow, 'bout one in the afternoon," one of the boys said.

'I'll be here at zackly one o'clock sharp," Mario said. "An' hey, when can I get inked up?"

"The tattoo only comes if we let you jump in."

As instructed, Mario reported to the alley behind the dry cleaners the next afternoon. One of the boys gripped a cat by the scruff of its neck. "Pop it," he said.

"You mean, like kill it?" Mario asked.

"Any way you like."

Without hesitating, Mario grabbed the cat by the tail, swung it around his head like a lariat, and smashed it, head first, into a brick wall. Fluffy stopped screaming at the precise instant her cranium exploded. Jagged pieces of her skull, mixed with chunks of gray matter, whiskers, and blood, stuck to the bricks. Flies swarmed as the gangsters gushed words of praise. "You're a right guy," they said, patting him on the back and punching him, with affection, on his shoulder.

In just a few days, Mario made dozens of new friends who taught him the correct way to make their hand signs. They showed him where the guns and drugs were hidden, and they demonstrated how to inject and smoke methamphetamine. He had become a BG, a baby gangster, who, with sufficient seasoning and unflinching loyalty, might move through the ranks and ultimately attain the elevated status of a hard-core gangster. Then, at last, he would have respect. Then, even though he still couldn't read, write a letter, or make change for a dollar, he would be someone to be reckoned with.

At home, Mario was happy. Rachel sensed his mood, and she was happy, too. She didn't question him; instead, she reveled in the levity of the moment and went about preparing dinner. *Maybe something good finally happened at school. Maybe he at least got through a day without causing any trouble.*

The next day her mood darkened when she saw the fake tattoos Mario had inked on his forearms. Equally apparent was the gang graffiti he had doodled on the pages of his three-ring notebook he was supposed to use for recording and completing his written assignments. Its pages were dog-eared and dirty, and except for the graffiti, they were blank.

"Why are you smiling?" Rachel asked.

"You shoulda seen it when I whacked that stinkin' cat, Ma. First she was screamin' her head off, then I popped her, and then there was nothin' but blood an' brains all over the freakin' place. You shoulda seen it, Ma; I'm tellin' you, we laughed our butts off."

Later, Rachel related their conversation to Angelo. "Our son did another cruel thing, a really cruel thing," she said. "It's like a part of him is missing, like there's a hole in his soul."

Angelo turned over in the bed but said nothing. *I lost it. I shook our child. Maybe my soul was leakin', too.*

Chapter 30

"How long has Mario been in special?" Angelo asked.

"It's coming up on seven years, now," Rachel said.

"Seems to me he's had a whole bunch of teachers."

"Yes, the one he has now makes number six."

"I gotta figure they didn't know what they were gettin' into."

"Well, they should have," Rachel said. "I'm told they all had Master's degrees from fine universities, and they all were interns for a year before they got here. But, four of them bailed on Mario and his classmates after a year and one of them lasted only two weeks. One of the moms said the last one vomited in the staff bathroom every day before school and finally took a job at a private girls' school in the suburbs."

"Jeez," Angelo said. "If this was a war, the kids won."

It's likely that the high rate of teacher attrition contributed to the dismal levels of academic achievement attained by Mario and his classmates. Or, it's possible that the unfortunate location of the classroom squelched learning. Perhaps, a limited school budget and the lack of modern teaching materials and equipment played a roll, as well, and certainly, factors the students brought to school with them, such things as brain damage, poor nutrition, chemical imbalances, the effects of physical and sexual abuse earlier in their lives, or limited exposure to English at home were operating to retard achievement in school.

Indeed, it's probable that all these factors, in various combinations, made important contributions to his failure, but what was known with absolute certainty is that at the end of eighth grade, Mario remained functionally illiterate. He still couldn't read the newspaper, order from a menu, or follow a series of written directions. He couldn't take public transportation or name three states other than his own. He had no idea what an opera was; he didn't know how far it was from New York to California, and he couldn't name the governor of his state or the mayor of his city. He couldn't name the planets, and he didn't know where north was on a map.

"Mario," his teacher said, "tell us what is important about the years 1492 and 1776."

"I don't think I was even borned yet, so why you askin' me 'bout that stuff?"

"Those are important dates from our history, and you should know why," teacher said.

"Well, I don't know 'em, but I could strip your car in 'bout twenty minutes," Mario said.

Basic multiplication and division facts were beyond him. His ability to tell time remained shaky, and using a ruler or yardstick was hit or miss. But, he was fourteen years old, so it was time for graduation from elementary school. Much like hide and seek, it was, "ready or not; here I come." Reluctantly, Mario dressed for the graduation ceremony and marched down the aisle, out of step with his partner, another weirdo and freak from Horror Hall. He walked onto the stage when the assistant principal called his name.

"I know what she's thinking," Rachel whispered, poking Angelo in the ribs.

"Whassat?"

"She's grateful that Mario and his mother won't be around to bother her next year."

At home, Mario stripped the blue and yellow ribbons from his diploma and spread it flat on his bed. "Do you want me to get a frame for it? We could hang it over your bed," Rachel said.

"For what?" Mario asked. "I can't read none of these words on here, so what's the use? I got a place for it right here in this dresser, under my spare blanket."

Sadly, the day he graduated from eighth grade, a significant event for most young people, was no different for Mario than any other day in his life. Except, he had to dress up.

To celebrate his graduation, the family went to an Italian restaurant for dinner. Mario unwrapped his presents, a lightweight shirt and a pair of sneakers. He liked his gifts, as much as he liked the prospect of another summer without school. He spent most of it at the movies, the beach, running errands for the gang, guarding their cache of weapons and drugs, and pulling the wings off flies.

Compared to elementary school, senior high school is an impersonal place with higher expectations for students and more demanding challenges. Teachers responsible for 150 students a day no longer teach children; instead, they teach their academic specialties.

"Here, in high school, we expect you to be able to work independently," the principal said. "You're supposed to have mastered your basic math and writing skills by now and be able to use them to complete your assignments."

Most students entering ninth grade were able to do what the principal expected of them. But for those like Mario, those whose potential for learning had been diminished due to brain damage and who entered high school functioning at the second grade level, the principal's goals were totally unrealistic. Indeed, expecting Mario to progress through high school subject matter in the same amount of time as his peers was out of the question.

Given Mario's academic and behavioral shortcomings, he failed all of his major subjects the first semester in high school. The next semester he failed them again. Finally, in the middle of a third dismal go at it, he stopped going to high school. During his undistinguished tenure, he had amassed a total of two credits, one in music and one in physical education. The National Honor Society would not be seeking him out.

Outside of school, however, Mario was a "quick study," indeed, an honor student. He attained fluency in "gangspeak" with a proficiency far beyond what he had shown for standard English. He learned to respond brilliantly, with appropriate force, to rivals foolish enough to disrespect or challenge him. He learned not to "rat" on his mates and to "juice" (respect) senior gang members. He became a master at keeping their secrets, running their errands, and terrorizing the community.

Chapter 31

Hard core gang members carry heavy "bread." They wear expensive "threads," drive souped up "iron," adorn their bodies with "brands," and like slick looking "foxes" on their arms. Mario wanted all of that, and he grew impatient. "I been a Baby Gangster long enough," he said. "I been good, I been loyal, and I done whatever they asked. It's time for me to move up."

"Jumping in" is the street gang's formal process of initiation, a ritual that culls apprentices whose motivation to join the gang is merely casual from those who sincerely want in. Only those who are willing to withstand abuse, humiliation, and pain and are not averse to committing criminal acts are deemed sufficiently sincere to be initiated.

The actual jumping in ritual requires that two to eight older gang members surround the would-be gangster, the initiate, and beat him for thirty seconds to a couple of minutes. Sometimes, the beating is timed, and it is always administered in a public place where there are plenty of witnesses, usually younger siblings and girlfriends of the older gang members. Little kids are present so they will begin to absorb this bizarre form of socialization and get started on their way toward a life of gang activity.

The severity of the beating varies. When crowd reaction is particularly raucous and the beaters are drunk or high on drugs, the beating will be worse. If the initiate takes his licks with nary a whimper or complaint, he's welcomed in.

124

Raphael, Mario's partner and mentor, said, "You're gettin' reborn tonight."

"Whatcha mean?" Mario asked.

"Think of it like a baptism. The beatin' is like a pretend murder, an' after, you get reborn as one of us. What I'm sayin' is that tonight, you're bein' born into a new family."

In gangs that have female members, getting "sexed in" is a cornerstone of the jumping in process. "Gangsta girls" either consent to sex with a number of gang members or they endure multiple rapes.

Fortified by alcohol and dope, and surely without concern for anything resembling tender, loving foreplay, the gangsters put their none-too-secure machismo on display. Only afterward are their girlfriends, now more or less qualified lust receptacles, granted membership in the gang. "Queens," they're called, and they always wear tight jeans and revealing blouses. Often, they wear overly large hoop earrings. Fake nails are very popular, as well as gold rings on every finger.

For Mario, the jumping in process required two sessions. First, he submitted to a savage beating. They punched him with their fists, and when he fell, they kicked him with their boots. They flogged him with their belts, and when he fell, they clubbed him with their sticks. They targeted his chest, legs, back, stomach, and groin, places where the bruises wouldn't be too obvious. Tough and motivated as he was, Mario took it all.

"Is that all ya got?" he screamed. Then he pulled himself to his feet, spit some blood and snot, and accepted hearty congratulations.

In a couple weeks, Mario had healed sufficiently to complete his initiation requirements. During his hiatus, he planned his "mission," an illegal activity sufficiently blatant and risky to catch the attention and warrant the admiration of his mates. It was a grand larceny he pulled off.

"What's your mission?" Raphael asked.

"I got my eyes on some iron, a silver Buick I'm gonna swipe. I prolly could hot wire it, but I been casin' it, an' the brother leaves his keys in it a lot."

Mario changed the license plates and ground down the serial numbers. He touched up the silver paint job, barely covering the scratches and rust spots. Now, he had his own iron, and he showed it off. His mates approved and showed their respect. Life was good.

He was promoted to associate gangster. He got his forearm tattooed with a gaudy, multicolored, six-pointed star signifying affiliation with his gang. Now, he was but one step removed from hard-core status, his most coveted goal. BS, MS, Ph.D.

To attain such lofty status, Mario would have to "bust a cap," that is, shoot a rival gang member brazen or foolish enough to stray beyond the boundaries of his home turf. Or, if his rival happened to be the cautious type, someone who restricted play to his home field, so to speak, Mario could venture forth and bust him wherever he pleased.

"My iron's been hard to start," Mario said.

"Yeah, an' I noticed the tranny slips in first and second, too," Raphael said.

"Yeah, but it's still good enough, leas' for cruisin' our turf on weekends." Raphael, flush from a sale of heroin, tied a band around his pony tail and graciously coughed up ten dollars for gas. "How we gonna know 'em?" Mario asked. "I mean, everyone with a slanty baseball cap an' low slung jeans that's wearin' a bandana ain't always no gangbanger."

"Yeah, onliest way to know for sure is if they're flashin' signs. See a dude flashin' signs, an' you know he's in a crew. Simple as that."

Raphael gestured toward two guys strolling down

the sidewalk flashing hand signs. Mario pulled the Buick to the curb, kept pace for a few yards, and watched them. Their signs were like nothing he had ever seen; thus, he naturally assumed they were rivals. He pulled a pistol from his belt and shot one of the boys in the back.

The Buick discharged blue smoke, and the tires squealed as Mario accelerated. A desperate high-pitched scream reminded him of the sound of an alley cat in distress.

Chapter 32

Hard-core status in the gang brought immediate benefits. At last, Mario had money in his jeans, more than he could possibly earn on any type of job, unqualified as he was. He was illiterate; he had no vocational skills; his social skills were practically nonexistent, and yet his cut of the drug money flowing into the gang's coffers every week was often twice as much as his father's take home pay.

"Hey, Raphael; I'm holdin' heavy bread, an' I need some stuff. Wanna come with."

"Whadya lookin' for?"

"Lotsa stuff. A stereo, some strobe lights, an' one of them big screen TVs, for starters. I wanna fix up my crib."

"You could use some new threads, too. Most times you're wearin' rags'."

"Yeah, I know. I'm gonna get me a coupla warm up suits, a coupla pairs of sneakers, an' some kicks with metal toes like you got."

"Yeah, these work nice durin' jump ins."

"I noticed." Mario bought all that, plus a digital wrist watch, three silk shirts, and a water pipe.

"What's it for?" Rachel asked.

"It cools the smoke from my reefer and cleans out the bad stuff so I won't get no cancer in my lungs."

Angelo, quite aware of the source of the money, would have none of it. He offered a firm ultimatum, "Take it all back; don't take no more drug money, and quit the gang."

"An' if I don't?"

"Then get the hell out of my house."

In the middle of the night, Mario unplugged the electronics and emptied his closet. He moved his possessions to the street where he and Raphael loaded the Buick. Rachel heard him leaving but did nothing; she knew any attempt to stop him would be futile. Their son was almost 17 years old, and he was lost. He was going away to live with his new family.

Lost too, was any semblance of the splendid hopes and dreams she'd had seventeen years earlier. In place of the research scientist, attorney for the indigent, pediatric brain surgeon, architect, or government leader she had envisioned, her fetus had grown up to be a gangster. He was flawed, broken, so inadequate she feared for his survival.

Mario moved into a house owned by three senior gang members who kept a room in the basement, a haven of sorts, for younger gangsters who would otherwise be homeless. Though spacious enough and equipped with a bathroom, the landlords had little concern for routine maintenance, clean sheets, or insect survival rates.

He slept late, hung around the neighborhood, ate junk food whenever he felt hungry, and developed a taste for cheap wine. The gang's stockpile of mind-altering substances included methamphetamine. Soon, it was Mario's drug of choice despite some nasty side effects.

I wish I could stop shakin'. My pillow is wet from sweat, an' there's this poundin' in my ears, my pulse, muss be. Stars with six points are floatin' through the air above me. Them cracks on the ceiling spell Harvey, I think. Bugs are crawling all over my nuts an' my butt, an' I'm bleedin' from scratchin' at 'em. I don't know the last time I slept or had anythin' to eat.

Jeez, there's a pack of hamsters walkin' around my bed. Where the hell did they come from? They're scary as hell, not like the neighbor girl's. Two got black and white stripes, and two got different color spots. The big one, muss be the leader of the pack, I figure, keeps changin' back an' forth from purple to orange. How does he do that? Now they're croakin' chatterin, and clickin'. Yellow spit's comin' out of their mouths an' burnin' holes in my mattress. They're circlin' me an' puttin' their filthy paws on my bed. They're smellin' me, too, prolly 'cause I stink so bad. They got them funny tongues with forks in 'em that they keep stickin' in and out of their mouths. They got bad teeth, an' they smell like old puke. Sweet Jesus, four of 'em are on me, each holdin' down my arms an' legs. The big one's on my chest with them bloody color eyes stickin' out of his head. I open my mouth to scream, an' he sticks a paw into my throat and pulls out a half rotten alley cat. I thought I popped it, but he's snarlin' and lickin' the skin off my cheeks.

Mario hadn't known that hallucinations, both visual and auditory, were one of the effects of methamphetamine overdose. Neither did he know that his drug of choice stimulated the production of dopamine and other neurotransmitters in his brain and that their excess could lead to impairment of his already diminished capacity to learn, remember and reason.

He didn't know that when he used, his body temperature and blood pressure would rise to dangerous levels. Nor, did he know that, beyond hallucinations, an overdose could lead to convulsions, repetitive motor activity, a stroke, kidney failure, a breakdown of his circulatory system, coma, and psychotic symptoms that might last for months.

In fact, none of these consequences mattered to Mario, because smoking, snorting, and injecting methamphetamine made him feel good. The word "euphoria" wasn't in his vocabulary, but it is what he experienced. He felt confident, powerful, focused and energetic. Like Superman, he could leap tall buildings with a single bound and stop speeding locomotives. In fact, there was nothing he couldn't do. Still uncomfortable in most social situations, a drug that made him feel like the "life of the party" was very seductive. So, it wasn't long before he was addicted.

Mario's highs, some of which lasted half a day, were always followed by lows.

"Crashing" from methamphetamine left him without energy and little motivation to keep himself clean or otherwise engaged in useful activities. He found comfort in repeating meaningless tasks, so he built houses out of playing cards. His record was a five-story house.

Without his fix, Mario was depressed, fearful, and he slept a lot. He awoke to nausea and tremors. Fantasies of homicide and suicide dominated his thinking. When he snorted and smoked again, it turned out that he needed more and more methamphetamine to get high. Five hundred milligrams a day is what it took, and the quantity grew larger every week.

Chapter 33

Some nights Mario played billiards at a local pool hall or went bowling. When he stayed in and tired of playing cards, he alternated between watching television, looking at the pictures in Playboy magazines, and devising new methods for capturing and torturing cockroaches. "I like to cut their legs off an' burn out their eyes," he said. "On a quiet night, I swear you can hear 'em scream."

He was a skilled shoplifter and purse-snatcher and better than most at rolling drunks, but fighting with rival gangsters, especially when he was high, was his real gift. Without apparent concern for personal harm, he waded in and attacked with a ferocity that was fearsome, even to seasoned veterans of dozens of brutal gang fights.

Once, after bludgeoning a boy unconscious, he sat on his chest and carved out his left eyeball with a switchblade. Upon completing the excision, he stood, pounded his chest, and roared like a beast. On another occasion, he amputated a rival's thumb, attached it to a shoelace, and wore it as a necklace. To amuse his mates, he manicured the nail with a file and kept it polished with red paint. Such behavior tends to create legends in no time at all.

Committing petty crimes was Mario's hobby, but his vocation was drug dealing. He was like a pharmaceutical supply house distributing a variety of product. "Rollin' good," was the street term for drug pushing. To stimulate sales, he made deliveries, "house calls," he called them, to addicts who were homebound. Success at these pursuits further enhanced his "rep" on the street, and within a few months, the only members of his gang who had higher status were those who had served time in prison.

Mario lingered in front of an electronics store deciding whether to purchase or steal a miniature radio and tape recorder. Distracted by a reflection in the window, he turned and saw his parents.

"Come home for supper; I'll make sausage and peppers," Rachel said. "I've got a chocolate layer cake and ice cream for dessert, and we can talk."

Mario sneered, removed a wad of bills from his pocket, and peeled off two twenties. To his father he said, "Take your wife out to a nice place for dinner and a coupla drinks on me."

Angelo's eye muscles twitched and sounds gurgled in his throat. He took the bills, tore them into pieces, and threw them at his son's face. Then, he grabbed him by the shoulders and shook him violently for 30 or 40 seconds. All the while, Mario did nothing except force himself to smile, thus baring a mouthful of brown teeth rotting from the battery acid, drain cleaner, and antifreeze he used to increase the strength of his methamphetamine.

Chapter 34

Mario and Raphael demonstrated their usual ineptitude at Friday night bowling and retreated to a booth in the lounge for their pizza and beer. To a couple of nice looking girls, Raphael said, "Hey, youse wanna join us over here?"

"Why don't *'youse'* consider getting lost?" the blond one answered.

Seth wondered what they would do if a couple of girls were actually desperate enough to accept their offer. Showering would be a good idea.

Seth looked toward the girls, now laughing and engaged in lively conversation with two young men, clean-cut, college types. He felt a yearning, not a sexual one, but rather a simple desire to be in the company of a girl again.

Mario jumped from his seat waving his arms frantically. He clutched at his neck, stomped his feet, and stuck his fingers into his mouth. Food had lodged in his throat; his airway was blocked, and he was suffocating.

A few onlookers fled the scene, frightened or unwilling to get involved. Raphael flitted about and screamed for help. When none came, he tried slapping Mario on the back, to no avail. The manager of the concession stand grabbed a telephone and called for an ambulance. Mario crumbled to the floor, dribbling saliva from his mouth and clutching at his throat. His face and fingertips turned blue, and his eyes bulged from their sockets.

Seth wheeled over and didn't hesitate. His unusual upper body strength made it easy for him to lift Mario from the floor. He sat him on his lap, head facing away, and locked his arms around his waist, just above his navel. He squeezed twice with quick, upward thrusts, and a morsel of mozzarella wrapped around a couple chunks of half-chewed Italian sausage popped out.

Mario breathed easier, and his color returned to normal. Seth lifted him from his lap and deposited him, none too gently, onto the floor. A team of three paramedics burst into the bowling alley and gave Mario additional aid. In the midst of the bustle and confusion, Seth and Jacob left.

Raphael ran after them, but by the time he reached the parking lot, they were speeding away. He couldn't identify the make of the car; all he saw was a Gallaudet University sticker affixed to the rear bumper.

Back in the car, Jacob asked, "Why didn't you just let him die?"

"It would have been too easy." Seth replied. "He hasn't suffered enough."

"Well, exactly what is it you're planning to do to him?"

Seth's reply was so malevolent, he frightened Jacob. "I'm going to torture and cripple him. Exactly what I'm planning to do is torture and cripple him."

Part III

Sam and Miriam

Prologue

Miriam delights in reminding me what a handful I was from the moment I was born. Apparently, I made a grand entrance, jaundiced, with a couple of black eyes, a mop of spiky hair, and sucking my entire fist. A nurse washed off all that white stuff, and I reached out to my mother. That, in itself, wasn't so unusual, but I'm told I reached out to everyone. Doctors, nurses, orderlies, and cleaning ladies—I didn't discriminate. In addition to my deafness, it seems like I inherited genes for boldness and extroversion. To this day not too much scares old Sarah. That's why I love skydiving and men, not necessarily in that order.

As I matured past infancy and entered "toddlerhood," stubbornness and creativity kicked in. On play dates, I got bored very quickly with the usual Ring Around the Rosy, Hide and Seek, and Duck, Duck, Goose. In their place, I made up my own games like "See How Far the Toilet Paper Stretches." My little friends loved it along with "Eat the Peanut Butter from Your Navel." Like they say, don't knock it 'til you've tried it.

I always went to special schools for the deaf. Mom knew a ton about them, because she has a brother who is deaf. She watched how well he did; he's a teacher now, and she insisted I get my education with other deaf kids while being taught by deaf teachers. She, and everyone else in the immediate family, learned to sign when Uncle Nick was born, so I learned ASL about as well as Deaf of Deaf.

School was an interesting time. I never had trouble with the work, but I didn't do so well conforming. Everyone drew their birds the same way, because they learned what birds looked like from coloring books. Well, I didn't like staying between the lines, and if I preferred four legged birds, what was so terrible, I ask? And, while I'm asking, what was so terrible about eating paste? It's not like it has artificial coloring or preservatives or other neurotoxins you find in most foods.

"Precocious" is an accurate adjective for my physical development. I've always been "well-formed," and I've never been shy with my *ass*ets. Hah! My older brother Anthony always had a lot of his jock pals hanging around; they tried to be cool, but a few of them weren't. It was great fun.

I did well in high school, and I had no trouble getting accepted at Gallaudet. My father Samuel is a huge benefactor, which results in my living in an apartment instead of a student dormitory. Of course, I would have lived in a dorm room if I had to, but hey, if you've got some clout, why not use it?

I've only been here at Gallaudet a couple of months, but I've already made a bit of a splash. I've colored my hair purple, and I wear matching contact lenses. My plan is to switch colors every semester, maybe every month. It's that thing about boredom, I guess. "Wanna taste my peanut butter?"

I've already had a fling with one of the profs. Nice enough guy, but a little stuffy and conservative for my taste. He's pro-life; one of those straight laced republican types without a lot of imagination. Very good dresser, too; it was hard to get him out of a suit and tie.

I'm majoring in rehabilitation therapy. It may be surprising, but underneath the surface glitz, there's a person here who likes other people and wants to help, and my brother Anthony specializes in rehabilitative medicine, "physiatry," it's called, so I'd like to be in a related field.

So far, I haven't been all that taken by the male population at Gallaudet. There are plenty of nice guys, but most are so serious, all caught up and concerned about their grades with little time left over for having fun. I'm keeping my eyes open though, and I've seen a guy who's real fine. He hangs out at a campus beer hall with a buddy, probably his roommate, and I'm planning to "run into him," maybe this week or next.

He's in a wheelchair, but I don't mind. Maybe I'll get to practice some of the things I'm learning in my rehab classes. By the way, there are about a dozen positions that are suitable for wheelchair sex, and some of them are really quite creative.

Chapter 35

Samuel was the seventh child of a seventh child, a rare occurrence that is supposed to foretell good luck. Early in her marriage, his mother, a descendent of strong stock from Eastern Europe, vowed to keep having children until she produced a son. His father, a medical supplies salesman whose commissions produced a nice income, was thrilled when Sam finally came along. Tired, too.

Except for the number of plates at the table, the family was rather typical. The sisters, to their credit, worked part time while completing high school, and each paid her way through college. As a result, three more teachers, two nurses, and a bookkeeper entered the workforce. All the sisters married, two of them to brothers. The weddings, small though they were, still constituted a bit of a drain on family finances.

In an impressive display of fertility, the sisters produced a veritable flock of nieces and nephews. "Are they a brood, a covey, or a pride?" Sam asked. In any case, when it got over twenty, he stopped counting, but his exceptional memory enabled him to remember most of their names and a few of their birthdays.

"Sammie, you're the brightest of all the kids," his father said. "Mom and me are proud of your sisters; they all did well in school, but you're the only one with really outstanding academic ability. You should think about going to an Ivy League School, maybe Harvard or Yale."

"They're a little snooty Dad, and don't they cost

a lot?"

"Let me worry about the cost; you get a degree from an Ivy League school and you'll be set for life. You could even pay me back if you want."

Indeed, Sam was a "superstar" all the way through school. The school psychologist ranked his intelligence in the top one percent of all children his age. His academic achievement, his drive, and his participation in all sorts of extracurricular activities got him financial aid to Exeter Academy, Yale Undergraduate, Wharton Business School, and Harvard Law.

At all levels, he qualified as a "big man on campus." National Honor Society, National Merit Finalist, president of Sigma Chi, captain of the crew team, Phi Beta Kappa, editor of the Business School Review, senior editor of the Harvard Law Review, clerk to a state supreme court justice—Sam didn't mess around. That he was going to make it big was apparent to anyone who took the time to look.

As if he were an All-American point guard, law firms began making offers his last year at Harvard. "A couple of Wall Street firms are seriously courting me Dad, but I'm not sure I'm all that interested."

"You accept their invitations and see what they have to say. You have nothing to lose," Dad said.

In general, Sam was seduced. He went to firm dinners, golf outings, and nightclubs. The potential for six figure salaries, along with perquisites like generous pension plans and memberships at exclusive country clubs, was very tempting. Sam, however, liked the idea of working for himself and building his own fortune. Dad wasn't so sure, but he went along, reluctantly, at first, but eventually with greater enthusiasm.

With money he borrowed from relatives, Sam established a financial management firm. He began by investing the assets of some of his well-heeled classmates. They got their money back plus profits in no time at all. So did Sam. "You don't have to be a genius," he said. "All you have to do is buy low and sell high."

He began dabbling in real estate as well. The idea was the same: Buy properties, rehabilitate them, and sell them for more money than you invested. Or, hire a manager, sit back, and collect the rent. With commissions from investments and returns from real estate deals he did on the side, Sam was a multimillionaire by the time he was 29 years old.

He paid his father back, with interest.

For a time, Sam partook of the free and easy life of a bachelor with deep pockets. He had a penthouse apartment in Manhattan, a condominium in Aspen, a winter home in Sarasota, a Corvette, and a Bentley. He had access to a private jet which he took advantage of on a regular basis. His wardrobe, exclusively custom made designer clothes, "threads," he called them, filled two walk-in closets, and his personal valet kept everything in order.

Despite huge success at such a young age and trappings some might have considered exorbitant, Sam had a conservative streak that kept him grounded. He watched his wealth carefully and put substantial funds into government insured investments. These, along with shrewd purchases of more stock and real estate, insured financial independence for his life and his heirs to follow. He "gave back," too, with very generous donations to a number of charitable organizations.

Sam was average looking at best. Fresh out of the shower at his health club one morning, he and a friend were dressing. "Sam, don't take offense, but I've got to ask you something."

"Fire away."

Your hair is thinning, you wear spectacles, you tend towards portliness, and you're short."

"All that is surely true," Sam said, "and you haven't even mentioned my chronic disease, yet."

"What is it?" his friend said, looking alarmed.

Sam, trying his best to maintain a somber expression, said, "My doctor is treating me for a serious case of Dickdoo."

"What in the world is that?"

Sam, no longer able to stop smiling, said, "It's when your stomach sticks out further than your dick do. Now what did you want to ask me?"

"Well, I asked you not to take offense, but I'm wondering how an average-looking guy like you makes it with so many pretty women?"

"I learned," Sam said, "just as soon as I started making big bucks, that most women, even the knockouts, don't mind average-looking men who are only five feet five inches tall, so long as they have tall stock portfolios."

One afternoon in April, before the warmth of the spring sun melted the snow on the slopes near Aspen, Sam was taking his last run down a black diamond hill. Though concentrating hard on the near vertical drop, he hit an icy spot, twisted his ankle, and landed on his face. He made it to the bottom on his own, in a fair amount of pain, not sure whether he had suffered a fracture or a sprain. A pretty young woman in the shelter taped his ankle. Her name was Miriam, and she towered over Sam by a good five inches.

Like Sam, Miriam had matriculated at the finest schools. Not a highly motivated student, she nevertheless scraped through Vassar for an undergraduate degree in Art History and Smith College for a Master's in Fine Arts. "If they offered a Ph.D. in "shopping," she said, "I would have been at the head of my class."

Miriam came from money; her father was Chief Executive Officer for the largest plumbing supply business on the east coast, flush, as it were. She was used to the good life—the family jet, lavish vacations, and unlimited charge accounts. She could spend faster than Sam, not an easy accomplishment.

Weekends in Paris, a river cruise down the Danube, black sand beaches on Santorini, a safari in Tanzania—all of these were part of Sam's persistent courtship. No expense was prohibitive, including a four-carat diamond engagement ring.

Some of their friends referred to the marriage of Sam and Miriam as a "merger." Certainly, they started off on firm footing.

"Sam, I just love the Bentley," Miriam said.

"Wait until you see the plans for our custom built estate house in Silver Springs I'm having drawn up. It comes with a pool, sauna, exercise room, and a 1600 square foot master bedroom with walk in closets. What do you think about hiring a chef, valet, maid and chauffeur?"

"I don't like ostentation," Miriam said, "but what about the gardener and masseuse?"

Chapter 36

Soon Miriam was "in a family way." She loved the idea of having a child, but the morning sickness and the effect on her figure were terrible inconveniences. She "abhorred" hospitals, so a midwife and two nurses helped deliver the baby at home. He was a perfectly healthy and robust newborn, and they named him Anthony.

Anthony was an easy infant—a good eater, not colicky, not predisposed to fussing, and quick to sleep through the night. He walked and talked early, well ahead of the norms. He had no problems adjusting to school; in fact, his teachers, without exception, offered glowing reports.

"Give me more like Anthony, any time," one wrote on his report card.

With such a competent child, Miriam convinced Sam that Anthony was enough. "He's everything we wanted in a child; I'm just getting my figure back, and why should we push our luck?"

Years later, they inadvertently pushed it. Miriam and Sam were "getting on" when Sarah was born. Mother contended that she was "a glorious gift from God." Father, slightly less spiritual, maintained they got careless on an extended weekend getaway to the White Mountains, and the Good Lord had nothing to do with it. Whatever the case, Sarah arrived when her parents were well into middle age, "forty-somethings," as it were.

Miriam devoted most of her time to the children,

running the house, and planning dinner parties. Fully occupied by business dealings, Sam was grateful. He had full faith in Miriam's mothering, well-organized and strict as she was.

"You do a terrific job with the kids, managing the house, and entertaining our friends," Sam said.

"Thank you, dear, I think of those things as my contribution to our wonderful life together." Sam truly appreciated Miriam, and he figured that any energy she expended managing things at home was less energy she'd have available for shopping.

Anthony grew into a bright, athletic boy who rather consistently delighted in testing the strength of his mother's firm hand. Once, after losing a particularly vocal disagreement over the nutritional value of brussel sprouts, he got up in the middle of the night, sneaked downstairs to the pantry, and steamed the labels off two dozen or so canned goods. Then, with devilish glee, he glued them back onto the wrong cans. To himself, Father admired his boy's chutzpah and creativity.

Miriam had a brother who was deaf. The cause was unclear, either a virus during infancy that the doctors couldn't pinpoint or, more probably, genetic. Given her brother's deafness, Miriam learned sign language at the same time he did. Twenty-five years later, she was a proud guest at his graduation from the University of Illinois. His master's degree and teaching certificate enabled him to work as a teacher of deaf children.

When baby Sarah's deafness was verified, Miriam decreed how her daughter would learn to communicate. "We will all learn American Sign Language," she said.

"And who are you referring to?" Sam asked.

"Our immediate family, our extended family, and anyone else who cares to be around baby Sarah."

When asked the reason for her firm resolve, Miriam said, "Sarah will be Deaf like her Uncle Nicholas, not handicapped."

Chapter 37

Sarah's formal education began at age three at a regional preschool program for deaf children. Miriam had little choice regarding Sarah's preschool, because it was the only such program available within a forty-mile radius. She would have chosen it even had there been closer programs, because the school provided instruction in sign language and the fingerspelling alphabet for those who preferred it.

That Sarah had inherited her mother's streak of stubborn independence was quite apparent from the day she entered school. She wouldn't stay within the lines in her coloring book and soon refused coloring books entirely. "I want to draw chickens my way," she said, stamping a foot. "With four legs and lips."

Similarly, Sarah didn't abide by the "Absolutely No Running" rule that was strictly enforced on the playground. She absolutely ran anyway, because running was what kids did. It was fun, mostly when dodging the playground monitor, a gray and blue haired matron who wasn't nearly as quick as Sarah and whose face turned purple when Sarah disobeyed. It was true, too, that from the first, Sarah preferred playing with boys.

She was particularly strong-willed when she didn't get her way. When Sarah wanted something and was refused, she relied upon one of two tactics. Most often, she crawled up on her father's lap and employed her seemingly innate ability to turn on a flow of copious tears at will. Typically, Daddy caved at about the two-minute mark.

On one of a very few occasions when Sam held his ground, Sarah turned to her second strategy. She threatened to run away from home. Miriam, a witness to these events, said "On your mark."

"That's it; I'm leaving this place," Sarah said, "and you'll be sorry. Don't even try to find me 'cause I'm going way far away, maybe even to California or Chicago, or even the North Pole." Determined as she was, she made it as far as the neighbor's back yard where she played with Isadore, their golden retriever, until she got cold and hungry.

The year Sarah turned six, she left home to continue her education at the Maryland School for the Deaf. With only a few tears, she handled the transition easily. On the other hand, Sam wept all the way home. Miriam, clearly the more stoic of the two, kept her emotions in check. "You'll see, Sam; our little girl is at an excellent school, and this will be for the best," she said. "Take it from me; this will be for the best."

It's difficult to measure how bright deaf children arc on standardized intelligence tests, but Sarah's work in class showed how gifted she was. Learning her basic academics—reading, math, spelling, and writing—came easily, but more enlightening was her ability to think creatively. One of her teachers said: "Sarah thinks like other smart children do, but she also thinks like other smart children don't."

One afternoon her teacher made a new kind of assignment. "Make a list of all of the uses you can think of for a brick," she said.

Most of the responses were ordinary and expected: to build a house, to build a garage, to build a barbecue pit, to use for a doorstop, to use for a paperweight, for example.

Sarah's answers were very different, though.

"Jewelry for a giant, a stage for a flea circus, and the third house for the three little piggies," she wrote. Such is the stuff of creativity.

Teacher posed what she called "thought problems" almost every day. "A truck is loaded up with boxes and it's ten feet tall," she said. "It comes to an overpass that is only nine feet ten inches. There is no room to turn the truck around or back up. How does the truck get through?"

Only Sarah and one of her classmates came up with the correct solution. "You have to let some air out of the tires," they said.

Sarah came home for holidays, spring break, and summer vacation. She had friends in the neighborhood, and despite the age difference, she was very close with Anthony. In fact, she loved him like a brother.

Anthony was an excellent athlete, graceful and accomplished at all sports, but especially gifted at football. Sarah learned the game, and whenever she was home during the season, she accompanied Sam to her brother's games. For Miriam, football was much too violent, so she stayed home or accompanied some lady friends to scour the women's wear departments at local department stores. "One can never have enough shoes," she said. In fact, she was fast approaching one pair for each day of the year.

Sarah cheered for Anthony and thought it was amusing when her father jumped from his seat and pumped his arms. Anthony was so good at football that he got a four-year scholarship to college. That made Father jump from his seat and pump his arms, too.

Sarah excelled at school, not just academically, but socially as well. Classmates admired her quirkiness and quick wit. Those traits, plus the fact that she was very pretty, brought her a large number of friends. One of them was Billy Calderelli, a boy her age from

Virginia.

Billy was tall, skinny, and had an Adam's apple the size of a ping-pong ball that bobbed when he got excited. His hobby was magic. "Ladies and gentlemen, boys and girls," he said. "Watch as I make this red handkerchief turn into a blue one, and now, for your pleasure and amazement, I will change this penny into a nickel before your very eyes."

As entertaining as those tricks might have been, his showstopper was turning a black and white spotted kitten into a tan cocker spaniel. When asked how he'd managed to master such incredible feats of legerdemain, he said, "Show business is my life."

# Chapter 38

Sarah was as precocious physically as she was academically. At first, she was embarrassed. She wore tight fitting tee shirts over her bra to flatten her breasts, and then covered everything with baggy tops. Nonetheless, the boys noticed, so it wasn't long before she shifted from chagrin to flaunting.

Billy divided his time into thirds: practicing magic, keeping up with his schoolwork, and lusting after Sarah. She, more single-minded with respect to her burgeoning sexuality, only lusted. Neither knew what they were doing, so they learned together. Often, she was the aggressor.

"Hey, Billy," she'd say, "let's sneak into the storage room and swap some spit."

In the face of such offers, Billy's Adam's apple commenced imitating a Halloween apple, and he was quick to stow his red silk handkerchief, at least for a time.

High school went nicely for Sarah, until a Sunday in October when her mother showed up unannounced. "Anthony has been injured playing football," Miriam said, welling up with tears.

"What is it?"

"He's paralyzed below his waist and may never walk again."

"It can't be, not my big brother, not Anthony, please, not him." Mother and daughter held on, each trying to comfort the other.

Sarah left school that fall. "I can't concentrate; I

can't study; and I want to be with Anthony," she said. "And what does it matter if I lose a semester, or even the rest of the school year before I graduate?"

At home, Sarah helped tend to her older brother. She sensed which days were better to be with him and which to stay away. She had never been around a depressed person before, and, at first, it frightened her. "Most of the time he sleeps," she said, "and when he's up, all he does is stare out the window. Sometimes his eyes are red, and I can tell he's been crying."

On one of Anthony's good days, they sat outside, she on the front steps and he in his chair. "Let's have a race," she said.

"Oh sure, that would be fair; you've got great legs and I've got dead sticks hanging useless in my pants. How much of a head start do I get?" Anthony asked.

"No, not that kind of a race," Sarah said. "You wheel to the corner and back, and I'll time you with my watch. Then, we'll switch places; I'll get into your chair, and you'll time me."

Anthony won by a full minute the first three days they raced, but after a week or so, Sarah cut the difference to thirty seconds. "When I beat you, what do I get?" she asked.

"I'm not sure; how about a new watch?"

Sarah never did beat Anthony to the corner and back, but she did get him out and exercising again. His efforts soon spilled over to the local YMCA where a wheelchair basketball team practiced a few evenings a week. With Anthony, they won every tournament they entered, and representatives from the United States Para-Olympic Team began scouting him.

Chapter 39

The following fall, Anthony, no longer depressed, returned to his studies, now determined to go on to medical school. Sarah returned to her school as well and found that Billy and the storage room were still available.

Her adolescent rebellious streak ran wide and deep. The school dress code mandated that skirts reach mid-calf and blouses be buttoned at the neck. To Sarah, however, "mid-calf" was synonymous with "mid-thigh," and "neck" meant approximately the same as "navel."

She was equally bold regarding her make-up. False eyelashes, heavy mascara, black finger and toenails, streaked hair—she tried them all. After some consternation, the headmaster said, "We must find a balance between student conformity to rules and allowing them to express their individuality."

The school administration planned a special event each spring. One year it was a field day with athletic competitions, and another year it was a treasure hunt. This year it was a barbecue dinner to be followed by a hayride.

Students and teachers looked forward to the event, as they did to anything that varied from the usual routine. The cafeteria staff set up tables outside and grilled hot dogs, hamburgers, and chicken. Heaps of coleslaw, potato salad, and baked beans were served up as side dishes, and chocolate ice cream sundaes made for a fine dessert.

The administration rented horses and wagons

from a company that also provided a trail leader and drivers. Things were proceeding nicely, until the leader, a short, skinny guy with bowed legs and a filthy cowboy shirt, pulled the headmaster aside.

"We don't cart no Nigras," he said. "If'n y'all wanna leave 'em behind, we can git along rat quick."

Along with the other students, Sarah wondered what was taking so long to get going. When she learned the reason for the delay, her response was immediate and firm. "Then none of us will go," she said. To a man, her classmates agreed and promptly vacated the wagons.

Sarah and two of her classmates confronted the trail leader before leaving. "You're a bigot and a shit head," she said, fully aware that he couldn't understand her signs. He did understand, however, when she leaned forward, spit all over his coke bottle spectacles, and delivered a well-aimed kick to his groin. Sarah feared no retaliation given that her sidekicks happened to be very big and broad. African-American, too. She would have held her own, regardless.

Sarah decided, during her junior year, that she would go to Gallaudet University and major in rehabilitation therapy. Anthony was going to specialize in physical and rehabilitation medicine, "physiatry," some people called it, and she liked the idea of studying something similar.

Chapter 40

During summer break between her junior and senior years, Sam and Miriam took a driving trip to the "left coast." Both had previously seen the Grand Canyon, Yellowstone, Los Angeles, San Francisco, Big Sur, and the Oregon Coast, but it had been a while and there were cousins to visit. Miriam planned a six-week itinerary, with a half-day each week set aside for shopping.

"Don't worry, Sam; AAA motor club gave me the route, so you just drive and I'll tell you where to go."

Nothing too different about that.

It was the first time in Sarah's life that she had complete freedom. With her parents away and Anthony enrolled in summer session, she was totally on her own. *Now is my chance to pursue an adventure, something I would never be permitted to do if my parents were home.*

Rock climbing was something she considered for an afternoon but rejected. *Not enough movement, and the view can't be that great, at least until you get to the top.*

She gave two thumbs down to scuba diving with similar dispatch. *Too many lessons are needed to get certified, and I've never felt completely comfortable in the water, especially below the surface.*

Surfing and white water rafting were geographically inconvenient, hot air ballooning was too leisurely, and bungee jumping was stupid. Finally, it came to her. *I'm going to jump out of an airplane. Just thinking about it sends a shiver up and down my spine.*

Under "Skydiving" in the Yellow Pages, Sarah

found a regional airport half an hour away that offered lessons. The advertisement specified that there was no minimum age limit for skydiving, but, she wondered if her deafness might disqualify her. Before setting out, Sarah took a piece of notebook paper and wrote, "I'm Deaf. Still want to give me some lessons?"

A guy with the word "Jumpmaster" embroidered on his shirt stood behind a counter in the office. Sarah smiled and gave him her note.

He read it and walked over to a telephone. Back at the counter, he wrote, "Boss says there's no rule against it, and we've had a few deaf folks before. Be here tomorrow about eight."

The next morning Sarah was at the airport at 7:45. Three others had arrived even earlier. As novices, each would take turns jumping in tandem with the jumpmaster. He pulled up ten minutes later, tossed what remained of his coffee in the trash, and got down to the business of training another group of beginners, "virgins" he called them, all pretending not to be scared.

Training consisted of much more than Sarah had anticipated; in her naiveté, she assumed she would simply strap on some gear, learn how to land, and jump. In fact, she spent almost the entire day becoming familiar with the aircraft, learning the procedure for exiting the plane, how to relax and assume the correct position during free-fall, and how to use the emergency handles. In addition, time was devoted to identifying hazards around the landing area, navigational skills, and proper landing technique.

After all of this, Sarah had enough and was ready to fly. *So much for this ground training; it's time for the friendly skies.*

Such was also the feeling among her fellow trainees, all of whom looked to be chomping at their bits. They were ready as they would ever be, except for one muscle beach type who was man enough to admit he was too fearful and went home. "Sorry, but I'm going to stick to water skiing," he said.

By luck of the draw, Sarah was first to climb into the small plane. The dry mouth and wide eyes syndrome hit her. *What am I doing here, inside this narrow metal tube, whose engine is missing badly, trying to imitate some goddamn birds?* Indeed, heretofore courageous in the face of all manner of danger, her heartbeat was approaching fibrillation.

The pilot, an uncleansed former hippie who wasn't into neat and trim coiffures, gunned it and climbed to 14,000 feet or so. He leveled off and the jumpmaster opened a door. A gust of at least 100 miles per hour distracted Sarah from her prayers. *I'm like the infantryman in a foxhole who suddenly finds God.*

Just a few seconds later, the jumpmaster barked, "STAND UP AND GET READY." Sarah read his lips at the same time she noticed her legs quivering like Jell-O and her bowels cramping.

"GO!" the jumpmaster screamed, and Sarah, securely in his grasp, quite literally took a flying leap. During her time in the air, she felt more exhilarated than at any other time in her life. All her nervousness vanished, and at 125 miles per hour, with the wind in her face, she experienced absolute bliss. She saw clouds approaching and passed through one. Her view extended for miles—patches of farmland, buildings, and glorious forestland.

Part of the euphoria came from meeting a challenge and overcoming the fear. A larger portion, though, came from getting as close to flying as humanly possible. Birds glided below her and hilltops rushed up to meet her. She hoped they would encounter a massive updraft that would sweep them upward for another descent.

160

Her chute opened at 5,000 feet and she glided to a soft landing, much too soon, she thought. After gathering her chute, she and the jumpmaster headed toward the training center. He didn't have to ask her how she liked it; there was joy all over her face.

The other novices congratulated her and shook hands. One of the guys, next up, looked at Sarah and said, "Y'all are goll durn brave, ah don't mine sayin'. Ah dint know, 'til jist now, that you was deef and dumb. Yessir, y'all are a real pistol."

Without understanding much of what he said, Sarah just winked and kept smiling.

She flew two more times before her parents returned from their trip. She would have gone again, but she ran out of the money Sam left her. She never told them; perhaps she would after she soloed.

Chapter 41

Back at school in September, Sarah was a senior at last. She had lived most of her life at school, and she learned much while maturing from a child to a young woman. She looked forward to moving on, but not before enjoying her last year in high school.

Billy and Sarah remained an "item," despite some fierce competition from other young men in the senior class. She liked him a lot, and he was good at necking. He added a "vanishing rabbit trick" to his repertoire, and classmates begged him to explain how he did it. "True artists never reveal their secrets," he said. "And, didya know that Harry Houdini is alive and well, living at an abandoned ski resort in Idaho? He's a bit of a flake, but we consult with each other all the time."

Thanksgiving was good. Billy and his mom came, and Anthony brought a girlfriend. Miriam and the cook did a great job with dinner complemented by Billy's entertainment afterward. "Good thing he didn't make the turkey disappear," Sam said.

Christmas was fun, too. Sam took everyone to Vail for skiing. It was one of a number of resorts in the Rockies that had a full line of equipment for disabled skiers. Essentially, Anthony sat on a chair that was mounted on skis. For additional balance and turning, he used specially adapted outriggers, short skies that he held in his hands. With only a few tentative practice runs, he was able to keep up with everyone else. Such is the way it is with natural athletes.

The coming of spring provided a welcome respite

after a surprisingly cold and snowy winter. Many of Sarah's classmates would not be going on to higher education. Some would be joining her at Gallaudet, and a few, including Billy, would matriculate at the National Technical Institute for the Deaf, a college at the Rochester Institute of Technology. He'd finally come to realize that a successful career in engineering was more likely than making it in show business.

Of course, there were the senior prom and graduation, both bittersweet times for Sarah. She felt as if she was just going through the motions. She loved these people, but she had been with them almost her entire life. She had an "itch," a strong yearning to spread her wings, to live on her own, and to test herself with new challenges.

"We'll stay in touch, dearest boyfriend Billy," she said after kissing him goodbye.

"Of course. We both know where the other will be. I'll write you letters with some special ink I just bought. By the way, how do you know when you're out of invisible ink?"

Sam, who had been busy with Sarah's luggage, signaled that it was time to leave. Through the passenger side window, Sarah took one more look at Billy. He waved, then put his fists together over his heart and wiggled his thumbs up and down. Thus, in their way, he said, "Goodbye, my sweetheart."

Chapter 42

Seth munched on peanuts and nursed a beer while Jacob phased in his coed of the week campaign. A few lovely looking ladies turned in his direction, but none walked over to investigate. He was about ready to stow his art supplies when a chesty girl with purple streaks in her hair bounced into the beer hall. "DEAF IS DANDY" adorned her tight, pink tee shirt, and in a few minutes, Jacob and Seth had company.

"I'm Sarah," she said, at the same time as she was swinging her curvaceous derriere into the booth. Jacob, given his eye for color, noticed that her eyes were purple too, a perfect match for her streaks. He admired women who attended to color coordination.

Sarah flashed a set of perfectly straight teeth and complimented Jacob on his artwork. "Looks like you've got a real talent there, buddy," she said.

"Yeah, I'm working on it; maybe I could do your portrait some time."

"I don't think so; I'm still way hyperactive, so I'd never be able to sit still long enough." She turned her attention to Seth and asked where he was from.

"A hundred or so miles west, small town you've never heard of," he said.

"I'll bet it's one of those places where everyone knows each other's business and gossips a lot. People sit around the village square in their bib overalls, smoking pipes, and pulling bugs out of their beards, and those are the women!"

"A little like that," Seth said, trying not to laugh

too hard. "How about you, though? Where did you grow up?"

"I'm from Silver Springs, Maryland; I've been deaf since birth; I graduated from the Maryland School for the Deaf; I believe sign language and skydiving are beautiful, I absolutely adore the Washington Redskins, and I'm majoring in rehabilitation therapy." As an aside, she mentioned that next month's streaks and contact lenses would be lime green.

Not wanting to cramp his friend's style, Jacob excused himself early for a dental appointment. Later, while getting his bicuspids buffed, he wondered how Seth was doing. *I think she'll be good for him, and I hope he likes her.*

Despite Sarah's aggressive approach, or maybe because of it, Seth was intrigued with her, but before he could get another word in, she slid into his chair, disengaged the wheel locks, and rolled over to the bar. She returned with two fresh beers, and he asked, "How did you get so good with a chair?"

"My brother broke his back playing football in college, and he let me wheel around once in a while."

"I'm sorry."

"Don't be. A couple years back, he was the leading scorer and most valuable player on the U.S. Para-Olympic basketball team, and now he's a physician here in D.C. He's got a knockout wife and two bright, beautiful daughters, too."

They finished their beers, and she invited Seth to her apartment for something to eat. "Slide into your chair," she said. "I live just two blocks away, and we can ride over together."

Seth wasn't sure what she meant until she eased onto his lap and said, "Roll 'em out, cowboy."

"How do you get to live in your own apartment instead of a dorm room like the rest of us?" Seth asked.

"Let's just say that I have a very close relative who tends to be extremely generous with his financial support to certain universities."

Sarah's apartment was much like she was—bold, bright, and a tad bawdy. Beanbag chairs and oversized cushions were strewn in bunches on a pink carpet in the living room. The walls were painted orange and pink, and the artwork was a curious mix of Monet prints, movie placards, African tribal masks, and two extra large tee shirts adorned with "Allow Me to Explain Myself through Interpretive Dance," and "Let's Hear it for Deaf People."

A painting of dogs waiting their turns at a fire hydrant hung on one wall in the bathroom across from a poster declaring, "I AM the Prettiest of Them All." Her bedroom ceiling was mirrored, and in one corner, an etching read, "Objects in this mirror are smaller than they appear."

In the eating area adjacent to the kitchen, a neon sign blinked, "Absolutely No Belching," and the table, nothing more than a thick wooden slab on legs, was pocked with dents and small holes.

"It was originally a door at the Alamo, and those are bullet holes," Sarah said. "You could ask anyone."

"What an amazing coincidence," Seth said. "Not too many people know it, but Davey Crockett was a third cousin, twice removed, on my mother's side. I've got the hat he was wearing when he died if you ever want to see it."

She tossed a salad and fired up the grill, and he set out some plates and opened a bottle of Cabernet. Each downed a couple of cheeseburgers and an excess of wine while discussing the need for a Deaf President at Gallaudet and the pros and cons of cochlear implant surgery for deaf babies. Seth was impressed with her opinions, especially since her views were essentially the same as his own. "It's that thing about great minds," he said.

Together in the living room, they drained what little remained of the wine. Seth's mind flashed back to Ellie and the last time he'd been with a girl. Such reverie faded fast, though, when Sarah asked, "So how long have you been a crip?"

Loose from the alcohol and feeling very much at ease, Seth spilled his guts. The shooting, his denial and depression, his rehab, and how difficult things were for Willa and Robert—for over an hour, he gave Sarah the details.

"You've left out one important thing," she said.

"What's that?"

"How's your sex life been?"

"Let's talk about it some other time," Seth said.

"Whenever you're ready," Sarah replied, "and how about we have a nice Italian dinner tomorrow night? I know a great place not too far from here, and we can split the tab."

Chapter 43

The head chef at Mamma Mangananzo's Ristorante was Mamma Mangananzo herself, a crusty, no-nonsense signora from Parma. Mamma was renowned for her oversized portions of veal and chicken parmigiana sprinkled with authentic Parmesan cheese. She also specialized in prosciutto di parma (ham), pasta y fagioli (white bean and pasta soup), straccota (beef stew), tortelle d'erbetta (stuffed pasta), and a variety of lasagnas and pizzas.

Her recipes had been lovingly handed down over three generations from her mother and grandmothers. Brilliant gastronomes as they surely were, it was clear that none gave a hoot about Jenny Craig or gastrointestinal reflux disease. Pappa Mangananzo handled reservations and functioned as maitre d', wine steward, and enforcer. He was not to be messed with.

Uninformed customers learned that their choice of wine was irrelevant, because Pappa dictated what went best with whatever dinners they had ordered. "You drinka what I'ma tella you," he ordered, "because I'ma da boss," and invariably customers were delighted, because Pappa really knew his wines. Or, they might have been fearful of what would happen to their kneecaps should they demonstrate any tendency toward freethinking.

Often frequented by senators, congressmen, and visiting dignitaries, the restaurant was a bustling place. The kitchen stayed open until one A.M. or until Mamma ran out of food, whichever came first. On those rare occasions when the larder ran to empty, Pappa told disappointed customers to come back the next night for antipasti and a glass of vino. "Onna da house. I'ma da boss and I'ma guarantee."

Rumor had it that it was easier to get a reservation if one's last name ended with a vowel. So, Seth stopped by before the lunch hour rush, and wrote "Pistaligliano" on the reservation list. Pappa raised an eyebrow but reserved a booth toward the rear below a large, autographed photograph of a countryman, with a menacing look, peering out from under his fedora. His name was Vincente Calabria; there was a bulge in his jacket, and he was sucking on a fat cigar. One might assume he made offers that couldn't be refused.

Sarah looked subdued and even prettier in a skirt, sweater and much less make-up. More than a few of the male patrons of the restaurant, even those who were with dates of their own, gave admiring glances. Seth was happy to be with her and at least equally pleased that she didn't insist upon rolling into the place on his lap.

Sarah scanned the menu, and when the waiter came by, she pointed to a salad, pasta y fagioli, veal parmigiana, and spumoni for dessert. Seth indicated he would have the same, but substituted straccota for his entree. Pappa "suggested" a bottle of Antinori Peppole Chianti Classico. It sounded expensive, but it was only ten bucks.

Dinner was delicious and informative. They discussed their coursework, families, Deaf theater, residential schools, and the possible advantages of manual methods of communication for hearing children who were slow to talk.

Over dessert, Sarah, direct as ever, said, "Enough with the small talk; do you want to be my boyfriend?"

"More than anything," Seth said.

Chapter 44

They began seeing each other two or three times a week, but soon, they were together just about every afternoon or evening. Often, they spent afternoons on study dates before having dinner at her apartment. Sarah had a connection for Redskin tickets, and they sat midfield at a couple games. They ate out on Saturday nights, always splitting the bill.

One night, after a matinee performance of Deaf Theater at the university auditorium and a nice Chinese dinner, they returned to Sarah's apartment for a nightcap. One drink turned into a few, at which point she suggested, with typical candor, "How about we retire to my bedroom and do our best to fog up the ceiling mirror?"

When Seth resisted, Sarah pulled back and said, "We're having a great time together aren't we? Our dates have really been fun, and there's no one else I care to be with. You, big fella, are one terrific boyfriend, and I think you feel the same about your girlfriend. Am I right?"

"Of course, you're right," he said. "You're the best thing that has ever happened to me."

"I believe it, and that's why I have a question for you."

"If you're going to ask me about sex again, I'm still not ready to talk about it."

"Then, allow me to pose another question," Sarah said. "If I were to tell you that we're done and I don't want to see you anymore, what do you think my

170

reason would be?"

"I'd think you decided you didn't want to be with a crip," Seth said. "I'd think you were rejecting me because of my body and the way I look, and that after giving me a shot, you decided the accommodations you'd have to make just weren't worth it."

"So my dumping you couldn't possibly have to do with anything else, maybe your personality, your manner of communicating, your grooming, or your interests. Is that what you're saying?"

"I really don't think so, but what are you getting at?"

"What I'm getting at is that you're still so wrapped up in your injury that nothing else really matters, not even making love to me. What I'm getting at is that you're not willing to talk about sex, because you're afraid you might have to perform. You're afraid of the total lack of feeling below your waist and how you're supposed to make love without an erection. You doubt if someone like me who can walk really finds you attractive."

"Is that all?" Seth asked.

"Nope. You're thinking that maybe you should only go out with crips. You're wondering if you'll ever find a girl who will tolerate a bladder or bowel accident in the middle of making love. You're not sure what you're supposed to do with your catheter when you're putting on a rubber. You're worried about where to put your urine collection bag when you're in the throes of passion. You don't know how passionate your throes will actually be. You're not sure if a girl who consents to make love with you really likes you or would just be supplying a 'mercy screw.' You don't know if you can father a child or whether guys in wheelchairs can make good fathers. I could go on, or is that enough?"

At the end of her litany, Seth was both amazed

and chastened. "How could you possibly know all that?" he asked.

"Sexuality after spinal cord injury is part of what we study in rehab therapy," Sarah said, "but I learned most of it from talking with my brother. Remember him, the crip doctor with the knockout, walking wife and two beautiful daughters? You need to make an appointment. If you'll go, I'll do what I can to get you an appointment sooner instead of later."

Chapter 45

Dr. Anthony practiced rehabilitative medicine at the George Washington University Hospital. Many of his patients were amputees or had sustained spinal cord injuries, strokes, or traumatic brain injuries. Others came to him because of arthritis, Parkinson's disease, chronic back pain, or intractable pain in other parts of the body. Many of these conditions presented multiple problems, so Dr. Anthony routinely teamed with professionals from other specialties, most often urologists, neurologists, and physical therapists.

Regardless of the nature or severity of their problems, his goal was to maximize what his patients could do physically and socially and help them adapt to what they couldn't. He did this by prescribing a wide range of treatments including prostheses, adaptive devices, therapeutic exercise, deep heat application, bracing, electrotherapy, and hydrotherapy. Because disabling physical conditions are so often complicated by emotional problems, he did a good deal of psychological counseling, as well.

Seth waited two weeks to see the doctor, a delay that would have been even longer had Sarah not wielded her clout. He arrived for his appointment, and a receptionist asked for a list of his medications and his health insurance card. After completing the paperwork, he suddenly felt a little tentative about what he'd gotten himself into. *How do I talk about sex with the older brother of a girl I'd like to have sex with?*

Judging from the furniture and artwork in the

outer office, Dr. Anthony was the conservative sibling. Earth tones took the place of pink and orange, and no mirrors were affixed to the ceilings. Instead, dark leather couches, chairs, and end tables covered with copies of "Sports Illustrated" and "Newsweek" filled the room. Seascapes, a couple of photographs taken during wheelchair basketball games, and some pictures of disabled skiers hung on the walls.

The carpeting was a low cut pile, and the doors were especially wide—both accommodations to make it easier for people in wheelchairs to maneuver. For the same purpose, ramps led in and out of the building, and stalls in the restrooms were larger than normal and equipped with grab bars.

The office was a cool, soothing place with soft lighting and a large aquarium stocked with tropical fish. Their languid movements were relaxing, and it wasn't long before Seth lapsed into a delicious nap. Fifteen minutes into a dream, which would have surely been X-rated, the receptionist rapped him on the shoulder and signaled that Dr. Anthony was ready to see him. She directed him to an examining room, and while he was scanning a wall full of diplomas and awards, the doctor, clad in the traditional white coat with a stethoscope around his neck, wheeled in.

"Hey, Seth; I hear you're dating my kid sister," were his first words. "Real firecracker, isn't she?" That Dr. Anthony had learned to sign later in life was obvious to Seth; nonetheless, he was quite competent and easy to understand.

"More like a five alarm fire," Seth said.

"You're my last patient of the day," Dr. Anthony said, smiling broadly enough to reveal the family inclination for perfectly straight teeth. "We've got plenty of time. Do you want to talk doctor to patient or crip to crip?"

"I'll go with crip to crip," Seth said, at once feeling more at ease. He liked the feeling of not being rushed; he liked that Dr. Anthony communicated in lay terms instead of medical jargon, and, more than anything, Seth liked the fact that he was seeing a medical specialist whose own injury and subsequent adjustments had to be somewhat similar to his own. *He's wheeled a few miles in my chair.*

Seth wasn't sure where to begin, so he was relieved when Dr. Anthony started their conversation. "Here's the deal," he said. "I'll start by telling you about my injury; then, you'll tell me about yours."

"Fine with me," Seth said. "All I know is that you got hurt playing football."

"Right, the guy who broke my back was an all-conference cornerback who was known for his 'physical' game, which means he played dirty. I was on my knees after a 12-yard gain up the middle. I turned to get out from under a large linebacker whose prominent butt was pinning my lower legs to the turf. There was no way I could have moved even if I had seen the cornerback coming."

"Where did he hit you?" Seth asked.

"In the chest, at full speed and helmet first, at least a full second after the referee blew the whistle. The force bent my body backward with such violence that I was knocked cold. When I came to in the locker room, I couldn't move anything below my waist."

"Yeah, scary as hell isn't it? Did they boot him out of the game, at least?"

"Yeah, for his brutality, he got kicked out for the last nine minutes, and I got kicked out for life. To lift my mood during the months that I was depressed, I dreamed about getting revenge. In my favorite fantasy, I'm looking at the sports section of the newspaper, and I read that he gets his neck broken in the Rose Bowl. He's quadriplegic and unable to breathe on his own. I immediately book a flight to Pasadena, sneak into the hospital during the early morning hours, and unplug his respirator."

"Beautiful!" Seth said, a little too gleefully. "I know the guy who broke my back, too. I was walking home from a restaurant with my roommate, and this punk leaned out of his car and shot me. I'm still not sure why; the only reason I can think of is that he might have thought we were flashing gang signs."

"I'll bet you have revenge fantasies like I did," Dr. Anthony said.

"Do I ever. In the latest one, I smash him between his legs with a sledgehammer. I hit him so goddamn hard that his scrotum bursts and his testicles rupture. Then, when he's down on the floor, squealing like a pig and grabbing at his crotch, I take the hammer to his kneecaps and shatter them. That, along with severing his hamstrings with a filthy butcher knife, will make it difficult for him to walk for the rest of his pitiful life. How's that for evening the score?"

Dr. Anthony said nothing for ten seconds or so, gathering his thoughts. "I haven't been doctoring all that long, but I've treated more than a few patients with spinal cord injuries inflicted upon them by others. Many of those people obsessed over revenge, just as I did after my own injury. With all of that, I'm quite certain that what you've told me isn't a fantasy at all. Nope, I believe it's reality for you, something you actually want to do, and we need to talk about it."

"Jeez. You and your sister are plenty damned smart," Seth said.

"Yeah, and you should know that she's even smarter than I am."

Chapter 46

At their next appointment and again over dinner at a Greek restaurant up the street, Seth and Dr. Anthony discussed revenge. Early on, the doctor asked, "Tell me what motivates you, as specifically as you can, to get even with the punk who shot you?"

Seth reeled off his well-rehearsed biblical justification. "An eye for an eye and a tooth for a tooth. As he has injured the other, so he is to be injured. Straight from the Old Testament, Doc."

"Right," the doctor said, "the quote comes from Leviticus, and people who have committed vengeful acts over the years usually refer to it when they are asked to justify their actions."

"So, I guess you're familiar with it," Seth said.

"Of course, just as I'm familiar with other biblical references that suggest a very different response to violence. Jesus, as I'm sure you know, advised his followers not to retaliate against violence but to turn the other cheek, and more recently, Mahatma Gandhi and Reverend King cautioned that seeking an eye for an eye will ultimately lead to everyone being blind."

"Come on, Doc. I'm about as far as you can get from Gandhi or Jesus or any other saintly kind of guy forgiving enough to turn the other cheek. I'm just a regular person whose entire life has been screwed up by an ignorant punk. I'm no different than anyone else; seeking vengeance is a natural thing. It's normal. Revenge is sweet and I'm looking forward to my just desserts."

"OK," the doctor said, "if Christ, Gandhi, and Dr. King don't suit you, let's talk about me again, a guy who is at least as unsaintly as you are. After my injury, I had a decision to make. I knew where the guy was; I could have easily devised a feasible plan and retaliated. Instead, with the help of wise counsel, I chose to put that instinct aside, difficult as it was, and pursue my career. In so doing, I've learned something you need to think about. In fact, what I'm about to tell you should become your mantra, something you repeat to yourself three or four times a day, or at least any time you find yourself in close proximity to a sledge hammer."

"I'm all eyes," Seth said.

"Huge success is the best revenge of all," Dr. Anthony said. Seth looked puzzled, so the doctor continued, "You may think I'm being immodest, but my success has truly been huge. I have a beautiful wife who's crazy about me. We have two great girls; we live in a modern, comfortable house, we have a wide circle of friends, we drive nice cars, we have traveled extensively, my daughters attend excellent schools, I have a very satisfying and successful medical practice, I'm a clinical professor at the university, I've published research articles and books, and I enjoy great respect from my professional colleagues and people in the community."

"OK, facts are facts; you've made it, Doc; you're a huge success," Seth said, "but don't you still want to get even?"

"There's no reason to, because Mr. All-Conference cornerback didn't make it in the National Football League. He's been chronically unemployed and has a criminal record for breaking and entering and grand theft. He lives on the street or in jail, except when he's staying at inpatient treatment centers for recovering alcoholics and drug abusers. Count on it; I have enjoyed huge success, and he's a homeless drunk. My desserts have been just; there's nothing more I need to do to him."

"I get what you're saying," Seth said, "but I don't think I can forget what the punk did to me and just wheel away, leaving him in a state of blissful ignorance. He needs to know, and he needs to suffer, just as I have."

Doctor Anthony kept at it. "What you don't get yet is that you'll be the one who suffers if you somehow succeed in carrying out your plan to get revenge. Instead of the closure you think you'll be getting, you'll never forget what you did. You'll never stop thinking about your act of vengeance, so you'll never stop thinking about your injury. Such thoughts will consume you, and you'll live out your life in despair, bitter and alone."

"You can't know that for sure," Seth said.

"Sure I can. You're giving the punk who did this to you the power to influence your future. Dwelling on getting even with him interferes with your life, clutters your mind with hideous thoughts, and saps your energy, and if you allow him to continue exercising that power, he will eventually make you sick. You'll become a permanent victim and never come anywhere close to meeting the considerable potential I think you have. You need to let him go, to move on and devote more time to thinking about happier things like my sister and what you want to do with your life."

Seth had entertained revenge fantasies for a long while, the better part of two years. Perhaps time had healed his wounds a little, but the scabs were slow to form and it didn't take much to rip them off. He'd see a guy jogging in the park, or playing a game of tag with his son, or jumping over a mud puddle, or skipping rope, or running to catch a bus, or kicking a can, or dancing with his sweetheart, and it hurt. It hurt him profoundly each time he was reminded that there were so many things he'd never be able to do again, so many joys he'd miss, and so many sidelines he'd never cross.

In his head, Seth grudgingly came to accept that Dr. Anthony had given him sound advice, but in his heart, he wasn't yet ready to accept it. What finally eased him around the bend was the doctor's vivid depiction of the even uglier consequences that would likely transpire should Seth go ahead and implement his plan. "Let's assume you're successful on your punk maiming expedition," Dr. Anthony said.

"You've effectively crippled him, destroyed his manhood, and made his voice an octave higher, and let's also assume that putting another crip in a chair gets you the closure you seek."

"Keep going," Seth said.

"At that point, or soon after, you will discover that even people with disabilities go to prison. A judge and jury will have no sympathy for your deafness or your paraplegia. Neither will they be swayed by the argument that a depraved gangbanger 'started it' and you were simply seeking to get even, as any right minded person would."

"So I go to the slammer, just for evening the score?"

"Count on it. Nothing your defense counsel says will convince the jury that what you did was justifiable enough to get you off the hook, and in the end you will be found guilty of committing a heinous crime."

"I still might be willing to go through with it if I get a short sentence," Seth said.

"I'll remind you of that when you're in your stinking eight by ten jail cell looking at fifteen years or so on a roach infested cot and a clogged toilet, and you get to shower once a week, and your meals consist of institutional slop, and there are more than a few perverted sociopaths lurking nearby who savor the idea of getting off on crips, and there is no one else around who knows sign language. How long do you think it will take before the sweetness of your revenge turns sour? And, by the way, Sarah will quickly tire of visiting a miserable wretch like you, let alone waiting for you to get out of jail."

Back at Dr. Anthony's office the next week, Seth yielded and promised to ditch his plan. "There is one thing before I forget it though," he said. "If I should ever run into him again, he's at least going to face me and see what he did."

"The cornerback knows what he did to me, so I suppose that's fair enough," Dr. Anthony said, "but I'm assuming that if and when you meet up with him, you won't happen to have, just by pure coincidence, a sledge hammer strapped to the bottom of your chair."

"Jeez, I was thinking more along the lines of a battery operated power drill to stick in his ear," Seth said. "Now, can we finally start talking about me and your sister?"

Chapter 47

Seth had enjoyed a full introduction to all matters sexual with Ellie. She was uninhibited and varied in her tutelage, and he was a "quick study." When it came to sex after his spinal cord injury, however, he was functionally illiterate, a rank amateur; indeed, somewhat of a dunce. With nowhere to go but up, as it were, he turned to Dr. Anthony for enlightenment.

"You've got what we call a 'complete' spinal cord injury, which means the bullets sliced all the way through your spine. The good news, though, is that your injury, like mine, is low, in the thoracic region, instead of higher in the cervical area, and the lower the spine is severed, the more function remains. That's why you can use your arms, why you have good upper body strength and control in general, and why you have no trouble breathing."

"I know most of that from the reading I've done," Seth said. "What I don't know is whether my injury, this low but complete kind, makes it impossible for my Johnson to stand up and stay that way long enough for me to do any good?"

"So, it's 'Johnson,' is it? Funny," Dr. Anthony said. "I discharged a patient last week who called his 'Luigi,' and another patient I'm seeing right now refers to his best friend 'Percy.'"

"I've got a couple you've probably never heard before," Seth said. "A guy who lives on my floor at the dorm calls his 'Private Eye,' and I remember a clown in high school who liked 'Stick Shift.'"

"My hunch is that the quantity of synonyms for

'penis' is more substantial than we think," Dr. Anthony said, "but whatever you choose to call it, whether your Johnson stands at attention, so to speak, and stays that way depends upon which type of two erections you're referring to."

"I didn't know there was more than one," Seth said. "What are they? I'll settle for either."

"The first kind, 'psychogenic erections,' they're called, happen when you think sexy thoughts. You may see a picture that arouses you; you may come across an erotic passage in a book, or you may be following a woman with an alluring figure. The thing to remember about psychogenic erections is that there is no need for touching, no need for direct contact with your penis."

"I used to get those all the time in high school," Seth said. "Just about every day and night, including weekends, for the whole four years, I would say. Looking at the girls, the teachers, the lunchroom ladies, dirty books, center page foldouts—I didn't discriminate. I'm telling you; I could have hung a wet bath towel on it. At times it was so embarrassing, I had to use my book bag to cover things up."

"Just like most of us when we were teenagers. I remember those days very well, too," Dr. Anthony said. "You know, are you glad to see me, or is that a banana in your pants?"

"You're OK, Doc; I don't care what anyone says."

"Kind of you. Anyway, reflex erections, the second kind, happen only with direct physical contact to the penis. Or, the touching may be to other erotic areas like your ears, nipples, or neck. A reflex erection is involuntary and can happen even though you're not thinking about anything that is sexually arousing."

"I can remember a few of those, too," Seth said.

"Men with complete injuries like ours usually

aren't able to experience psychogenic erections," Dr. Anthony said. "So, no matter how many steamy issues of 'Penthouse' you look at or how many movie starlets you fantasize about, your Johnson isn't likely to perk up. With low injuries, though, even those that are complete, direct physical stimulation sometimes does the job."

"I've tried it, Doc, but nothing happens."

"There are things available that may help you," Dr. Anthony said. "Take these booklets back to your dorm. Reading them is your homework assignment between now and next week. We'll talk about your alternatives then."

 # Chapter 48

Seth completed his homework assignment and wasn't happy. Nothing he read about vacuum pumps, penile injections, or penile implants—all ways to help paraplegics produce and sustain erections—was encouraging.

"Hey, Jacob," he said. Would you like to see some ways that crips can get it up?"

"Why not; it's either that or read more of this organic chemistry."

"OK, first, there's the vacuum pump. 'Hoover,' I call it. To use it I'd have to insert my Johnson into this cylinder, pump out all the air, and hope that blood flows into the vacuum. Then, I'd have to tie it off at its base, like using a tourniquet, to keep the blood from flowing back into my body. Having sex for a long time is out of the question, because if you don't loosen the tie after twenty to thirty minutes, there's a risk of sores and infections."

"I'd give it a pass," Jacob said. "What else is there?"

"Well, we've got penile injection therapy which requires jabbing Johnson in the side with a needle. A drug or combination of drugs flows in causing an erection that lasts for an hour or so. What happens is that the drug dilates the arteries in the penis, blood rushes in, and after fifteen minutes or so, Voila!"

"That sounds a little better if you can stand the thought of sticking a needle into a very sensitive part of yourself," Jacob said.

"Fact is, I don't like needles of any kind, even thin ones," Seth said. "No way I'm going to stick myself down there. Bruising, scarring, and small growths on the penis are side effects, and the rule is no more than one injection per week. 'Sorry, my dear, but we've got three days to go.' So much for spontaneity."

"Anything else?" Jacob asked.

"Yes indeed. There's the penile implant approach. The doc actually inserts a reservoir and a pump into your body, just below your nuts, and when the need arises, you squeeze the pump, or your partner does, fluid flows out of the reservoir, and there you have it."

"Kind of like fill it up with regular, Ma'am," Jacob said.

"Yes, and like any other surgery, there's a risk of infection, as high as four to five percent in guys with spinal cord injuries. Also, implants have been known to erode over time and require replacement surgery after ten years, more or less."

About the only material in the booklets that Seth enjoyed were graphic pictures of the numerous positions for wheelchair sex. What was depicted was a truly creative display of movement worthy of a blue ribbon at a competition of acrobats.

Back at the office, Dr. Anthony showed up more than an hour late. "Sorry," he said, "but there was an emergency, and I had to stay at the hospital longer than usual."

"Mind if I ask what happened?" Seth asked.

"Not at all. A urologist and I prescribed penile injection therapy for one of our patients with an injury similar to yours. He's supposed to inject a drug into the side of his penis which produces an erection that lasts for about an hour."

"Yeah, I read about penile injection in one of

your booklets, and I don't mind saying that jabbing Johnson with a needle isn't a pleasant thought, but what happened to the guy?"

"He made a mistake with his dosage and injected more drug than he should have, I think almost twice as much. Five hours later, still stiff as a carp and in great pain, he showed up at the emergency room. It's a serious condition called 'priapism,' and without immediate attention, the result can be permanent damage to the penis."

"Jeez, what did you do for him?"

"First, we aspirated. That required numbing his penis with a local anesthetic and inserting a small needle and syringe to drain the excess blood. It didn't work.

"Then we medicated. We gave him a drug, several doses over a couple hours that were supposed to stop blood from flowing into his penis and cause the blood already there to flow out. That didn't work either.

"Finally, we operated. The urologist inserted a shunt into his penis. It rerouted the flow of blood allowing it to flow in and out normally. That worked."

"Will the poor guy have to stay at the hospital?" Seth asked.

"No, he's probably already on his way home, and if he's more careful with his dosage, it shouldn't happen again."

"Wasn't he embarrassed in front of all those nurses while his Johnson was flapping around in the breeze?"

"He might have been had he known what the nurses called him behind his back."

"What's that?"

"An all day sucker." Both had a good laugh, after which Dr. Anthony returned to Seth's homework assignment. "I guess you completed your reading assignment. What do you think?" he asked.

"The truth is I didn't like any of it; it was a total downer, and it left me with a 'what's the use?' sort of feeling," Seth said.

"Tell me more."

"My sex life hasn't been all that much, Doc, but what little I've had was natural and spontaneous. It was fun," Seth said. "The stuff in your booklets, though, the vacuums, the injections, and the surgery, make it seem so mechanical and scheduled. It was really a depressing read."

"What else bothered you?"

"Jeez, right now, all I want to do is make love to Sarah, whenever and however we like, without all that paraphernalia and all the planning and interruptions required, and there's more, too."

"Like what?"

"Well, even if I try the vacuum pump or penile injection, and one of them works, I still may not be able to make babies."

"You're right," Dr. Anthony replied. "You might not be able to ejaculate. Even if you can, you probably have fewer sperm than normal, and a lot of those may already be dead, and to complicate matters even further, whatever live sperm you have may not be sufficiently motile; that is, not good enough swimmers, to make it upstream and fertilize an egg."

"So, like I said, Doc; what's the use?"

"What it all comes down to is a personal decision on your part," Dr. Anthony said. "Do you want to have a sex life or don't you? Do you want to have children or don't you? Answering 'no' to those questions is OK, as long as you make an informed decision. Answering 'yes,' though, means you have to be motivated enough to make some adjustments. Guys like you and me simply have no choice; we have to make adjustments.

"Take some time to think it over; maybe talk to

Sarah about it, and next week, or whenever you're ready, we can discuss your decision."

Chapter 49

Seth went back to the dorm where Jacob was working on a plaster cast for a sculpture.

"You got a phone call from your father," he said. "He wants you to call him back as soon as you can."

"You're mother is ill," Robert said. "Can you come home for the weekend?"

Seth called Sarah to explain what was happening. "Do you want me to come with?" she asked.

"Probably not a good time to meet my parents; I'll go by myself, and I'll call you as soon as I find out what's going on."

He threw some clothes and toilet articles in a duffel, and Jacob drove him to the train station. Robert was waiting for him, and after a long, tight hug, he said, "Your mother has lumps in her breasts."

To Seth, Willa looked thin and a little pale. "Don't you worry," she said. "I'm fine. The doctors know what to do, and I'll be better real soon."

She didn't get better.

She tired early in the day, and she was unsteady on her feet. The doctors did their probes and tests; they cut her, injected chemical poisons, and burned her with radiation. The days grew shorter, and she got sicker.

Robert fed her, cleaned her vomit, and bathed her. When she was too frail to walk, he carried her through the woods she loved so much. They sat in the sun and remembered their youth. Each night, he massaged her back and legs until she slept. Only then would he gather her hair.

Seth came home as much as he could, and with each visit, he saw that his mother had deteriorated. "She's dying," he said, when Sarah asked about her. The cancer spread to her lungs, liver, and brain. Robert and Seth watched in horror, helpless, as she wasted away. Limp skin sagged from her rib cage and pelvis. Violent coughing spells exhausted her. The whites of her eyes turned yellow, and open sores festered on her tongue and scalp. Still, when her pain eased, she smiled for them.

Robert held her in his arms and soothed her, cooling her fever with a moist cloth. She faded in and out of consciousness, a bald, shriveled shell of what she had been. In her last lucid moment, she thanked him for being her husband. She told him to be brave, and she promised she would love him and watch over him. Slowly, the light left her eyes. At last, she sighed once and died, no more to suffer.

Robert dressed her in a fresh gown. He dabbed her with drops of her favorite scent and put a black orchid in each of her hands. He kissed her on the lips, made the sign of the cross, and wept. Then, he started to die.

He grieved for eighteen days. A profound despair crushed his spirit and beat him down. He ate little, his sleep was brief and fitful, and he shut himself away from all others. He would not see himself in a mirror, and he grew gaunt and slovenly.

At dawn and dusk, he placed yellow roses on her grave. He sat on the ground and rocked, alone, except for the butterflies and squirrels. Between visits to the cemetery, he stayed in their bedroom. He looked at her pictures, and he smelled her clothes. He would not change their bed sheets.

Seth and Sarah found him, cold, eyes fixed and vacant, on Willa's side of the bed. His knees were drawn to his chest, and his hollow cheeks were streaked with dried tears. Her pillow was in his arms, close to his face, and, tight in one hand, he held a sheaf of her hair.

Seth closed his eyes and covered him with their quilt.

Chapter 50

Sarah was a steadfast source of comfort and support, as were Dr. Anthony and Jacob.

Given the enormity of his loss, Seth held together well. For sure, he had his moments, but for the most part, he mourned his parents with great dignity, as they would have wanted.

He inherited the house and its contents, along with the car and a few thousand dollars. He put the proceeds from the sale of the house and car into a government insured certificate of deposit, and he donated the furniture to Good Will Industries.

In the days following his parents' deaths, Seth discussed his time at Gallaudet with Jacob. "When I came here, I had two great parents and two great legs. Now I'm an orphan and a crip," he said.

"You're not thinking of leaving arc you?" Jacob asked.

"No, I figure I've got my 'bads' out of the way, and things will start evening out for me soon."

A message from Dr. Anthony printed out on the teletypewriter. "Drop by the office tomorrow afternoon if you can; I've got some news I think you're going to like."

"What did I tell you," Seth said. "Things are starting to even out."

During his afternoon break between abnormal psychology and physical science, Seth got over to see Dr. Anthony. "What's up?" he asked.

"Well, what's up is precisely what we're going to find out."

"OK, Doc. I give; what's going on?"

"Just sit tight and see me out. There's a pharmaceutical company in New York planning a clinical study of a new drug. They're doing the study with scientists who work with the National Institutes of Health and the Food and Drug Administration, and they're looking for volunteers."

"I'm all for new drugs, but what does this have to do with me," Seth asked.

"Actually, it has to do with both you and me, because they want to include paraplegics in the clinical study sample, and I'm certain I can get us in."

"Jeez. Slow down, Doc. In for what? It would help me a whole lot if you told me what this new drug is for."

"Sorry. It's a drug for men with erectile dysfunction, and they want to determine if it works for guys with spinal cord injury at the same time as they're looking at how it works for guys with erectile dysfunction in the general population."

"Are you telling me there's a chance for crips to have sex without vacuum tubes, injections, or implants?" Seth asked.

"Yep, as I understand it, you just swallow a couple of pills and you'll be ready to go in minutes."

"Jeez, where do I sign up?

"I've got your medical history, and everything else they need. I'll submit the paperwork and keep you posted."

"About how long do you think it will take?"

"I'd like to say no more than two weeks, but you never know with these kinds of studies. It's always possible there could be delays or other kinds of bureaucratic snafus."

"You going to apply too?" Seth asked.

"Why not? I've still got plenty of lead in my

pencil."

Ultimately, the results indicated that slightly more than half the men in the clinical study with low and complete spinal cord injuries benefitted substantially from the drug. With the pills, each was able to obtain and maintain an erection for a satisfactory length of time. Seth was one of them. So was Dr. Anthony. Both reveled in the miracles of modern medicine.

"So, are you going out with Sarah this weekend?" Doctor Anthony asked.

"Yes, we have a date, but I'm reasonably certain we won't be going out."

Chapter 51

The "sweet spot" on a baseball bat is about six inches from the end of the barrel. Should a batter connect with a ball at that point, a minimum amount of vibration is transferred to his hands, and the ball leaves the bat at maximum velocity. Home runs or hard line drives are usually the result. It is precisely that part of the bat that struck Mario on his left temple.

In a well-planned assault, a group of rival gangsters jumped him. Four of them held him to the ground, face up, and the fifth wielded the Louisville slugger. After a few practice swings, he got right up in Mario's face and said, "This is for taking out my eye."

A hard wooden bat, whooshing at 80 miles per hour, shattered his eardrum and the bones in his middle ear. His cochlea and auditory nerves were mangled, as were his semicircular canals, and facial nerves. The force fractured Mario's skull, and neurons were ripped apart. His brain swelled, oozed blood, and pressure built up from a clot. Cerebral spinal fluid leaked from his nose and ears. To complicate matters, Mario began having seizures. The neurosurgeons didn't expect him to survive.

Out of alternatives, the doctors induced a coma. "Why must you do that?" Rachel asked.

"We hope that by giving his brain a rest, it will lead to a reduction in swelling and give his brain time to heal," the doctors explained. They attached him to a respirator to make it easier for him to breathe, monitored his vital signs, and waited.

Rachel was at his bedside every day, and Angelo came after work. For two months they watched their son hover between life and death in what was essentially a vegetative state. When they weren't at Mario's bedside, they were praying in the hospital chapel. At last, the doctors decided it was time to reverse the coma.

When he came to, Mario's pupils were dilated, and his vision was clouded, as if a piece of gauze had been placed over his eyes. At times, he saw a whirling kaleidoscope of color that sickened him. Pinpoints of complementary colors, yellows and violets for example, flashed across his visual field at random. What felt like electric charges "zapped" through his head and made him twitch, often violently. Any verbalizations tended to be repetitive and nonsensical. "Chumbalone" and "stink slinger" were the most prevalent.

His arms and legs were so weak he couldn't lift them from the bed. Often, he thought he heard the voices of his parents, but he was too exhausted to open his eyes. When he did, he saw the Virgin Mary and the Christ Child hanging on the wall, and confused as he was, he wondered what he was doing in church. *I guess it's OK for me to come to a holy place again, 'cause guys that get hurt real bad are forgiven. Chumbalone.*

A priest stood at his bedside, between his parents. He spoke, but Mario couldn't understand. Neither could he remember his father's name. While they were making the sign of the cross, he gazed upward toward a fluorescent light on the ceiling. *Maybe I'm dead, but where are the angels? Maybe there are no angels. Sweet Jesus, maybe I'm in hell. Maybe Satan is here to jump me in. Chumbalone.*

Doctors came into his room every morning and examined his head. They changed his dressings and probed his wounds. His head hurt all the time, not merely an ache, but a persistent, pounding throb that made him sick to his stomach. The strongest narcotics helped some but only for a while.

Nurses turned him over in his bed and stuck him with needles. Vomit rose from his gut and exploded out of his mouth. "Stink slinger," he said. "Folk singer, humdinger." They cleansed him with warm water and changed his bed sheets.

Several weeks passed. Mario's level of consciousness increased, and he was awake and lucid more often than not. The pain was less acute, and, although his balance was poor, he tried standing by the side of his bed several times a day. Slowly, he and his parents came to grasp the full consequences of his injury.

He spoke very little and when he did, his speech was slurred. This, in combination with the soft, raspy quality of his voice, made his speech unintelligible much of the time, and he had other kinds of language problems that were subtler and more difficult to remedy.

For Mario, like most people, the left hemisphere of the brain is the language center. Thus, damage to his left temporal lobe left him with language disabilities; most notably, problems comprehending the speech of others and problems finding words to express himself. Regarding incoming speech, he often asked people to repeat themselves. "Say that again," he said, or "Whadya mean?" Experts in the field call it "receptive aphasia."

Language problems having to do with Mario's ability to express himself were troublesome as well. Often, he couldn't match the meaning of what he was trying to say with an appropriate facial expression. He would smile when conveying a sad thought, for example, or frown when communicating a happy one. To make things even more difficult, he sometimes forgot the rules about taking turns when communicating with another person.

He had, too, what the language therapist called a "word retrieval problem;" he often couldn't come up with the word or words necessary to express an idea in his head. Instead of saying the correct words, the words he wanted to say, "peanut butter," for example, he would describe them. "Y'know, that brown stuff that sticks to the top of your mouth an' tastes good with grape jelly."

Some of Mario's visual perception abilities, already deficient before the trauma to his brain, were even weaker now. His ability to discriminate a figure from its background was particularly poor. When asked to look at a picture of various letters of the alphabet and pick out all the "e's," for example, he had trouble finding them. "Everythin' looks the same," he said, "like it's all one big blur." His short-term visual memory was poor, too. When presented with a series of three random numbers for five seconds, he couldn't remember them when they were removed from sight.

His memory of events around the time he was beaten was gone. He couldn't recall his assailants or anything about the time right after the doctors reversed his coma. "About all I can remember from those first days in the hospital is standin' at the side of my bed an' bein' held up by a very cool lookin' nurse," he said.

Remembering anything he'd learned during the weeks after his brain damage was hard for him, too. The name of the hospital, the names of his doctors and nurses, the days and times he was scheduled for language therapy, the exercises he was supposed to do on his own for physical therapy—all those things slipped his mind just seconds after he had learned them. Even the location of his room eluded him. After short walks in the halls, he would get disorientated and need help finding his way back.

One of the nurses was the first to comment on

Mario's mood swings. "One minute he's smiling and projecting confidence, and the next he's sad and withdrawn. He'll giggle, then weep, even when there is no good reason for either. It's called 'emotional lability,'" she said, "and it's a common characteristic in patients who have sustained severe brain damage."

Mario became obsessed with trivial details, too. The window shade in his room had to be at exactly the right height. He insisted that the arrangement of food on his dinner plate each night be precisely the same, and that the visitors' chairs be placed at the same angle to his bed each morning. Any change in routine irritated him, for example, meeting a new nurse or orderly. He meant no disrespect, but his responses to these changes were often tactless and impolite. "Who the hell are you?" isn't particularly welcoming.

A sickening combination of vertigo and nausea warned him of the onset of his epileptic seizures. Often, he saw a pattern of lights or heard buzzing noises. Then, as if in the midst of a panic attack, his breathing turned rapid and shallow, and just before he lost consciousness, he screamed.

His muscles seized and excess saliva dribbled from his mouth. He clenched his teeth and thrashed out with his arms and legs at the same time that his head and neck lurched up and down on his pillow. His bowels and bladder evacuated, and his lips and fingertips turned blue. After fifteen minutes or so, Mario quieted down, and his color and breathing returned to normal. He regained consciousness, confused and exhausted. If he seized in the evening, he usually slept the clock around.

Medication helped reduce the frequency and violence of the seizures, but other problems remained. He had lost some hearing in his left ear, and he had recurrent ringing in his right. He had bouts of dry heaving, sometimes three or four times a day. On rare occasions when he felt like eating, nothing smelled or tasted right, as if those senses had somehow been turned off or contaminated, and the damage to his facial nerve made it hard for him, at least at first, to voluntarily close his eyes, to smile, or to keep food in his mouth when he was chewing.

A social worker at the hospital warned Rachel and Angelo that personality changes were common in people who have suffered brain injuries as severe as Mario's. "You've already noticed some changes in your son, and more may show up, even months from now. When he discovers he can't do some of the things he used to do, he's likely to get frustrated or hostile. He may exhibit an increased level of sexuality, including inappropriate remarks to women and touching. There may be times when he's anxious and withdrawn, and many patients get so depressed they don't want to do anything."

"What are we supposed to do if he acts that way?" Rachel asked.

"There isn't much you can do," the social worker said. "You have to accept the idea that the old Mario is gone, and the new one is a different person. The doctors will prescribe the right medicines and therapies, and you need to be patient. Be supportive and give him as much love as you can. You and your husband will have difficult days and nights, but try to remember that your son has survived an injury so terrible, so severe, that one bit more and he would have died. His brain will continue to heal, but it will take some time."

"We will do our very best," Rachel said. "My husband and I will take care of our son, and, with the help of the Good Lord, he will get better."

"There is one other thing," the social worker said. "The doctors here are the best; they know as much as anyone in the world about traumatic brain injury and its effects, but even they will tell you that our brains are very hard to understand. There are no hard and fast rules. Every patient is different and what is true for one isn't always true for another. There is always the chance that Mario, even though his injury was certainly very extreme, will make a recovery better than any of us expect."

Mario was as tough in the hospital as he had been on the street. He worked hard in daily sessions with physical, occupational, and language therapists. To nourish himself and grow stronger, he ate the hospital food without complaint. He never grumbled during countless examinations, some of which were quite painful. "Is that all ya got?" he asked, even as he winced. It was a time in his life that Mario behaved valiantly.

"Our son is a warrior," Angelo said. "He's fightin' back from the worst hurt anyone could possibly stand. I'm not sure I wouldn't have tossed in the towel if it happened to me."

On the four-month anniversary of his admission to the hospital, Angelo drove Mario home and helped him to his bed. When Rachel took out an extra blanket to warm him, she found his diploma from eighth grade graduation. Thinking back and reflecting upon all that had happened since that evening, she sunk to her knees and wept.

Usually, when Angelo came home from work, Mario was asleep. "How did he do today?" he asked Rachel over dinner.

"I think he's doing a little better each day, but he's still so weak and so sick."

"Does he ever ask about me?"

"Let's go upstairs," Rachel said. "Sometimes he wakes up to go to the bathroom." Rachel and Angelo approached his room and saw a light shining from beneath the door. "Go in and talk to him," she said.

Angelo knocked on the door to his son's bedroom and found him awake, thumbing through a Playboy magazine. Mario put it down and motioned for his father to sit at the side of the bed.

"I'm sorry, Dad. I'm so sorry for everythin' I done."

"As I am too, my son."

"Say that again, Dad."

"I'm sorry for what I have done, too, my son." They held each other, rocking back and forth.

Chapter 52

Mario gained strength, and the nausea and vomiting ceased. His speech wasn't as halting or slurred, and walking every day helped his balance. Thanks to Rachel's meals, he gained some weight. Only rarely, perhaps once every couple of weeks, did he have a headache severe enough to force him to bed, and by carefully complying with his dosage, his epileptic seizures were equally infrequent.

Thus, Mario, a young man who had already been limited by neurological deficits and learning disabilities before being beaten, survived, and, to a degree, he healed. With his injury, however, and the subsequent physical problems and changes in his personality, his future was questionable, at best.

Angelo and Mario took walks every day. At first, they settled for making it to the corner and back. Gradually, they worked up to walking around the block, and their goal was to make a mile.

They sat outside in front of the house, resting after one of their walks. Together, they saw Raphael come out of the candy store on the corner and walk in their direction.

"You want me to send him away, Mario?"

"Say that again, Dad."

"You want me to send Raphael away?"

"Nah, Let him come; I wanna hear what he has to say." Raphael noticed them and paused before proceeding. He might have been wary of Angelo, or perhaps he was uncomfortable seeing Mario, given that he'd never made it to the hospital for a visit.

"Hey, my man," Raphael said, simultaneously flashing one of their gang signs. "Glad to see you up an' at it again."

"Yeah, how you doin'?" Mario asked, not even attempting to smile.

"We're havin' a session tomorrow night," Raphael said. "We're jumpin' in three new dudes. Wancha pull on your boots an' come?"

"Say that again," Mario said.

"Three new guys are jumpin' in tomorrow night. Wancha come?"

"Nah, I don't want no part of that."

"Say what, man?"

Mario got close enough to spit on Raphael's face when he spoke. "You listen to what I'm sayin' to you," he said. "You tell 'em for me I'm through with them and gangbangin' and ain't nothin' ever gonna bring me back. You tell 'em for me, straight up, that I'm droppin' the flag."

Raphael's eyes narrowed. During all the time it had taken him to move through the ranks, plus the years he had enjoyed hard-core status, the only gangsters who dropped out were those who died of natural causes or were killed in gang fights. Otherwise, quitting the gang wasn't an option without paying a price.

"You can't drop the flag, just like that," Raphael said. "It's 'beat in an' beat out,' an' you know it. Just like we beat you when you jumped in, we're gonna beat you, only worst, if you try an' get out."

"Say that again," Mario said.

"Whadya deaf? I said there's no way you can quit the gang without takin' another poundin.'"

"Yeah, well you take a good look at us, me an' my dad I'm talking about, 'cause we're right here. You know where we live, an' if you wanna come after me, we're waitin'. Ain't no way you can hurt me more than I already been hurt." The muscles around Angelo's eyes twitched and guttural sounds rose from his throat.

Raphael turned toward the noise, and Angelo leveled him with a stare that was so fearsome, so fierce and chilling, that he averted his gaze, something gangbangers must never do in the face of a challenge.

Angelo calmly gripped Raphael around his neck with his thumbs squarely on his Adam's apple. He smiled, as sweetly as an altar boy, and squeezed until some of Raphael's acne pustules popped and he sunk to his knees. "You come back with your three toughest punks, an' one by one I'll rip your lungs out."

No one ever came after Mario.

Chapter 53

Rachel was happy with the way the men in her life were spending time together. Usually, they went on long walks, but sometimes it was a ball game or a movie. Angelo rented a rowboat and some bamboo poles, and the two of them fished a lagoon at the municipal park. They took in a circus and marveled at the trapeze act and lion tamer. They even went to a live rock concert, something neither of them had ever done.

"Loud enough to wake the dead," Angelo said. "Everyone stands up and waves their arms at the same time they're screamin' their heads off. I mean, you can barely hear the music most times. You couldn't tell if they came to hear the music or jump up and down and scream."

On one of their walks, they came to the Holy Family Children's Home. "Wanna see where your mother an' me grew up?" Angelo asked.

"Yeah, I heard you talkin' 'bout it a lot with Mom, but I never been inside of it."

A receptionist and security guard, upon verifying that Angelo was an "alum," allowed them in. Angelo showed his son the rooms he and his mom lived in, the cafeteria, the classrooms, and the chapel where he first made love to his mother.

"Mom an' me left here when we turned eighteen, not that either one of us knew what we were doin'. I mean, we didn't even know how to write a check, buy groceries, or keep a budget."

"I don't neither," Mario said. "Maybe you and

Mom could teach me pretty soon."

Outside again, Mario asked, "How was it growing up like a...y'know that word that means you don't have no mom or dad?"

"You mean an orphan?"

"Yeah, that's it."

"Bein' an orphan wasn't that good," Angelo said. "I was only three when I got here, so after a while, I couldn't remember my parents; I even forgot what their faces looked like. The people here took decent care of us, but I was lonely. Some of the kids had visitors, and some even went to live in foster homes, but not me. We didn't get out much, an' there weren't many laughs or good times.

"School was the worst thing, 'cause I wasn't good at reading or much else, except the shop courses. I mean, it wasn't near as bad as bein' cooped up in a hospital, but it wasn't good."

"Say that again, Dad."

"I was sayin' that when I was in school, I never learned to read very good, so I didn't like bein' there. It wasn't as bad, though, as you bein' stuck in the hospital for all that time."

"The hospital wasn't so bad," Mario said, "leas' after I started feelin' a little better. I had lots of time to think, an' I don't know if you know it, but me an' the social worker spent more than a few hours talkin' 'bout the kind of person I was. So, at leas' I learnt some of the real reasons I acted up so much, joined the gang, an' left the house."

"I'm listenin' if you want to tell me about it."

"I was a loser Dad, a flat out loser. There was nothin' I was good at. I stunk at school, I was lousy at sports, I couldn't get a girlfriend or any kind of part time job if I tried, an' I knew, in my head, how much I was lettin' you and Mom down. So, it was easier to run away an' be with other losers than to stay home an' grow up like a real man is s'posed to do."

"Y'know, I'm no shrink," Angelo said, "but what you're sayin' seems just about right to me, but all that's done now; it's over, an' what you gotta start thinkin' about, whenever you're ready, is how to turn the leaf an' make a life for yourself now. Got any ideas?"

"I been thinkin' 'bout it some," Mario said, "but before I do anythin', I gotta find someone."

"Who you lookin' for?"

"There's this guy that saved my life. Me and Raphael was at the bowlin' alley, an' we was havin' some pizza. Some of it got stuck in my throat, an' I couldn't breathe. This guy I'm talkin' 'bout did that maneuver, whatever you call it, an' saved me from croakin'. In the old days, it wouldn't have mattered all that much to me, but now I'd really like to find him an' thank him."

"It's a big city, Mario. How you gonna find this guy?"

"It's gonna be hard for sure, 'cept I know a coupla things about him. I'm almost positive he goes to some college in town here, an' he gets around in a wheelchair."

That night, at the kitchen table, Angelo and Mario practiced writing checks and making out budgets.

Chapter 54

"How we gonna find out what college this guy goes to?" Angelo asked.

"Raphael seen a sticker on his car, one of those things you glue on your rear bumper that's got the name of your college on it. I can't remember the name of the college now, 'cept I'm sure, almost positive, it starts with a 'G.'"

"Coulda been George Washington University," Angelo said.

"Nah, I'm thinkin' it only had one word."

"Then maybe it's Georgetown."

"Could be, but I don't think so," Mario said. "It just don't sound right to me, like ringin' a bell, or nothin."

"Well, we could try the yellow pages, Angelo suggested. "There's gotta be a list of all the colleges in there." Mario pulled the phone book from the cabinet under a kitchen counter. It soon became clear that the concept of alphabetical order was something Mario hadn't mastered, either in or out of school. So, gently and without a hint of criticism, Angelo taught him.

Under "Colleges and Universities," Angelo read "Gallaudet University" aloud.

"That's it!" Mario said. "I'm sure that's it. What street's it on?"

"It's over on Florida Avenue, a forty-minute ride or so if there ain't too much traffic. I gotta work tomorrow, but I'm off Friday, so we can take a ride out there if you want." Mario asked Rachel if she'd like to come with, and she was enthused. "It's a college for deaf people," she said, "and I think I once heard that it's the only one like it in the world. If the weather is nice, we'll make a day of it. We can walk around the campus and eat lunch at a nice restaurant, too."

Finding the campus was easy. Angelo stopped for a permit and parked in the visitors' lot. Mario exited the back seat and stared, open-mouthed, as a group of students, actively engaged in animated sign language, passed by. He looked puzzled, as if trying to recall something he couldn't quite remember.

"It's sign language," Rachel said. "It's how deaf people talk to each other."

Mario fell silent. *I know I seen those kind of hand signs before. My memory ain't so good now, but I know I seen it. Maybe it'll come to me.*

"Whatcha thinking about?" Angelo asked.

"Nothin' really, 'cept how cool it looks to talk with your hands like that. Jeez, look how fast they move. I think I could learn to do that if I tried really hard," Mario said.

"Let's walk this way, toward the library," Rachel said. "We'll get some sun on that bench over there and do some people watching. Look at that. Kids sure dress funny these days. I wonder if they rip those holes in their jeans on purpose? And look at the hairdos. Those are boys with hair past their shoulders, and there's one with only a strip down the middle. He looks like an Indian."

Had they been in a comic book, a light bulb would have flashed over Mario's head. *I got it. It was the day me an' Raphael was cruisin' in the Buick, 'cause I was lookin' to bust a cap. We seen two guys walkin' down the street an' thought they was flashin' gang signs…Sweet Jesus; I think I busted a deaf guy.*

The campus was quiet while classes were in session. Occasionally, individual or small groups of students entered or exited the library, along with a few older people, probably professors. At ten minutes to the hour, however, hundreds of students poured out of classroom buildings, hustling on their way to other classes, or lunch, or maybe an early start at their favorite beer hall. During the better part of three hours, they saw four people in wheelchairs. Three were women, and the other was a morbidly obese man who had somehow trained his golden retriever to pull him along in his chair.

"Looks like we struck out," Mario said.

"Yeah, it was a long shot to begin with," Angelo said, "but there's no reason you can't come back on your own if you wanna."

Angelo drove his family home after a late lunch at a deli. Mario didn't eat much and was as quiet as he had been since his injury. Rachel hoped it wasn't the kind of withdrawal the social worker had warned them about.

Chapter 55

That night, Mario slept about an hour. His mind raced, and he couldn't get comfortable.

Maybe I should juss forget the whole thing. I don't even know for sure if I busted him, or maybe I juss winged him in the shoulder or the leg, an' he was fine after a few days restin' and gettin' stitched up in the hospital. No harm, no foul, like they say durin' them professional basketball games.

For sure, I don't wanna go to jail, so maybe I should juss clamp up and forget the whole thin'. I mean, no one's ever gonna know what I done but me, so maybe I should juss let it be. Chances are if anyone else knew about it, the police woulda come after me by now, so why not juss let a sleepin' dog rest, or somethin' like that.

But, what if I busted him or at leas' wounded him real bad? If I turn myself in to the cops, maybe they'll juss put me in Juvy Hall for a little while then give me probation 'cause of my age an' 'cause I been hurt so bad, an' 'cause I never had a record or nothin'. I mean, it's not like I been a good person, but maybe they'll give me a second chance.

But, if I turn myself in, I'm gonna have to tell the truth an' the whole truth, so they're for sure gonna find out about my drug dealin', and maybe even the shopliftin', an' who knows how much time I'll get for that. Sweet Jesus, I sure don't wanna go to jail, so maybe I should clamp up an' let it be.

But, if I wind up in jail 'cause I hurt the guy real bad, it would be fair, sort of like makin' the score even. An', whenever I got out of jail, an' that could be earlier than I think 'cause of good behavior, at leas' I'll feel better 'bout myself with a clear conscience, an' I wouldn't have to be thinkin' 'bout what I did to another person an' keepin' it quiet for the rest of my life. I mean, shootin' another human bein' who prolly never hurt anyone else an' was juss walkin' down the street talkin' to his deaf buddy an' mindin' his own business is a whole lot worst than poppin' a cat; that's for sure.

But, done is done, like they say, an' even if I cop to the shootin', it's not gonna make anythin' better for the guy I shot. I mean, let's say I shot him in the leg an' he lost a ton of blood, or he got an infection and they had to chop his leg off or he would die. If I spill my guts an' wind up in jail, it sure ain't gonna get him his leg back. If it would get him his leg back, chances are I would turn myself in without a doubt, but if he ain't never gonna ever walk again, nobody wins. I rot in jail an' he's still walkin' 'round on one leg an' a peg or sittin' in a wheelchair. So, what's the use; nobody wins.

But, Raphael knows what I done. I doubt he'll rat, though, 'cause rattin' ain't somethin' that gangsters do, even on guys that drop the flag. An' even if he was mad enough to rat on me, he'd be stupid to do it, 'cause he was right there in the Buick with me, an' that means he'd for sure get in some serious trouble too, even though he didn't pull the trigger or nothin'. Raphael's a pretty smart guy, so he's got to know better than that. Come to think of it though, I'm not sure zackly how smart Raphael is; I mean, he may be smarter than me, but that still leaves a lot of room to be smart. It might be, too, that neither one of us, or anyone else in the gang, for that matter, was too long on smarts.

Sometimes, I wish it was like the old days when I didn't give a darn about other people. I remember those days pretty good; back then, I never woulda gave this whole thing a second of my time, let alone the whole night. It woulda been like what's the big deal; I shot someone, so that's his problem. Screw him, an' that woulda been the end of it. Case closed.

It's kind of hard for me to figure, but ever since my brain got hurt, I've noticed that I feel sorry for other people a lot more. It's sort of like the golden rule that I learned way back there in grammar school. Not that I ever followed rules too much, but it tells you to treat other people like you want them to treat you. So, I never shoulda killed that little girl's hamster neither, an' if I could ever find her, I'd sure get her a new one. Or, at leas' a golden fish. Sweet Jesus, now I got two people to find. An' a golden fish.

It muss be mornin' or nearly, an' I still don't know what I should do. All night long I been tossin' an' turnin' an' thinkin' 'bout this, an' I still don't know what to do. I'd say 'bout half of me thinks I should just clamp up an' say nothin'. Another half is tellin' me to cop to it an' lay everythin' on the table. An', the rest of me is so freakin' tired from not sleepin' that I wish I could juss stop thinkin' about it an' leas' catch a little sleep.

Mario decided what to do at about the same time the sun came up. He would sit with Rachel and Angelo at the breakfast table and tell them everything. He hoped his parents, older and smarter and with more experience, would be able to advise him.

"You look tired, Mario. Didn't you sleep well?" Rachel asked.

"Say that again, Mom."

"I said you look tired, like you didn't sleep very well."

"Boy, you notice everythin', Ma; truth is, I was up most of the night wrestlin' with a problem I got. I was hopin' to talk to you an' Dad 'bout it, an' maybe you could help me out with some advice."

"Dad will be down in a couple of minutes, and you can tell us what's bothering you while we have breakfast. Here's pancakes, eggs, and bacon. Come, sit down and eat."

Chapter 56

"It's good you came to us," Angelo said, after listening to Mario's story. "Calm down an' think real hard. Try to pitcher everythin' that happened from the time you saw the guys walkin' on the sidewalk to the time you drove away. There might be somethin' you forgot."

Mario closed his eyes and rested his chin on his hands. "There is somethin' I forgot to tell you," he said, after a minute or two. "When I was peelin' away, I heard a loud scream."

"That prolly means you busted him," Angelo said. "My guess is that nobody woulda screamed 'less you busted him."

"So, what do I do now?" Mario asked.

"What you did was bad son, really bad. You shot a guy for no reason 'cept to prove you were tough enough to jump in with the gang. Now, you have to pay the price. Otherwise, if you do nothin', you'll never be able to put what you did out of your mind, an' it will eat at you for as long as you live, like a sore that don't heal up."

"I know you're right, Dad, but I don't want to go to jail. It scares me real bad."

"It scares me an' your mother, too, so before we do anythin', I think we gotta talk to someone that knows more about these things. We gotta talk to a lawyer first. I'll ask around at work to see if anyone knows who we should talk to. 'Course, in the meantime, zip it up an' don't say nothin' about this to no one else but me an'

Mom."

Angelo's boss had a brother-in-law who was once a criminal lawyer. He had been disbarred because he was caught bribing judges, but he was available for consultations at a fee much less than Angelo would have had to pay to a practicing attorney who bribed judges but hadn't been caught. For Angelo, their meeting was disheartening.

At dinner that evening, Angelo explained what he had learned. "Here's the deal. If you turn yourself in an' cop to what you did, you'll be tried as an adult. What you did was so bad, there will be no Juvy Hall, no release to the community when you're twenty-one years old, an' no probation.

"Even though you're a first time offender with serious health problems, chances are you would serve heavy time, twenty years or so, maybe more, at a maximum security prison. Right now, the way things are with gang violence an' drive by shootings, judges and juries are bein' real tough on gangbangers, even the ones who quit."

"Christ, Dad, I don't have no record; the doctors say I'm disabled an' prolly ain't gonna get much better, no matter how hard I work at it. Ain't there no chance I might get a little...y'know, that word that means people feelin' sorry for you? An' wouldn't I get a lighter sentence for cooperatin' with the police?"

"I think the word you're lookin' for is 'mercy,' Son, and the other lawyer, the DA who prosecutes you, is for sure gonna point out that you didn't have much mercy for the guy you shot. I'm not gonna lie to you, Son; if you confess, chances are you'll prolly be goin' away for a long time."

"Say that again, Dad."

"I said if you stand up an' tell the truth, chances are you'll be goin' to jail for a long time."

Both turned toward Rachel. To this point she had listened carefully but hadn't contributed to the conversation. She put down her coffee cup, smoothed her hair, and took her turn.

"Mario, my son, it's true that you did a terrible thing. Shooting a gun at another person, perhaps killing him, or even wounding him is a mortal sin. All of us understand that and agree that you made a very bad mistake, a terrible mistake, but I am your mother; I gave you life, and I will not let you go to prison. Your injury has made you softer. You've changed since they beat you so badly. Your brain is different, and you're a different person. You feel for others, and you're sorry for what you did. I believe in my heart that the hole you once had in your soul has knit."

"All that's true, Mom. I am a different person now, an' maybe that's why I need to stand up an' be a man."

"No! We're not even sure you can take care of yourself yet, and we have no idea of the kind of doctors and therapy that would be available while you're in prison, if any. What good will come from your going to jail? Haven't you suffered enough?

"Yeah, me an' you an' Dad know how much I suffered an' how hard it's been for all of us, but I can't stop thinkin' about the guy I shot. Sometimes I wish I was like I used to be, y'know, not carin' 'bout no one or nothin', but now I can't help thinkin' that I owe him 'cause he's been sufferin' too, maybe even worst than me."

"You know there are gangbangers in prison, and I bet they have long memories," Rachel said. "They're going to come after you. Do you want to trade saying you're sorry for your life? How will it be for your father and me when you're gone, and all we can say is that you were sorry for what you did right up to the moment they stuck a knife in your belly? No! We will keep this quiet. I'm telling you we will keep this quiet, and that's the way it's going to be. Eventually, the Good Lord will judge you."

"An' us," Angelo added.

Thus, Mario's dilemma went unresolved. For three days it went unresolved, until the doorbell rang early the next morning. Two policemen, a young man in a wheelchair, and a sign language interpreter waited at the front door. An anonymous snitch had provided the address.

Chapter 57

Angelo pushed aside the drapes covering the living room window to see who was there.

He couldn't know who the interpreter was, and, at first, he suspected the young man in the wheelchair might be the person who had saved Mario's life, but why the police?

Wait a second. This could be trouble. This could be the guy that Mario shot. He opened the front door. "How can I help you?" he asked.

One of the policemen, a tall, barrel-chested man, about six foot four, asked Angelo if he were Mario's father. "We need to talk with him, and with you and his mother, about the possibility of criminal behavior."

Angelo ushered everyone in, pausing to help Seth over the threshold. At the same time, Rachel and Mario entered the living room.

Seth looked toward Mario, and his adrenaline kicked in. A surge of strength coursed through his body, and he clenched his fists involuntarily. The hair on his arms rose, as did goose bumps. His pulse pounded in his ears, and the muscles in his neck and shoulders tensed. Sweat covered his brow, yet he felt chilled and clammy. Later, he would discover that he ground his teeth so hard he'd fractured a tooth.

This is the punk who shot me in the back. Here he is again, standing right in front of me, with his goddamn birthmark and tattoo, probably scared out of his mind, because even with half a set of wits, he's got to know why I'm here with the police.

220

He's probably thinking about how I found him and where these policemen are going to take him. Maybe, he's considering the living conditions in prison and how long he'll be there. Or, he might be concerned about perverts who have a voracious appetite for "fresh meat," guys who are a whole lot tougher and sicker than he is. I hope he's thinking about all those things and contemplating, if he can, how dismal his pathetic future is about to become.

All the time Seth was ruminating, perhaps thirty seconds, Mario was staring back at him. He stuffed his hands into his pockets to hide his trembling and tried to stifle one of his inappropriate smiles. He shuffled from one foot to the other, resisting an urge to flee and a need to urinate. For a few seconds, he felt nauseated and heard the buzzing sounds that typically signaled the onset of a seizure, but the sensations passed.

Sweet Jesus. This is the guy I busted on the sidewalk. With the cops here, it can't be no one else; it's gotta be him. Someone must of ratted. An', I figure he's sittin' in that wheelchair 'cause I put him there. Without a goddamn care in the world, I shot him down an' crippled him, prolly for the rest of his life. What the hell was wrong with me?

What am I gonna say to him? There's nothin' I can say to him that's gonna matter, anyhow. Truth is, when I shot him, he didn't mean any more to me than that freakin' alley cat I popped. Sweet Jesus. Whatever the hell was wrong with me, I deserve what I get.

If I was him, I'd sure wanna get even; I'd wanna put me in a wheelchair, too, or at leas' put me back in the hospital after layin' some kind of serious hurt on me. What am I gonna say to him? I wish someone here would say somethin', at lease.

Finally, the second policeman, a short guy with a gravely voice, spoke up and read Mario his rights. Mario and his parents listened intently, only briefly shifting their attention from the policeman to the interpreter.

"We have reason to believe that Mario acted to

satisfy a street gang induction ritual by participating in a drive-by shooting," the policeman continued. "As a result, this young man suffered a spinal cord injury that caused him to be paralyzed from the waist down. As you can see, Seth is deaf as well, a problem severe enough by itself, let alone in combination with paraplegia." Turning to Mario, he said, "Is there anything that you would like to say?"

"You don't need to say anything, Son," Rachel said. "You heard your rights; you don't have to say anything until we get a lawyer to represent you. Whatever you say, they can use it against you, just like the officer said."

"No, Mom. I ain't gonna clamp up no more. I'm tired of livin' the lie. It's time for me to stand up an' admit what I done. I don't want no sleaze bag lawyer tryin' to get me off. I'm ready to go to jail for what I done if you an' Dad will get me the help I need when I'm in."

"What kind of help would that be?" Seth asked.

"Mario was beaten by other gangsters," Rachel said. "They hit him in the head with something hard, maybe a club or a bat, and fractured his skull. He was in a coma for two months and almost died. The doctors tell us his brain is healing, but it will take a long time. He doesn't hear so well out of his left ear, and he has a hard time understanding what people say to him."

Rachel dabbed a handkerchief to her eyes and faltered, looking toward Angelo and urging him to continue. "Whatever he learns, he forgets very quick," Angelo said. "Sometimes he can't control his emotions or impulses, I think you call 'em. His medicine helps, but he still has those epileptic seizures. We been told that people whose brains have been damaged like Mario's often get depressed, sometimes so bad they commit suicide. Even if he don't get depressed, he'll need all kinds of therapy for a long time. God help him and us."

"Forgive me, sir, but I'm going to need a wheelchair for a long time, too," Seth said. "Forever, in fact."

"My mother an' father know that, an' so do I," Mario said. "I know you won't believe me, man, but I'm sorry for what I done to you. I'm really as sorry as anyone could be for what I done to you. If I could, I would trade places with you in a second. For sure, I would sit in your chair for the rest of my crummy life if it would help you walk again."

Seth sat and thought. *These aren't bad people. I actually believe this punk; I actually believe he's sorry for what he did.*

Huge success is the best revenge of all.

Finally, he turned toward Mario and asked, "How's your bowling game?"

"Say what?" Mario asked.

"I asked you how your bowling game was."

"I don't get it," Mario said. "Why you askin' me that?"

"I'm asking because I'm the one who saved your life when you were choking at the bowling alley."

"For real?" Mario asked. "That was after I busted you on the sidewalk. Are you sayin' that you saved my life after you knew I shot you?"

"That's right," Seth said. "I knew you were the one who shot me before I saved you. In fact, I was looking for you at the bowling alley the night you choked."

Huge success is the best revenge of all.

"Then, why did you even bother helpin' me?" Mario asked. "Why didn't you juss stay out of it and let me flop around on the floor 'til I croaked?"

"An' why didn't you go to the cops when you

first figured out it was my son that shot you?" Angelo added.

"The truth is that I saved your life and I didn't go to the police, because I believed that choking to death on a chunk of pizza was too easy a way for you to die. It was too quick. You hadn't suffered enough, and you hadn't felt enough pain. I hated you, Mario; I hated you so much that I wasn't going to let you get punished by anyone but me. Not the police, not the Good Lord, only me."

Mario felt tears welling up; still, he maintained eye contact with Seth.

"Your two bullets hurt me real bad, Mario. They disabled me forever; they took years out of my life; they broke my parents' hearts, and they put me into a black depression, a hole so deep and ugly I thought I'd never climb out."

"God, I'm so sorry, Seth. What can I do?"

"Your two bullets made me less of a man, a man who probably won't be able to father children, and for a while, they turned me into a stinking beast whose main purpose in life was revenge. You did all of that, Mario; you did it with your two goddamn bullets in one selfish moment when you were somehow convinced that joining up with a bunch of gangbanger losers was more important than another person's life.

Huge success is the best revenge of all.

"I won't tell you what I had in store for you, Mario, except to say that the consequences would have been at least as bad as those you suffered from your beating. I had it all planned, and I promise you that when I was finished, you would never have been the same. Down to your very core, you would never have been the same."

"I get all that," Mario said. "Whatever you had planned for me, no matter how bad it was, I had it comin'. I know that, an' juss like you, I woulda been lookin' to even the score if someone shot me an' screwed up my life the way I done to you. An', I wouldn't have gone to the police, neither. An eye for an eye, just like it says in the Bible, I think. I'm tellin' you, though, straight up as I can, that there ain't nothin' I wouldn't do to make you whole again. An', if me goin' to jail will at leas' make you feel better, I'm ready."

"You're going to have to come to the station with us," the taller policeman said. "You'll be held in the lockup until a preliminary hearing, and my hunch is that it's going to be very difficult for you to make bail."

"Wait a minute," Seth said, signing slowly and carefully so the interpreter would get everything exactly right. "I've changed my mind; I don't want Mario to go to prison."

Mario, his parents, and the policeman stood mute, jaws agape. A full ten seconds passed before Angelo gathered himself and asked, "What's that you're sayin', young man? Maybe I didn't hear you right."

"What I'm saying is that I've changed my mind. I don't want Mario going to prison. I think a juvenile detention center, a place where he could continue receiving therapy, would be better than a prison. While he's there, he could go to school and maybe even learn some kind of trade. That way, when he gets old enough and is released, he'll be equipped for some type of job other than pushing dope and rolling drunks."

"No way in hell that's going to happen," the shorter policeman said. "His crime was so serious that no judge will refer his case to juvenile court. He'll be tried as an adult, and if he's found guilty, he'll be going away for a long time. Yeah, he may have some physical and mental problems from the beating he took, but prisons have doctors who help inmates who are sick."

"Then, let me put it to you another way," Seth

said. "If Mario isn't tried as a juvenile, I won't press charges. He's already paid a huge price; and given the trauma to his brain, he's going to keep on paying for a long time. The only thing prison will do for him is make him a more effective criminal. He'll just get better at conning people, and he'll make more drug contacts."

"Unbelievable," the policeman said, veins now clearly visible on his forehead. "He maimed you and put you in that chair for no good reason, for Chrissakes. We've got him right here; he deserves to be punished, and you want to let him off with Juvy? Unbelievable."

"We do it your way," Seth said, "and chances are Mario gets out of prison without the skills necessary to survive on the outside. He'll be exactly like three out of four other prisoners who have served their time and wind up back in prison less than a year after they've been released. If you're looking for something unbelievable, officer, you ought to consider those numbers.

"We do it my way, and at least there is a chance Mario turns the corner and makes some kind of decent life for himself. So take your choice, officers. Either Mario's case is processed through the juvenile court system, or he walks."

Chapter 58

Seth was correct about adult prisons. That Mario might simply mature into a harder criminal was a valid concern, and his statistics regarding the recidivism rate were right on the money. What Seth didn't know, however, was that the situation in most juvenile detention centers wasn't much better. The reality was that most of them were run exactly like adult prisons, their sole difference being that they housed a younger crop of inmates.

"You know," he said to Jacob, "it's amazing, but in the typical juvenile detention center, 'Juvy' it's called, orange jump suits and sandals are the required dress, the same as it is in adult prisons. Kids live in cells, spending most of their time isolated from others. Cell doors are locked, and watch towers, even dogs, are used for security."

"Seems like the only thing they're doing is preparing young criminals to be older criminals," Jacob said. "I thought the main idea was supposed to be rehabilitation."

"Well, their mission statements say that rehabilitation, not punishment, is their goal, but without well-trained counselors and teachers, it's pretty hard to pull off."

"What about daily living?" Jacob asked. "How do they spend their time and who are they responsible to?"

"From what I've read, they eat in large cafeterias, institutional style," Seth said. "Vocational training programs, if available at all, are taught by poorly-qualified teachers using substandard equipment. Recreation and physical fitness programs are unstructured, often consisting of nothing more than an hour or two of free time in the 'yard' without any sort of organized activity. Supervisors, a euphemism for guards, assume punitive roles, and with their billy clubs and harsh demeanor, they tend to be feared rather than trusted."

"How many are released and wind up back in adult prisons?"

"It's called the 'recidivism" rate," Seth said, "and it's almost as high as it is for adults coming out of prison. More than half, in some places as high as eighty percent, of the kids who spend time in Juvy, wind up back in jail as adults."

Mario, however, was fortunate to be placed in a juvenile detention center that broke the rules. It was in a jurisdiction where authorities had studied centers in other states and identified their strengths and weaknesses. Subsequently, with more knowledge of best practices, they modified their own system.

Their new mission statement indeed stressed rehabilitation rather than punishment, but here, the philosophy was supported by a slew of very real reforms. Architectural changes offered a new style of living—dormitory rather than cellblock. Health and wellness strategies stressed nutrition and disease prevention.

Participation in structured physical education and fitness programs was required every morning, as was involvement in a competitive sport. Group counseling provided a mechanism for countering anxiety and depression and helped with the resolution of conflicts, and certified school teachers helped residents attain literacy and prepared them for higher levels of academic achievement, even college.

Data gathered over a twelve-year period subsequent to these reforms indicated that only ten percent of those released from juvenile detention had been incarcerated in adult prison, the lowest recidivism rate in the country. This is the center to which Mario was assigned.

He was arrested and transported in a police cruiser to his place of confinement where he would remain for the next four years. Upon arrival, no one took his street clothes and exchanged them for an orange jump suit and sandals. With a few others, he spent an hour taking part in an orientation to the facility. Then, he was given clean towels and a fresh bar of soap before showering and washing his hair with delousing shampoo.

Dinner consisted of hamburger sandwiches, french fries, salad, canned peaches, and a glass of lemonade. He ate at a table with three others, and the food, while far from gourmet, was appetizing and good enough. After dinner, he watched TV for an hour before sleeping in a holding area with six other "newbies." Like dinner, the bed was good enough.

Adjudication and detention hearings were held, and Mario moved to his permanent quarters. His room was one of only ten in a dormitory style building rather than a cellblock. Mario had no way of knowing, but it wasn't much different from typical dorm rooms at colleges and universities everywhere.

It came furnished with a dresser for personal belongings, a double decker bed, a sink and mirror, two desks, two closets with adequate space, and two small windows covered with wire mesh. Nowhere were there bars, barbed wire, watchtowers, or Dobermans.

Fluorescent bulbs controlled by wall switches lighted his room. Thus, unlike other juvenile detention facilities in which the lights were kept on all night long,

Mario slept in the dark, and if he wanted, he could have a phonograph or radio to listen to music.

For the first two weeks, Mario's roommate was a sixteen-year-old skinhead with swastikas tattooed on his back and biceps. "Adolph," as he chose to be called, shunned clean clothes and soap. Apart from desecrating synagogues, his main claim to fame was seemingly endless flatulence. "I been tape recording 'em, and if I can cut one longer than twenty seconds, I'm going to submit my tape to Alec Guinness; you know, the dude that keeps track of all them world records."

Adolph was transferred to another facility before attaining his goal, much to Mario's delight. It took about twelve hours for the redolence of bowel gas to fully dissipate. Then came Tavadas. He was a young man whose passions in life were bodybuilding and shoplifting; in fact, he had been apprehended while attempting to shoplift a Lexus from a dealership in the suburbs.

Tavadas was fastidious about personal hygiene and didn't have much to say, characteristics which delighted Mario, as well. Additionally, he was capable of doing 75 one armed pushups followed by a perfectly executed 60-second handstand during which time he supported himself entirely on his fingertips. Both athletic feats were admirable and Mario told him so. "Jeez, you're one strong dude," he said.

"You ain't seen nothin' yet," Tavadas said in a rare burst of chattiness. "When things are just right, like with the atmosphere, the humidity, the air pressure and that, I can float." Things never turned out to be just right.

Mario adjusted to his new routine easily. He ate in the dining hall, participated in structured physical education and fitness programs on the athletic field before breakfast, telephoned Rachel and Angelo once a week, as allowed, and saw them on visiting days. He cleaned his room, laundered his clothes, and purchased toiletries and other personal items at the center store.

On weekdays, from 9 until 3:30, he went to school. Classes were small, no more than eight students in a class. Teachers used high interest but low reading level teaching materials. Twice a week, after dinner, he participated in mandatory group counseling sessions. These ran for at least an hour, but lasted twice as long when residents were concerned with difficult issues and needed the extra time. The counselors, like the teachers, had college degrees and were state certified in their fields.

Part of the philosophy at the facility was that residents would profit from extracurricular activities, something they might find enjoyable and in which they might continue to participate once being released. Learning to compete in a sport was one possibility, and everything from archery and boxing to tennis and wrestling was available. For residents less athletically inclined and energetic, chess, yoga, meditation, and breathing classes were offered. Whatever his choice, one evening a week, Mario was required to show up for "extracurriculars."

He would have chosen boxing if he were allowed, but with his medical history, particularly the brain damage, the staff wouldn't allow it. "Not a chance," the coach said. "With your history, the trauma to your brain and all that, there's isn't a chance in the world we'd expose your noodle to any more hits."

"Look, I just wanna get in better shape, an' I think the best an' fastest way to do it is to box," Mario said. "How about if you work with me. You could teach me to throw punches the right way and how to move around the ring without bein' so clumsy. The only difference is that we'll work side by side in the ring an' never throw punches at each other."

"Lemme talk to my boss, first," the coach said. "I'll let you know tomorrow."

The answer was a flat out negative. "We understand your point about sparring side by side and not punching each other. But, boxing for you, in any form is still something we're not comfortable with. There's no way to predict what can happen in the ring, and honestly, besides the chance of falling on your head, there are legal issues of liability we don't want to expose ourselves to."

Mario went back to the list of activities available and gave it another look. *I know I already stink at most of these, though I never tried badminton. I'm not even sure of what it is 'cept hittin' somethin' over a net. Wait a minute. Here's yoga and breathing exercises. It says it's relaxin' an' makes you less tense. I could use some of that.*

Mario's teacher was an avid believer in the value of what she taught. "Advanced breathing practices and yoga will cleanse your body and mind," she said. "You'll each learn how to use your breath to get relief from all the effects of stress and negative emotions you have. You'll become calmer and more alert, and I promise that you'll sleep better, beginning as soon as tonight. Also, you'll learn practical life skills that enable you to accept responsibility for your past actions and to handle future conflict and stressful situations successfully. When you've learned everything in my program, you'll have something that will benefit you for the rest of your life."

That kind of sales pitch was irresistible for Mario. He attended regularly, participated enthusiastically, and although all of the benefits his teacher cited weren't immediately noticeable, he did, in fact, begin sleeping better, right from the first.

At all other settings outside of the boxing ring

and wrestling mat, Mario and his fellow residents were required to solve their problems civilly, with words instead of physical force. If there were a conflict, anyone could call for a "circle," a talk session, at any time. The rest had to stop whatever they were doing and discuss the issue with a counselor.

Thus, Mario had a full day; in fact, he had never been so busy in his life, and along with all of his other activities, he had an after-school job—mowing and maintaining the grass and landscaping on the detention center grounds with a team of others.

Three of Mario's more distinguishing characteristics when he entered the juvenile justice system were a set of rotten, brown teeth, a "loud" tattoo on his forearm, and illiteracy.

To his yoga instructor, he asked, "Any way I can get my choppers fixed? They're so bad, I don't wanna smile."

A state-employed dentist fixed his teeth, extracting the bad ones and inserting substitutes. "Also, I'd like to ditch my tattoo, if I can. It reminds me of too much bad stuff," he said.

A dermatologist sandblasted and removed his tattoo, at least to the extent that it wasn't recognizable as a gang symbol.

Teachers, however, found it more difficult to remedy his sundry academic deficiencies.

In Mario's case, the barriers to academic achievement were indeed formidable. Neurological deficits from infancy, perceptual and language delays during early childhood, the poor quality of his "special" education, the brain trauma he sustained during his beating, the subsequent language, perceptual and memory problems—all these factors, alone and in combination, limited his learning capacity to a minimal level. Nevertheless, each of his teachers assumed he had the capacity to become literate.

"Lease they give me a chance," Mario said; "None of 'em thinks I'm gonna flunk, even before we start."

Given his teachers' optimism and conscientious efforts and Mario's sincere motivation to improve, he did manage almost a three-year gain in academic levels during his four-year stay. More important, however, was the curriculum he was exposed to. Mario didn't need to learn how to divide fractions, diagram sentences, or read English literature. Nor did he need to know physics, world history, or a foreign language. Instead, it was crucial that he learn practical knowledge and skills, the kind of information that related to everyday living and basic facts that most people were familiar with.

Reading the daily newspaper, filling out a job application form, how to conduct oneself during a job interview, how to make change, to order from a menu, to read a bus and train schedule, to complete an income tax form, to compute a tip, write a letter, calculate a discount—these things, more than achieving a certain grade level on a standardized test, were emphasized.

Similarly, necessary information, for example, the names of important governmental figures, the structure of the government, basic geography, at least of the United States, and exposure to art other than graffiti and music other than heavy metal were stressed.

There was even more reason for optimism, too. Besides coming home with bright, new teeth, a winning smile, and basic literacy, Mario returned with the ability to operate, maintain, and repair every piece of lawn and landscaping equipment currently in operation.

His knowledge of gardening had become fairly extensive; some might even say "expert." All things botanic, from tea roses to maple trees, grew for him, and he had become equally expert at trimming large trees and repairing small engines, too.

Mario had found his niche, an area of endeavor in which he excelled, an area that was not heavily dependent upon academic excellence.

Five Years Later

Chapter 59

Seth completed his Master's Degree in a year and a half and was accepted into the doctoral program in clinical psychology immediately thereafter. "This is a different ball game," he said, "the equivalent of the academic major leagues." Seth fully understood he was in for a much more exacting challenge; in fact, the barriers for Ph.D. candidates were many and high, designed to be hurdled by only the brightest and most motivated.

"What are your courses going to be like?" Sarah asked.

"Well, for starters," he said, "the courses and seminars require a ton of reading and lengthy term papers as well as individual and group presentations. My professors are serious scholars, and they expect no less from us. My advanced statistical methods and experimental design courses look like real doozies."

Fortunately, for Seth, he had taken some math, including calculus, as an undergraduate. He had developed good study skills; he was well organized and managed his time well, and most importantly, he was determined to earn a doctorate. He was quite aware, too, that no one at Gallaudet would grant him one simply because he was good looking.

Sixteen courses after his Master's and a one year internship at the university mental health clinic preceded written comprehensive examinations—eight hours a day for three consecutive days. He passed those and presented his dissertation proposal to a committee of six professors in clinical psychology and related fields. His committee readily accepted his topic, "The Comparative Effectiveness of Cognitive-Behavioral Therapy and Antidepressant Medication for Deaf Adolescents and Young Adults with Clinical Depression."

After his research proposal had been accepted, he said to Sarah, "I can't be positive, but I think the committee's quick approval of my research topic might have something to do with the fact that at least three of the members are depressed themselves. Maybe heavy teaching loads, two percent annual raises, and crotchety department heads do that."

Seth anticipated that at least two years would be required to gather and analyze data and write his dissertation. The final hurdle would be defending his dissertation during a three-hour session, open to the public, at which committee members would be free to grill him upon any aspect of his research. "Final orals" they're called.

Other graduate students who had recently earned their doctorates assured him that the oral defense was the easiest part of the process. "By that time, you'll know more about your research topic than your professors, so it's a snap, nothing more than a formality," they said.

"Easy for you to say," Seth said.

Seth and Sarah lived in a ranch house a comfortable distance from campus. During the process of redecorating, Sarah consented to pastels and earth tones, except for one bedroom done in her preferred pink and orange. But, even that room had no mirrors affixed to the ceiling.

The house had three bedrooms, two and a half bathrooms, one off the master bedroom, a family room, mature trees, and a large back yard. Sarah purchased ramps for the entrance and exit doors, and Seth hired a contractor to make the modifications he needed in the master bath.

"Do we really need a steam shower?" Sarah asked.

"Hey, I checked it out," Seth said. "It has therapeutic value, so it's tax deductible." The previous owner certified that the roof was only two years old and the basement had never flooded. The lawn in the back yard had been resodded the previous summer, and the exterior of the house had been repainted. Nice, too, was the fact that Seth had the money from his inheritance to cover the down payment and remodeling costs.

His position as research assistant professor at Gallaudet brought in a modest salary, and Sarah helped by working as a rehabilitation therapist at the student health center at Gallaudet. Together, they supported themselves nicely, much better than the large majority of doctoral candidates and their wives, most of whom lived in graduate student housing and ate a lot of bologna sandwiches and Ramen noodle soup.

Seth and Sarah had married two years earlier. Although no one asked for her help with planning, Miriam seized the reins. "We'll have a lavish affair at the country club with at least 300 attendees, including the governor and a congressman or two," she announced. "We'll need a twelve-piece band, hot and cold hors d'oeuvres accompanied by Champagne cocktails, and a filet mignon dinner served on tables covered in Irish linen and laden with fresh orchids."

"Have you run it past the kids?" Sam asked.

"Not yet, but don't you think they'll love the idea of waiters sporting tuxedos and white gloves? For dessert, we'll have a sweet table with exotic fruit everyone can dip into rivers of milk chocolate flowing to and fro. Matrons will help Sarah change, and we'll hire limousines to deliver out-of-town guests to and from their hotels."

Sam, of course, was prepared to accommodate Miriam's every whim and would have but for the bride and groom nixing such ostentation and opting for a smaller, more "dignified" wedding. Only the immediate families and closest friends would be invited.

Miriam pouted for a time, but ultimately gave in. "I guess it's their wedding, not mine," she said, "but so many of our dear friends and acquaintances will be disappointed. It might have been the social event of the year. I will at least inform the society page reporters at the Post and Times."

Sarah's guest list consisted of 47 people and Seth added another 20. It was a mixed crowd; 42 were people who could hear, and 25 were Deaf. Jacob and Dr. Anthony were co-best men, and Sarah's cousin, a child prodigy on the harp who spoke fluent French, as well, was flower girl. Another cousin, a disagreeable six year old from Poughkeepsie, with attention deficit disorder and rampant mucous rather constantly leaking from his nose, was the ring bearer.

Sam popped for the entire affair, but Sarah called many of the shots. "I want the procession to the altar to be led by two American Sign Language interpreters. They'll proceed down the aisle, before the officiate, so that all of the guests will know that Deaf are an important part of our wedding.

"The officiate will stand between Seth and me, and everyone will face the guests. We'll exchange our vows and love poems in sign, and the interpreters, one standing at the side of the altar facing the guests and one facing the officiate, will translate.

"Our guests who are Deaf will sit with hearing guests for dinner, and at every table, at least one hearing person will be fluent in sign language. That way, no one will be left out of conversations that might be hard to follow, and everyone will be comfortable."

Sarah met with the florist before the wedding and instructed her to provide centerpieces that were not so tall as to interfere with anyone's line of sight and serve as a barrier to signing. Similarly, the photographer and videographer agreed to work unobtrusively, not getting in the way of anyone's vision.

The wedding turned out to be delightful, or, as described by the society page reporters, "an intimate and elegant affair, tasteful and dignified." A steady flow of alcohol helped to loosen any inhibitions. People mingled nicely; some spoke, some signed, some danced and some didn't. A few too many asked Sarah to dance and for kisses, requests she graciously honored, all the while thinking of a foot rub and hot bath.

During dinner, the guests who were Deaf took turns standing at their tables and waving white handkerchiefs, the Deaf way of encouraging the bride and groom to kiss, in much the same manner that hearing newlyweds are urged to kiss in response to the tinkling of glasses.

A band played during dinner and dessert, and some of the guests who were Deaf chose to dance. Their participation on the dance floor surprised most of the hearing guests. "How can people who are deaf hear music?" they asked each other.

They can't, of course, but not hearing music doesn't preclude "feeling" music. What happens is that deaf people sense vibration in the part of the brain that other people use for hearing.

The brain is incredibly adaptable when it is young. If the part of the brain responsible for processing sound isn't called to action, it doesn't sit idly by and do nothing. Instead it takes over the job of processing vibrations. This is why deaf people enjoy concerts, other musical events, and even become performers.

Miriam at least had her way with the sweet table. Indeed, tens of thousands of calories, mostly sugar, were consumed. It's safe to say, with only slight hyperbole, that a couple of the guests developed adult onset diabetes right there, while gorging on profiteroles, éclairs, and chocolate covered fruit.

"It's a river of chocolate," one man said. "What a terrific idea."

"Yes," his wife replied. "If you happen to have quick access to a cardiologist." Soon, the crowd began to thin as people said their good-byes.

On the ride home after the wedding, Miriam turned to Sam. "Our little girl has chosen a fine young man for her husband," she said. "He's bright, extremely good looking, well-mannered and respectful, and with his Ph.D, I'm certain he'll be able to support her nicely—perhaps not entirely in accord with the manner to which she's accustomed, but nicely, nevertheless."

"Yes, I agree on all counts," Sam said. "Our son-in-law is a terrific guy, but I have to wonder if he'll be able to provide us with a grandchild or two? Now that would be a real blessing."

Chapter 60

Seth didn't disappoint. On the first anniversary of their marriage, Sarah delivered a healthy baby girl. They arrived at the hospital with about three minutes to spare, and the baby popped out even before the obstetrician was fully gowned. Back in her room, she handed Seth their child. The baby was eagerly sucking on her fist and already sporting almost a full head of fine, black hair. "Look at our daughter," she said. "She is very beautiful, just like your mother."

"Yes, she has the same coloring, the same wide set eyes, full lips, straight nose, high cheek bones, and even the same silver streak in her hair. It's really amazing; I'm overcome with joy; thank you my precious wife for bringing her into our lives," Seth said.

"We will call her Willa," Sarah said.

"That would be beautiful," Seth said, cradling his child. "My parents, may they rest in peace, would like that."

It was beautiful indeed, and it only happened because of the miracles of modern medicine. Back from their honeymoon, a week in Maine, Seth and Sarah visited a physician who specialized in fertility issues for people with spinal cord injuries. After gathering Seth's case history and conducting preliminary examinations, he advised them, with the help of an interpreter, of three alternatives.

"You can apply a vibrator to the underside of your penis. Some men, about half of those whose injuries are above the 12th thoracic vertebra, are able to ejaculate this way. You can try this technique at home, and if it works, we'll bring you in, collect a sample of your sperm during the time that Sarah is ovulating, and artificially inseminate her uterus."

"And if it doesn't work?" Sarah asked.

"Then we'll try electroejaculation," the doctor said.

"I don't like it already," Seth replied.

"Yes, the name has a scary ring to it, but it's really not so bad," the doctor said. "What I do is insert an electrode in your keister and electrically stimulate your prostate gland and seminal vesicles. If you've forgotten your physiology, your seminal vesicles are a pair of tube-like glands that are found behind your bladder. Think of them as a sperm production factory.

"During the process of electroejaculation, we hope that your muscles contract and you ejaculate, or in the vernacular, come. We would, once again, time the procedure with Sarah's ovulation in order to artificially inseminate her uterus. With this procedure, successful pregnancies occur about forty percent of the time."

"And if it doesn't work?" Seth asked.

"Then we do microsurgery. I use a tiny needle to penetrate your scrotum and withdraw some sperm. As you probably know, you may only have a small amount of live sperm and some of them may not be sufficiently motile to swim upstream.

"The advantage of this procedure is that even if we can only extract a few sperm, each one of them can be injected into one of Sarah's ripe, fertile eggs. It's an easy procedure done under local anesthetic right here in my office. There will be very little disruption in your normal activities, although you might want to wait a couple of days before playing any rigorous sports."

"OK, if those are our alternatives, which of these procedures do you recommend?" Seth asked.

"I'd suggest trying them in the order that I presented them to you. If the vibrator doesn't work, we'll go to electrical stimulation, and if that doesn't work, we'll turn to the needle. Of course, I can't give you any guarantees, but I'm confident things will turn out well for both of you."

Using the vibrator was pleasant enough, especially when Sarah took over with some encouraging words. The good feelings, however, did not lead to the desired outcome. Electroejaculation did, though. The artificial insemination took, and after an uneventful pregnancy, except for Miriam's constant nagging over what Sarah should eat and drink and the kind of wood the crib should be made of, beautiful Baby Willa made her appearance.

Everyone was smitten, of course, but none more than Sam. "What a blessing," he said. "Let me hold her; her skin is so soft, like velvet, and I can't get enough of her smell in my nose. There has never been a more beautiful child. A grandchild is a blessing. Thank you for her, dear children. What a blessing."

It wasn't long before a pediatric otologist verified that Willa was profoundly deaf. Seth and Sarah had wished for it all along.

Chapter 61

Seth completed his dissertation and defense with only a moderate amount of difficulty.

One of the faculty members on his committee, Professor Morely, a stickler when it came to the interpretation of data, would have preferred multiple statistical analyses be applied in addition to the single one Seth had chosen.

"Young man," he said, "your analysis is assuredly correct. However, in the true spirit of scholarly rigor, I contend it would have been prudent had you applied additional statistical analyses thus lending even more vigorous support and credence to the verification of your hypothesis."

That's how some professors talk. Others on the committee politely overruled the pedantic prick.

The committee adjourned and informed Seth that he had passed. To the chairperson, Seth asked, "Can I have people call me 'Doctor' now?"

"You insist upon it for six months," she said. "If you do so after that, we will call you in for an ego adjustment, and, by the way, Professor Morley says precisely the same thing at every doctoral candidate's dissertation defense. You did a great job, Doctor."

In fact, the protocol with respect to calling people who have earned the Ph.D. "Doctor" is that the title only be used at university settings or at professional conferences. Seth, however, still flush with his success and feeling somewhat puffed up with himself, insisted that Sarah use his title at all three meals, at the grocery store, while doing the dishes, during sex, for restaurant reservations, at family picnics, and at all other family and social gatherings. In fact, he required it of her during every conscious moment of interaction.

Seth was pleased to accept a tenure track position at Gallaudet. Such positions are not available that often; they are highly competitive, so attaining one was a real plum. He spent half his time teaching graduate courses in psychology and the other half doing research and therapy at the university mental health clinic. If he could provide evidence of excellence in teaching, research, and service to the university and broader community over the subsequent six-year period, he would be granted tenure, thus assuring a job for as long as he wanted it.

Sarah, too, progressed nicely in her career. "Hey, Doctor," she said. "I'm getting a promotion at work!"

"I'm not surprised. What will you be doing?"

"They're making me Director of the Rehabilitation Therapy Department, and I'll be in charge of supervising six therapists. I'll keep seeing my own clients, though, at least a couple each week."

"I couldn't be more proud," Seth said. "You deserve the promotion."

Seth's schedule at his job was flexible, so he was available to take care of Willa one or two days a week. Miriam "donated" one day a week, and on days when neither could make it and Sarah was busy, they utilized the services of Katurzyna, a nanny.

Katy, as she liked to be called, was a Polish immigrant in her middle thirties. She provided childcare every day, working for several families. Willa liked her, and she had her own car, so neither Sarah nor Seth had to pick her up.

Baby Willa thrived. As expected, she began signing very early, and her development in other areas was accelerated, too. Her uncanny resemblance to her paternal grandmother, both in looks and manner, increased as she grew older. It was eerie to Seth, almost like a reincarnation.

Jacob was also doing well, to no one's surprise. Armed with his bachelor's degree from Gallaudet, he attended graduate school at the National Technical Institute for the Deaf, part of the Rochester Institute of Technology. It is a diverse place with students from all 50 states and more than 100 foreign countries. Almost 1,500 were either deaf or hard of hearing.

Jacob majored in architecture, graduated with honors, and took a job with a firm in Manhattan. Although they designed a few upscale residential properties, most of their projects were commercial, especially office buildings, hospitals, and schools.

As nicely as Jacob was doing in his career, his love life suffered. He'd dated a series of women, none of whom sparked any real interest. Regarding set ups, he learned that every one of his friends had a nubile, young cousin who was a knockout. "You've got to meet her," they said. "I'm telling you she's a combination of Penelope Cruz and Julia Roberts."

Of course, such splendor never materialized when they greeted him at the door. Then, he met Carla, the computer geek from Keokuk, Iowa.

"She was truly a rare combination," he told Seth. "Beautiful, extremely bright, profoundly deaf, and sexy as hell. Things were going along great. We were seeing each other regularly; there was talk of meeting family and sharing an apartment, and I was secretly saving for a ring. Then, early one morning, after a round of particularly kinky sex, she told me that she couldn't possibly even think about getting married without first becoming established in her career. 'I'm just not ready to commit to taking the next step,' she said."

"Ouch," Seth said.

"Yeah, this I took as a dump, and I split rather than prolong the agony. Of course, it hurt for a time; I'd say about six weeks. I mooned and moped around, all the while developing a taste for Chivas Regal, foreign films, and Thai food."

"Why am I just finding out about all of this now?" Seth asked. "I'm sure me and Sarah could have dulled some of the pain."

"Well, the bad feelings are fading, and I'm getting back to the dating scene again. I'm telling you; it's really expensive. Do you have any idea about how much dinner and a movie cost in Manhattan? You could always ask one of my dates. Hah!"

Chapter 62

On an unpleasant Sunday afternoon, unseasonably cold and windy with a persistent drizzle, Sarah and Seth lounged in front of the fireplace reading the newspaper. Baby Willa alternated between playing with a puzzle, her dolly, and drooling big gobs of spit on the area rug.

"We've got a little problem," Sarah said. "One of the families that Katy works for offered her a full time job, and she's going to take it. I guess she'll be making more money and won't have to drive around so much, so I can see her point."

"Maybe your mom will give us another day, or I may be able to find a student who needs some part time work. I'll put a notice on the department bulletin board first thing tomorrow," Seth said.

"Sounds like it might work, Doctor. Anyway, do you think it might be fun to take a short driving trip? We could leave after your class Friday morning, find a nice motel for a couple of nights, and drive home on Sunday afternoon."

"Great idea. Where would you like to go?"

"I'd like to see more of where you grew up, the town and the school you went to. It would be fun to roll up and down Main Street and do a little people watching and window-shopping. We'll find a forest preserve nearby with some accessible walking trails and do some hiking. This will be Willa's first time hiking, and I think she'll love it."

Seth thought he was particularly inspiring during

his Friday morning lecture on bipolar disorder. He met with a few manic students after class, and then swung by the house to pick up Sarah and Willa. Lunch was at a roadside diner where the Friday special was "Fish and Chips, All You Can Eat."

Willa pulled her nose up at the fish, but it was the first time she sampled a bacon, lettuce, and tomato sandwich followed by frozen custard. She dived in with gusto. A few hours later, Seth parked on Main Street in front of Ellie's Eating Establishment. "Let's have some coffee here," he said. "I have a feeling I know the owner."

Seth wheeled his chair into the diner behind Sarah and the baby. Everything looked a little worn around the edges—the linoleum floors, the wooden tables and chairs, the round, padded stools at the counter, the fake antique clock on the wall, and Ellie.

At first, probably because he was in a wheelchair, she didn't appear to recognize him. She did a quick double take, however, and Seth read his name on her lips.

"Oh dear, what happened, Seth?" she asked, using the finger spelling alphabet and a sign or two he had taught her.

"I had an accident a few years back, but I'm fine now. How have you been?"

"Actually, I've been well; I've met a nice man, and we're engaged to be married."

"That's just terrific, Ellie. By the way, this is my wife Sarah and our daughter Willa."

"So nice to meet you both; please sit down anywhere you'd like, and whatever you have to eat and drink is on me." Ellie visited with them over coffee.

"What happened to Round Rosie?" Seth asked.

"Oh, the old gal retired, moved to Las Vegas, and sold the place to me. She took a small down payment, and I'm paying her the rest in monthly installments. It's working out great. I've added a few new items to the menu, and business is steady. If it continues, I'm thinking of hiring a second chef and staying open through the dinner hour, but enough about me. Besides getting married to this pretty lady and having a beautiful little girl, what have you been up to?"

"Actually, I've been in school most of the time, and now I'm a university professor, if you can believe it."

"Well, I seem to remember that you were a quick learner," Ellie said with a sly smile.

Seth felt a little awkward and began to wonder if the old adage about never being able to return home were actually true.

Back on the road, Seth explained who Ellie was and what their history had been. "You should be thankful," Sarah said. "She's an important person in your life."

"Yes, I know it, and I really hope she'll be happy now."

"Before we do anything else, let's check in at a motel," Sarah said. "We'll nap the baby for a while, then swing by the cemetery to visit your parents' graves before it gets too late."

"Seems like a plan to me," Seth said. "I could use a little nap myself."

Of course, Willa didn't know what a cemetery was, but she liked the open space and trees and delighted in chasing the squirrels and butterflies. She noticed the headstones and touched a few, but couldn't know their significance, as she played among them.

The maintenance people had done their jobs well. The gravesites were neat, the lawn had been mowed, and flowers had been planted. He and Sarah placed bouquets on top of the graves and stood awhile, alone with their thoughts. "Nana and Poppy," Sarah finally said, but Willa only looked puzzled.

"They were sweet people," Seth said, "and they loved each other from the time they were children."

The house was much as Seth remembered it, although its dimensions seemed smaller and the front yard had been fenced. "Maybe we remember things bigger than they actually are because our memories of them are from a time when we were smaller," Seth said.

"Yes, I've noticed the same thing," Sarah said. "Or, maybe it's our memories of happy things that grow and our memories of sad things that shrink over time. Do you want to knock on the door and see if they'll let us in?"

"I don't think so; the last time we were here was when my father died, and before that, I was watching my mother die. I'd just as soon leave all that alone. Come on; I know an accessible trail with a waterfall at the end where we can still have a nice hike before it gets dark."

The next morning the three of them rode out to the residential school. Seth was shocked to discover that it wasn't there. When he pulled up to the gate, a sign read "The Stonybrook School for Girls." Curious, because there was nary a brook around let alone a stony one. Armed with a pad of paper and pen, Seth took his family inside.

A receptionist asked if she could help them. Seth wrote, "Please tell me what happened to the school for the Deaf? I was a student here many years ago."

"Yes, I started working here just after it closed," she wrote back. "It seems as if enrollment had dwindled to the point that it was no longer sustainable. My understanding was that more and more parents chose to keep their deaf children at home and send them to their neighborhood schools. 'Mainstreaming,' I think they called it."

"Thank you for your time, and enjoy the rest of your weekend," Seth wrote, before they left.

"What a horrible mistake," Sarah said.

"Yes, it is a horrible mistake, but I guess I shouldn't be surprised that my school no longer exists. Residential schools have fallen out of favor. There's been a movement across the whole country to close them down, maybe because they're too expensive or because parents have been convinced that raising their children at home has advantages, or because of the old notion that they segregate us."

"It's so ignorant," Sarah said. "Whatever the reason, closing schools for the Deaf is ultimately going to hurt a lot of Deaf kids, not just academically, but socially as well. They will have few friends to share their childhoods with and no one to share their hopes and their secrets and their fears. Many will be isolated; they will not learn to sign, and most will be illiterate. Too many hearing parents of deaf kids just don't get it. If only they would talk to some Deaf people before they make their decisions."

"One thing for sure," Seth said. "Willa will go to a residential school, maybe the Maryland School where you went. Who knows; there's always the chance she'll be a less rebellious resident, although I'm not really sure I'd like it should that turn out to be the case."

It turned out that Willa wasn't all that fond of hiking, except for those segments where she saw wildflowers growing or saw a snake on the path. She hadn't learned to be afraid of them yet. Sarah, however, shrunk from garter snakes as if they were boa constrictors.

They went to a playground and children's museum before driving home, stopping only once for frozen custard. After her treat, Willa slept like a baby. It hadn't been impossible to return home, merely difficult.

Chapter 63

Sarah was very happy in her marriage to Seth; in fact, she couldn't imagine being happier. He was considerate, attentive, and loved her "to pieces." They had a large number of friends and pursued an active social life, almost as active as their sex life. Energetic as they were, they enjoyed tennis, softball, bowling, swimming, and golf.

Golfing was difficult for Seth until he figured out an easy modification. In place of standard sized adult clubs, he bought a set of shorter, junior sized clubs. These allowed him to sit comfortably in his chair and whack away. It wasn't long, given his upper body strength and eye- hand coordination, before he was knocking balls well out onto the driving range.

"Y'know, I shoot in the 70's," he said to a deaf friend.

"I couldn't be more impressed," the friend said. "Can you do it consistently?"

"No, if it gets any colder, I don't play," Seth said. They and their friends never missed Deaf theater, ballet and folk dancing performances, or art exhibits at Gallaudet. Everyone enjoyed captioned films and dinners out. Their social circle was tightly knit, and they were comfortable with each other, a nice situation for young married people getting established and raising their families.

Once, after taking a particularly merciless thrashing from Seth on the tennis court, Sarah suggested he try a new sport.

"What have you got in mind?" Seth asked.

"You've got to try skydiving," she said, without hesitating.

"You're thinking I'm scared, aren't you? You're thinking the good Doctor doesn't have the spine for it, as it were."

"Yep," Sarah said. "You'd be a fool not to be scared, but it's worth it, because it's the most exciting experience you'll ever have, short of being my husband, of course."

"I'll tell you what." Seth said. "You find a skydiving place equipped to handle deaf paraplegics, and I guarantee I'll jump out of an airplane with you and beat your butt to the ground."

Finding such a place didn't take Sarah very long, because she had done her research even before raising the question with Seth. "After training, you'll do a few tandem jumps, then, it may even be possible for you to solo. Very few paraplegics have done it. Are you game, Doctor?" she asked.

"You can bet the house on it," Seth said, secretly kicking himself for such totally unwarranted braggadocio. *Looking out of windows above the third floor makes me weak in the knees. What the hell am I doing?*

Seth's training was longer and much more exacting than Sarah's had been. Special attention had to be devoted to canopy and landing skills, because a hard or an offsite landing could be disastrous for a person without full use of his legs. A precise free fall and accurate landing were demanded rather than simply soaring off into the wild blue yonder.

Additionally, Seth needed to participate in wind tunnel training to simulate high altitude free fall while he was still on the ground. Such a controlled environment would help Seth relax and learn how to maintain a stable position in the air. Also, wind tunnel training identifies those novices whose disabilities or temperaments are such that they should go no further with skydiving. "Hey, there's always skiing or tennis," his instructor said.

Initially, Seth tried low air speed in the air tunnel in order to familiarize himself with the effects upon his stability. Gradually, the air speed was increased until it reached 120 miles per hour, the approximate speed he would encounter during free fall. From this, his instructor would determine whether Seth was able to maintain the correct body position in the air after exiting the plane.

Attaining full stability in the wind tunnel was impossible for Seth. The correct position required that he arch his hips forward, hold his head back, pull back his arms and stretch them out, bend his knees to a 90-degree angle, and hold his legs apart. He couldn't keep his knees bent and legs apart without special equipment. When his instructor furnished it, however, it was sufficient, and he was ready to go. His first jump would be in tandem with his instructor.

As Sarah had done, they would exit the airplane at 14 thousand feet, free fall to about four thousand, at which point the canopy would open and they would drift to the ground. The instructor's legs would take the jolt of the landing, and they would both roll together.

Sarah and Willa waited on the ground while Seth went up. The rush of adrenaline masked his trepidation, an outcome that surprised Seth, who ten minutes earlier had been squelching his gag reflex. He and his instructor hooked up, and, in moments, Seth came to understand the exhilaration that Sarah had talked about.

"Look up in the sky. There's Daddy flying," Sarah said, and indeed, Seth felt like he was.

"I think it's the total freedom," he said on the ride home. "It's a long time since I've felt so unleashed, unbound from my chair and everything else. Being up there is a great equalizer, it seems to me. We're going to keep doing this until I learn how to solo; then you and me will fly together. You've heard of the mile high club haven't you?" he asked.

"You bet I have," Sarah said, "Think we can pull it off, Doctor, or should I say 'pull it out' at 120 miles per hour?"

It isn't too often that paraplegics solo, so to document the event and get some much needed publicity, the owner of the facility alerted the newspapers regarding the date and time of Seth's scheduled jump. Seth got a refresher course on the ground, since on his previous jumps, he had essentially been a passenger, along for the ride without any real responsibility. Now, he had a huge responsibility. His life.

The jump went well. Seth did everything he was supposed to do, and his gear worked perfectly. He executed the proper type of low angle approach to the ground; his special equipment kept his legs up and apart, and he skidded along on his well-padded butt for a perfect, if somewhat undignified, landing. "I'm sure I'm hooked for life," he said, after hugs from Sarah and Willa.

"Daddy like birdy," Willa said.

A full-page article and picture of the entire family was in the papers the next day. "Paraplegic Professor at Gallaudet University Sky Dives" appeared at the top of the page. Many of their friends asked about the experience, and two went so far as to sign up for lessons. Both backed out, one for fear that the rush of air would bring on a migraine and the other concerned about the landing's effect on his sciatica.

Chapter 64

Seth was happy to be married too, with good reason. He had a wife he adored, a healthy, beautiful child, and a fine career ahead of him. Sarah's family treated him with love and respect; he enjoyed socializing with friends, and there was always the possibility of more children in the future.

He foresaw no financial problems, especially since Sam had already advised him on investment opportunities that were profitable. Seth bought low and sold high. What could be better?

He was doing well at the university and would soon be up for promotion to associate professor. For the most part, he liked his colleagues; there were a few Morley types who were a little too stuffy and pedantic for his taste, but for the most part, he admired their work and enjoyed their company.

As for teaching, he was well organized and thorough, truly an interesting and engaging lecturer. His classes were among the first to fill at registration, and the word was out. "This guy ought to sell tickets," students said.

Seth found his work at the clinic particularly stimulating. "What kinds of problems do you work with?" Sarah asked.

"Most of the students I counsel are freshmen in minor kinds of funks due to being homesick or struggling with first year adjustments to college life. A few, however, have much more serious problems; they are truly mentally ill and hanging on by some very thin threads."

"Tell me more," Sarah said.

"Well, one young man has many of the characteristics of paranoid schizophrenia. He has auditory hallucinations, for example. On occasion, he hears voices; some are harmless, almost like imaginary friends, but others are hostile, threatening, and persistent in urging him to do bad things to himself.

"Delusions of reference and grandeur are parts of his behavioral repertoire, too. He tells me that the voices are coming to him from old mercury fillings in his molars. Other messages come from the inside of mailboxes or from Julia, a raven haired vixen who materializes at his bedside each night and emits a green glow from her navel and an aphrodisiac mist from her ears."

"Wow. Is there anything else?" Sarah asked.

"Yes, a lot. He says he's the brightest student at the university, fluent in five sign languages, expert in subatomic particle physics, author of six textbooks, and a candidate for a Rhodes scholarship."

"Docs hc havc fricnds in high placcs?"

"How did you know? Last week, while looking over his shoulder to make sure no one was listening, he said that he regularly speaks with the president."

"The president of the university?" Sarah asked.

"No, the President of the United States," Seth said.

"Does he give you any details of their conversations?"

"You bet. They're usually between two and four in the morning on a private line. Nobody but he and the president can use it, and mostly they consult over matters of foreign policy, particularly nuclear disarmament. The president is urging him to be his Secretary of State during his next term, but he's still considering his options.

These behaviors, along with chronic anxiety and depression, anger, insomnia, argumentativeness, a condescending attitude toward others, and an almost total lack of concern for personal cleanliness make it hard for me to know how he manages to stay in school."

At the clinic, they devised a team approach in an attempt to help the young man. A psychiatrist prescribed anti-psychotic medication, Seth provided cognitive-behavioral therapy, and a social worker helped by getting his family involved in the treatment regimen.

Three months into therapy, the student executed a perfect swan dive from the top of the tallest building on campus. He landed on his head, thus depositing a good deal of his gray matter on a paved pathway that served as a shortcut between the math building and the biological sciences building. Among the more cynical, it became known as "dead man's alley."

Seth was disconsolate. During his training, he had been advised that all doctors, no matter their skill level or specialty, lose patients. This was his personal initiation to that kind of tragic reality, though, and it was so sudden and so dramatic that he had a difficult time coming to terms. Speaking with senior therapists at the clinic helped, but it was a while before the nightmares ended, and he was willing to wheel past the site of the student's demise.

Seth made a habit of stopping at the department office every day to schmooze with colleagues and check his mailbox. Typically, his mail consisted of announcements of committee meetings, notices from publishers urging him to adopt new textbooks, invitations to faculty social gatherings, or similar types of university related correspondence. This day, however, there was a personal letter mixed in with all the other envelopes.

Dear Seth,

I am Rachel. Angelo is my husband, and Mario is our son. We met when you came to our home after our son hurt you. From the newspaper article about skydiving, I learned that you are a professor at Gallaudet University, and I hope my letter reaches you.

The picture in the newspaper shows you and your beautiful family. You look very healthy and happy, and it must be so if you can jump out of an airplane. What a brave man you are.

I would like you to know that Mario has been home for a while now. He's doing very well, I'm so happy to say. Of course, some of the problems from his brain injury remain, but he has improved very much.

Mario has a job now. He works for a landscaping design and lawn maintenance company, and Angelo and I are very proud of him. He's already been promoted once, and he's saving money so he can open his own company. He's like a new man with a fine set of teeth, his own place to live, and he even has a very nice girlfriend.

We want you to please know how important you are to us. We know in our hearts and in our minds that everything good that has happened to our son is only because of you. There is no way we can thank you enough, because without you we are sure that Mario would either be in prison or dead.

Angelo and I have moved to a nicer place with some flowers and trees and room for a vegetable garden. I have enclosed our address and telephone number, and if you ever want to, it would be a very special gift for us to see you and meet your wife and little girl. It would be an honor if you would allow me to make dinner for all of you. It's so very

important for me to thank you in person.
Angelo and Mario would like that, too.
May God bless you and your family,
Rachel

Seth read the letter a second and third time, then placed it in his briefcase to take home and show Sarah. On the way, it occurred to him that Rachel was right. Everything she had written was right. In fact, he had saved another person's life, a person who, at one time, he was prepared to maim or murder. How much better things had turned out.

Chapter 65

Sarah read the letter twice herself. "We must go," she said. "We must go and have dinner with them as soon as possible."

"I'm sure you're right," Seth said. "I'd like to see for myself how things have turned out for Mario. If it's even close to Rachel's description, it will be a success story that is hugely gratifying."

"I'll ask my brother to call her and see if he can come with to interpret. Or, maybe we should all go to a restaurant instead of having Rachel go to the trouble of cooking for us. I'll think about it before I talk to Anthony."

"They might be more comfortable in their own home rather than a restaurant," Seth said. "If she wants to prepare dinner for us, we could bring some side dishes and some wine and dessert."

"Don't worry. I'll work on it," Sarah said, "and I'll run the plan past you before deciding on anything."

Two weeks later, Seth drove to the address Rachel had sent him. Rachel and Angelo had moved to Columbia Heights, one of the most ethnically and economically diverse neighborhoods in the Washington area. People lived in a mix of expensive condominiums, townhouses, and middle-income housing. Some public housing was available for low-income people, too. Recently, a revitalization effort brought in a large shopping center and several new restaurants. Some of the old housing stock had been torn down and new apartment complexes were being built, as well.

Sarah sat in the passenger seat, and Dr. Anthony was delighted to sit next to Willa in the back, next to a large bowl of salad and a banana cream pie. Judging from the lack of conversation, everyone was a little nervous. "Perk up," Seth said. "Let's consider this an adventure," and so it was.

Angelo, Rachel, and Mario were waiting in front of the house when Seth pulled up. Seth transferred to his chair, and Mario was the first to greet him, a wide smile on his face. "Hey, Seth," he said. "I made it through Juvy, an' now I'm home again. I thank you every way I can, with my whole heart an' with everything that's in me, for savin' my life a second time."

"I'm happy for you, Mario. You look great, a little more meat on the bones, and that great smile. Your mom tells me you're a working stiff like the rest of us now. Hey, this is my wife Sarah and our daughter Willa, and this lunk here is Sarah's brother, Dr. Anthony. We brought him along not because we like him but because he can interpret for us."

Seth turned to Rachel and Angelo. She hugged him for a long time before standing straight. "We are so pleased to see you again. This time it will be much better, a festive occasion when all of us are all happy, and I didn't invite any policemen, either."

Angelo's hug was equally enthusiastic. "Like my dear wife, I thank you for everythin,' an' I'm very happy you an' your family are here. If a man comes to know even one person in his life like you, he is very lucky. Please come into our home an' share our feast."

The rest of the introductions were made, and everyone proceeded inside. Sarah and Rachel took the salad and pie into the kitchen, and Dr. Anthony poured the wine. Mario gave Willa a gift from the family, a picture book and a stuffed animal. She was content to play with them on the living room floor while depositing only a minimal amount of drool.

With everyone gathered back in the living room, Seth proposed a toast. "This is to Mario," he said. "May your health continue to improve and may you enjoy a full and happy life. You have turned the leaf and everyone here is thankful and proud of you for that. You've taught us all that no matter how far down a person may be, if he tries hard enough, he can always change for the better. Here's to your finding a woman like mine and giving your parents the joy that only comes with grandchildren."

"I'll drink to that, an' I've got a toast of my own, even though I'm not so good at public speakin' yet," Mario said. "To Seth, the man that changed my life around, a man that's got more guts than anyone I'll ever know, a man that cares about other people, even bad guys that hurt him, an' a man I'll never forget. Thank you, Seth, for everythin' you done for me and my parents, an' may your life be filled with joy an' happiness, too."

"Thank you, Mario," Seth said. "That was plenty darn good for a guy who says he's not so good at public speaking."

Angelo raised his glass, as well. "All of you grace our home with your presence. May God bless Seth, Sarah, Baby Willa, and you, too, Doctor Anthony, with good health an' happiness, an', if it is your wish to have more children, may the Good Lord watch over them. Come, let us break bread."

Rachel had gone all out in her preparation of a sumptuous Italian dinner. Full platters of antipasti, veal parmesan, sausage and peppers, spaghetti with meat sauce, grilled vegetables, salad, and potatoes weighed on the table along with several bottles of chianti. The banana cream pie complemented the cannoli and gelato nicely.

During dinner, Seth asked Mario about his job. "What are you doing to keep busy?"

"Well, right after I got home, I got hired on by a landscapin' company," Mario said. "They were working right here in the neighborhood, an' I was still stayin' with Mom and Dad. I figured I had nothin' to lose, so I walked straight up to the boss an' tol' him I'd work a coupla days for free so he would see what I could do an' think about givin' me a job. Lucky for me, it juss so happened that durin' the first day, one of their mowers quit. When no one else could fix it 'cept me, the boss hired me on the spot."

"Good for you," Seth said. "It's great you were willing to show him what you could do. Is it mostly talking care of lawns?"

"I do lawn maintenance, tree trimmin', plantin' an' prunin', an' they're teachin' me how to lay brick pavers for patios and driveways. Yep, I do all that, an' I'm also one of the two guys in charge of keepin' everythin' in tip-top workin' shape. Anythin' that goes wrong with the engines, I can fix, an' believe me; I learned all those things when I was at Juvy."

"How's the pay?" Seth asked.

"I'm makin' a good salary; they pay me time an' a half for overtime an' somethin' toward health insurance, too. After I pay my rent an' utilities an' take care of my other bills, I have money left over. I been puttin' it into the bank an' not too long down the road, I'm hopin' I'll have enough to start my own business."

"That's terrific," Seth said. "You're really doing great. Actually, you're doing better than great; 'fantastic', is more like it. When you have the time, why don't you come over to our house and give me a bid? A neighbor kid has been mowing and edging our lawn, and he does a fair job, but I think it's time for us to hire a professional. We need some landscaping and tree trimming, too. Maybe, after you see our lot, you could draw up a design for some flower beds, new bushes, and a couple of evergreens."

"I'll do it. For sure, I'll do it. You can always count on me," Mario said, "an' I guarantee my work will be the best there is, the best you could find anywhere. I'll talk to the boss, too, an' see if I can get you a special price; y'know like a family discount."

"You know, now that I think about it," Seth said, "I know at least three or four other families, a couple of them right across the street from us, who aren't all that happy with their lawn service. When you come over, you can drop by and see them too and maybe pick up a few more clients."

The rest of dinner went smoothly. Mario and his family were attentive hosts; they asked about skydiving, Seth and Sarah's work, and how Willa was doing. "Look at how she already does sign language," Mario said. "Man, she's still a little baby and she knows so much."

"Yes, she learns it automatically, by imitating her dad and me, just as you learned by imitating your parents," Sarah said.

"Well, I can tell you one thing for sure," Mario said. "Willa's learnin' to do sign language a whole lot faster than I learnt to talk. Mom tells me I didn't have much to say when I was little; truth is, I didn't say nothin' 'til I was past my fourth birthday. Dad all the time jokes around, y'know. He says I didn't have nothin' to complain about 'til then."

At the same time, Willa made it known that she would like a second helping of gelato. She put her fingertips together and quickly moved them apart—the sign for "more."

After conversation over coffee, some of it concerned with growing up in an orphanage, and some of it about Dr. Anthony and his wife and family, Sarah said, "It's getting late, and Baby Willa needs to go to sleep. Thank you for this delicious dinner and for being such wonderful hosts. We're so happy we were able to be here with you. You must visit us at our home soon. I promise to have Dr. Anthony call you so we can decide on a date that will be convenient."

"That would be our great pleasure," Rachel said. "We will bring the wine, and maybe Mario will bring his girlfriend, if it's all right."

Before leaving, Seth gave Mario their address. "Come by any night next week, after work. We can seal the deal on our house and set up appointments with the neighbors." On the way out, Baby Willa stretched out her arms to Mario. He blushed a little but still managed to gave her a hug and kiss.

Chapter 66

Mario's boss was pleased with the prospect of new business in "virgin territory," a neighborhood where they hadn't previously worked. "You take my car and head out there," he said. "Spend a whole day seeing these people if you need to. Don't rush; if you need it, take two days. Here's a bunch of brochures so you can cover the whole neighborhood. Put one in everyone's mailbox, even people you don't have appointments with."

So, for a full day and a half Mario became a sales representative for his company. When he was finished, he had acquired Seth's business and the business of four neighbors also ready to change their service. Ultimately, the brochures brought in seven more clients; thus, Mario, all on his own, was responsible for twelve new customers.

"Not a bad day's work," the boss said. "These new people will be your responsibility; you will be in charge of the crew we send out to their houses, and you will get a good raise for your efforts."

Soon, Mario was spending all of his time working in Seth and Sarah's neighborhood. He devoted special attention to their landscaping needs, and, in a few months, their front and back yards were the envy of the area. This, along with an article and pictures in a lawn and gardening magazine, brought even more clients to the company. Business was so good that the boss hired three more workers, bought a new truck, and added a slew of new equipment.

After work one evening, the boss called Mario into his office. "Please sit, Mario," he said. "Here, have a nice glass of cold lemonade."

"What's up, boss? You look a little tired."

"Yes, it's true. Working full days is harder for me than it used to be."

"You can always give me more work; I never mind workin' overtime, even at regular pay," Mario said. "I'm in great shape; you should kick back an' take it easy a little more."

"That's what I wanted to talk to you about. I'm happy to say that you are my best employee, Mario. You never miss a day of work; you have excellent skills, the best I've ever seen, you bring in new business, and you stay out of trouble. For all of that, I would like to make you an offer."

"Thank you for your kind words, boss. What is it?"

"In a little while, I think about two years, I'm going to have to retire. I have no sons, and I don't trust any of my other relatives enough to have them take over my business. So, what I would like to do is make you a one quarter partner right now, and a one half partner next year. That way, when I retire, you'll know everything you need to know to run the business on your own. What do you think?"

"Are you kiddin'?" Mario said, a little too loudly. "I think I'm gonna say yes! I know I'm gonna say yes! I love my job, an' if you're sayin' this business will be mine one day, there's nothin' in the world that could make me happier. You can count on me boss. I'm your man. I'll learn everythin' I need to know, an' after you retire, you'll be happy when you come back here an' see how good the company you started is doin'. I won't let you down. I'm your man. You can count on me boss."

So it was that Mario, the former gangster, dope

pusher, shop lifter, purse snatcher, drunk roller, drug addict, learning disabled, dyslexic, socially maladjusted, attention deficit disordered, hyperactive punk who murdered cats and hamsters and carved guys' eyeballs out became a respectable businessman.

Where was the assistant principal now with her phone calls? Where was the social worker to evaluate Mario's coping mechanisms? Where was the school psychologist to test his intelligence? If Rachel had her way, she would have scheduled one more "multidisciplinary staffing" and invited all the experts. This time, though, she would do the talking.

Mario always stopped in to see Seth and Sarah on Fridays, the day he worked at their house. He never forgot to bring something for Willa, a chocolate bar or a small gift. Of course, he kept them informed of developments at work, his partnership and impending ownership. "You're the man, Seth," he said. "You're the man who made it all happen."

"Actually, I might have helped a little, but it's really Dr. Anthony who is responsible," Seth said. "He was the one who straightened out my thinking. We both owe him."

Chapter 67

Willa was almost four years old, at an age when Seth and Sarah wanted to find an appropriate preschool so she would begin relating with other deaf children. Activities requiring her learning to take turns and share with other kids were sorely needed. Everyone, especially Poppy Sam, had done an excellent job doting on her to the extent that Baby Willa would benefit from discovering there were other kids apart from her in the universe. She was ready, too, to begin learning pre-reading and pre-math skills.

Sarah, with Miriam's help, scoured the area for a preschool. Finding something suitable was difficult. The trend toward mainstreaming deaf children had reached all the way down to early childhood education; thus, schools, or even individual classrooms, in which the enrollments were exclusively deaf and the manual methods of communication were valued had become rare.

The choice came down to home schooling or placing Willa in a new program housed in a church basement about a mile away. The teachers were inexperienced but enthusiastic, and they were strong advocates of signing and finger spelling. So, Seth and Sarah decided to give it a shot.

"We've very little to lose," Sarah said. "If it doesn't work out, we'll teach Willa ourselves until she's older, and at least this preschool is close by."

Over dinner, Seth looked up from his beef stew and said, "So what do you think about my forming another intimate relationship with an electrode?"

"You serious, Doctor?" Sarah asked.

"Yeah, I'd really like a son, not that another one like Willa wouldn't be great, too."

"Seems like a terrific idea to me," Sarah said. "I've got some eggs that could use some scrambling, so let's get after some of your spermies while they can still do the backstroke."

It wasn't so easy this time. Electroejaculation worked, but insemination in Sarah's uterus didn't. They tried for five months, before getting impatient and frustrated. In consultation with the fertility specialist, they considered microsurgery. "Let's give electroejaculation a couple more shots," he said. "We can always resort to the needle later on."

Later on, the microsurgery resulted in the desired outcome. In fact, two of Sarah's eggs were fertilized and implanted. At the three month mark, though, just after bidding a grand slam during her afternoon bridge game, she hunched over the table in pain, started bleeding, and promptly miscarried.

"We're so sorry," Miriam and Sam said. "These things happen, we know, but it's so much more difficult when it's your own family. Are you going to keep trying?"

"The little guys probably weren't developing normally," Seth said. "It's hard now, but in the long run it's probably for the best. We're going to rest for a while, then decide if we want to try again."

Seth plunged into his work at the university with renewed vigor. He published several articles in professional journals, read papers at conventions, took over the chairmanships of two university committees, and helped organize local competition for the Special Olympics. These activities, along with consistent evidence of superior classroom teaching, resulted in his promotion to associate professor. The advancement brought a nice raise, too.

Working at the mental health clinic was always stimulating and often enlightening. Seth suspected, after getting to know more patients—their histories, diagnoses, and responses to various kinds of therapeutic interventions—that people were ashamed to be mentally ill. They still attempted to deny that mental illnesses existed, or, if they were at least willing to accept their reality, they tried to hide them. Seth assumed it was the lingering stigma and negative attitudes as yet associated with mental illness that gave rise to their humiliation.

To test his assumption, Seth conducted an informal experiment in two of a colleague's classes. These were graduate classes in interpretation, a degree program in which participants learned to translate back and forth between English and American Sign Language. Armed with their degrees, they would work in schools, medical and legal offices, in the arts and business; in fact, at any setting where information between hearing and deaf people needed to be exchanged.

The students Seth met with were pursuing their master's degrees, and they had limited backgrounds in psychology. The total enrollment in the two classes was 34, and all could hear.

Seth raised two questions with these students: "How many of you have ever taken an antibiotic drug for a bacterial infection of any type?" All 34 students raised their hands. "Now, how many of you have ever taken Prozac or a similar antidepressant drug?" Nobody raised their hands. Zilch, zippo, nary a one.

Now, it might have been that these students were telling the truth. Perhaps there really wasn't a single graduate student in either class who had ever taken an antidepressant. Improbable as it was, it was still possible.

Seth didn't buy it. He believed some students had indeed taken antidepressants and that at least a few still were. But in front of their classmates and professors, at the risk of having the perceptions others had of them diminished, they chose to lie when answering his question. They lied because the prevailing attitude, not just among students at Gallaudet, but throughout the population at large, was that to be physically ill is OK, but to be mentally ill isn't.

"Physical illnesses are common and expected," Seth said. "They are accepted as a routine part of everyday living; everybody gets them; thus, they are no cause for shame. Mental illnesses, however, are rare, not at all routine, and because the behaviors associated with them are perceived to be weird and unacceptable, they are shameful."

"It's true," Sarah said. "People readily admit to their diabetes, even wear bracelets to advertise it, but seldom, if ever, do they admit to their obsessive compulsive disorders unless they're prepared to be ostracized or taunted. This has been the case throughout history, and it seems as if it remains the case presently."

Seth learned that health insurance companies didn't get it either. They provided full coverage, albeit sometimes reluctantly, to people with physical illnesses. However, people in need of psychiatric care paid out of their pockets after only five visits to a mental health professional. Why in the world should it matter?" Seth said. "Sick is sick, and whether it's kidney disease or schizophrenia, it shouldn't make a difference."

Willa adjusted and progressed nicely in her preschool. Her teacher kept her busy with a wide variety of projects; she benefitted from associating with her peers, and her knowledge of sign language expanded. Sarah was amused one day when Willa brought home one of her drawings—a chicken with four legs and what looked like udders.

Better if it had lips.

Instead of having Willa ride a school bus, Sarah drove her to school in the morning and picked her up at noon. Each enjoyed being alone with the other and stopping for lunch or some other kind of treat after school, and it gave Willa a chance to show Mommy the work she had completed each day before having it pinned to the bulletin board in the kitchen.

Driving Willa to the preschool and back had become a routine and fun part of the day for Sarah. Then one morning, a rainy Wednesday, while stopped at a traffic light just a few blocks from home, she had a peculiar feeling. A black pickup truck eased up behind her. Two young men, who looked to be in their late teens, were in the car. The driver maintained a reasonable distance and wasn't aggressive or rude in any way.

What bothered Sarah was that he stayed with her, turning when she did, slowing when she did, speeding up when she did, and never attempting to pass. For the rest of the way to school, he stayed directly behind her, pulling away only when she stopped at the entrance to the school.

The incident nagged at Sarah for the rest of the morning. She returned for Willa at noon and stopped for sandwiches at a restaurant that had an outside eating area they both liked. She happened to glance to the street while applying ketchup to Willa's fries, and she was certain she saw the black pickup slow and drive by. When the driver stopped for a red light, she made a note of the numbers on the license plate.

"It's probably nothing," she told Seth. "Maybe I'm just being paranoid and overreacting for no good reason."

"Maybe," Seth said, "but I've always trusted your instincts. What I'm going to do is follow you and Willa to the preschool tomorrow morning to see if there is anything unusual going on. If you're still uncomfortable, we'll let the police know."

So, Seth "tailed" his girls on their way to school Thursday morning. Traffic was heavier than usual. Construction crews were out pretending not to waste time. There was a lot of bustle as people hurried to make it to their jobs on time. During the ride, Seth stayed a car length or two behind Sarah. Checking his rear view mirror every few seconds, he didn't notice anything out of the ordinary. Neither did he when he looked ahead.

The heavy traffic caused Sarah to be a little late. By the time she got to school, most of the children had already entered; in fact, Willa was one of the last. Sarah deposited her where she always did, an entrance to the playground in front of the school, and kissed her goodbye. She watched as the same two playground monitors greeted and welcomed Willa. They were an elderly couple, friendly and outgoing as could be, who volunteered their services every day. She called them "Ma and Pa Kettle."

Sarah flashed the OK sign to Seth and waved goodbye. She drove toward home feeling very much relieved, confident that she had simply been imagining things the day before. Her bridge group would be coming by later in the day, so she stopped at the grocery for some fresh fruit and snacks.

When she walked through the garage door into the kitchen, the light indicating a phone message was blinking. The call was from the principal at Willa's preschool.

So it was that the nightmare began.

Chapter 68

"We're calling to remind you that parents are required to inform us when their child is ill or going to be absent from school for any other reason. We assume that Willa is at home with you. Please call in to verify."

Sarah didn't like it. *This can't be; it has to be a mistake. Of course, Willa's at school. I dropped her off at the exact place I always do. Maybe she went to the bathroom and got locked in a stall, or maybe she's hiding behind a tree on the playground because she didn't feel like going in today.*

She called the school and got the principal on the telecommunicator. "Willa went in through the same entrance she always does, and I saw the playground monitors greet her. Have you looked in the bathroom or out on the playground?"

"Those we're the first two places we checked," the principal said.

"I'll call my husband, and we'll be there right away." On the phone with Seth, she said, "Willa is missing. You saw me drop her off at school, and now they can't find her."

"Leave right now, and I'll meet you there," Seth said.

A dreadful wave of fear and foreboding overcame her when she saw two police cars in the school parking lot. *This can't be happening. Not to our baby. Oh please, Willa. Where are you, baby? Please God, where is she?*

Seth pulled up a few minutes later followed by a police car with blinking lights and a very perturbed officer who had been trying to stop him for speeding and running stop signs the last two miles. Three policemen, a policewoman, and an interpreter stood with Sarah in the playground and introduced themselves.

"I'm Officer Ramon Rodriguez," one of them said. "We've conducted a thorough search of the building and grounds, and we haven't been able to find your daughter, we need you to give us some identifying information, a recent picture, for example, would help. Our next step will be to canvas the neighborhood."

At that point, Sarah lost it. She might have collapsed had not the policewoman steadied her.

"I'm sorry. I know how difficult this is," the policewoman said, "but to help us find your little girl, you've got to try your hardest to stay calm and not panic. Tell us, as best you can, everything that happened this morning from the moment you left home with Willa until the moment you got the call from the school. Take your time, and try to remember everything."

With trembling hands, Sarah fished through her wallet for a picture. Then, in detail, she recounted everything that had happened between leaving home with Willa and driving up to the playground. "I was a little late getting Willa to school because of the traffic," she said. During her description of events, Officer Rodriguez took copious notes.

"Why did your husband follow you to school this morning?" he asked.

"I felt as if someone was following us yesterday, and my husband rode behind me to see if anything unusual was going on. Nothing was, or at least, he didn't see anything."

"What about the ride home?"

It was then that Sarah remembered the license plate. "Wait," she said, "how stupid of me. When I was driving home with Willa yesterday, we stopped for lunch, and I thought I saw the pickup truck again. The driver stopped for a light, and I wrote down his license number. Here it is in my purse."

"We'll check it out right away. This might be our first useful lead, and we sure need one." In a few minutes, the police knew the identity of the person who owned the pickup. He was Mr. George Wellburton, a 52-year-old carpenter and general contractor. Upon questioning Mr. Wellburton, they learned that his son and a buddy had been driving through the neighborhood near the preschool the day before.

The boys were delivering bids to several homeowners in need of room additions. One of the officers said, "They're talking to them at the station right now; our guys say they seem like good kids. My feeling is that you're seeing them twice yesterday was just a coincidence, and they had nothing to do with your little girl's disappearance."

"OK then," Officer Rodriguez said, "what is certain at this point is that your child is missing. It's possible that she might have wandered off and is lost somewhere in the neighborhood, but we also have to accept the possibility that someone abducted her."

"Have you folks dealt with these kinds of problems before?" Seth asked.

"All the officers here are part of our department's special unit that handles missing persons and kidnapping cases. We'll begin by questioning the playground monitors, Willa's teacher, the janitorial staff, the principal, and everyone else that works here. If they don't provide us with anything useful, we'll talk with the other parents, the ones who dropped their children off this morning."

Seeing the word "kidnapping" made Sarah swoon. The ground beneath her seemed to tilt, her vision faded to black, and she fainted. She came to in Seth's arms, head down, with a cold compress on her brow.

"This can't be real," she said, looking directly into his eyes. "It's every parent's worst nightmare, and it's happening to us."

Seth did his best to comfort her without revealing his own emotions. *I've got to be strong for both of us, and I can't let Sarah see how frightened I am. I pray they find our little girl before it gets dark. She'll be so scared if they don't. How will she make it through the night, and how will we?*

What Sarah didn't know, at least not yet, was the brutal truth about kidnapping. About three out of four children who are abducted are between 3 and 11 years old, and 75 percent are girls. The number of children kidnapped had doubled in the last ten years. Criminal gangs, well aware of the possibility of lucrative ransom payments, were active in the child abduction business. Of those children kidnapped, over 80 percent are physically assaulted, and nearly half are sexually abused. Four percent are never found, and 90 percent are dead within 24 hours of being taken. These are the facts, the cold reality. Mercifully, the police kept them to thcmsclvcs.

Canvassing the neighborhood and interviewing school personnel weren't helpful. The playground monitors affirmed they had seen Willa. "We hugged her as we always do, and she was one of the last kids to get here. After that, we didn't see her again. What can we do? We'll do anything. We've got sixteen grandchildren of our own."

"I was in the basement fixing some leaky pipes when the kids got to school," the janitor said. "I was down there from the time I punched in at 7:00 until about ten in the morning. I didn't see anyone except the principal who came down at about nine, I would say, to see how I was doing."

"I noticed Willa was absent right away," her

teacher said. "I have only eight children in my class, so it's obvious when someone isn't here. Of course, I immediately checked with the front office to see if one of her parents had reported her absence, and that's when we called Willa's mom."

Four other parents either walked or drove their children to preschool every day. None of them reported seeing or hearing anything unusual. "My little boy was right in front of Willa when the playground monitors greeted them," one of them said, "but after that I didn't see her."

"I don't know what to say," the principal said. "My heart breaks for these people. Our school and everyone in it will cooperate in every way we can with your investigation. I don't know how this could have happened. We pride ourselves in our security; the safety of our children is our highest priority. I simply don't know how this could have happened."

Chapter 69

A patrol car escorted Sarah and Seth home. *Maybe she's here. Maybe a neighbor found her wandering on the street and brought her home. Maybe her teacher or a policeman found her and brought her back to Seth and me.*

When Sarah went upstairs and saw Willa's empty bed, pajamas, and dolly, it was almost more than she could bear. Only Officer Rodriguez and his partner were able to hear the awful keening sounds issuing from her throat.

Seth looked up and saw her leaning on the banister. "Come downstairs, Sarah. We have to tell your parents and your brother and his family," he said. "It will be difficult for them, to say the least, but we can't protect them any longer. They need to know, and I think sooner is better than later."

Seth made the calls, and Miriam and Sam, ashen faced and disheveled, arrived some twenty minutes later. As if they had aged prematurely, they pulled themselves out of the car with difficulty and slowly made their way into the house. Sam, hunched over and unsteady on his feet, clutched Miriam by the arm. It was hard to tell who was supporting whom.

"It's because of me," Sam said. "It's my fault. Everyone knows who I am, and they know how wealthy I am. Someone has taken my precious granddaughter, because they're after my money. Did you get a ransom note yet? I guarantee you it will be here soon. We'll find out who's doing this, and I'll kill him. He doesn't know who he's dealing with, and I swear, with these two hands, I'll kill him."

Sam lurched into a coughing fit, and his face turned lilac. His eyes were bloodshot; he was perspiring profusely, and with his blood vessels pulsating on his neck and forehead, his blood pressure had to be 200 at a minimum.

"Please, Sam, try to keep calm," Seth said. "This is bad enough without you having a heart attack. We're all in this together. Sit here and I'll bring you some water."

Calmer now, at least a little, Sam, the patriarch, tried to reassure his family. "I know a lot of guys, very tough guys who owe me favors. I can call on them any time. They know how to deal with punks like this."

Miriam was as anxious and distraught as Sarah had ever seen her. Unlike Sam, however, her method of handling her feelings was to remain quiet and move around. Back and forth she paced, wringing a handkerchief, only occasionally wiping away a tear.

"Did anyone call Anthony yet?" she asked. "He needs to be here with us. This is a terrible time, a family crisis, and the whole family needs to be together."

Sarah, somewhat back in control of herself too, checked the mailbox and found nothing except a few bills and some junk mail. While outside, she noticed an unfamiliar car parked across the street, a couple doors east. It was an unmarked police car manned by two officers doing surveillance. Should there be need for it, they would stay all night.

A couple of hours passed, about as quickly as a glacier. Except for greeting Dr. Anthony and filling him in, nobody spoke, nobody ate, and nobody drank. They took turns sitting, standing, and pacing, alone with their thoughts.

Finally, Seth turned to Miriam. "You and Sam need to go home. There is nothing you can do here, and both of you need to eat and get some rest, and if Sam is right about their motivation, the ransom note may very well be at your house. We'll call you just as soon as we learn of anything new, and, you do the same."

"I've called home, and all the girls send their love and prayers," Anthony said. "They know I'm staying here for the night, so don't even think about asking me to leave. You guys need to eat, too, so how about I run over to the deli and get some soup and sandwiches. Nobody is hungry, I know, but we need to keep our strength up."

Seth and Sarah tried to swallow some soup and each nibbled at a roast beef sandwich. Despite Anthony's urging to eat, the food was totally unappetizing; worse than that, it was nauseating. So, too, did everything nearby sicken them. The air they breathed, the hollowness in their stomachs, and the taste in their mouths—all of it sickened them. The house and everything in it had become very ugly.

In their entire lives, neither Seth nor Sarah had ever been afraid of the dark, but this night, as the sun went down, they were. Each couldn't help but think the same kinds of sad and frightening thoughts: *Is anyone feeding Willa? Who is keeping her clean? Where will she sleep tonight? Will she be alone in an unfamiliar room? Will she be warm enough? Is she crying? Who will give her milk? Is she wondering where her cookies are? Is she tied down with tape over her mouth? What will she do without her dolly? Is anyone holding her? Is anyone abusing her? Is she wondering why we've deserted her? Is our baby in a hole? Is our baby already dead? Please God, she's not even four years old.*

Now it was Seth who lost it. Seething inside, he turned to Dr. Anthony. "Let's say a miracle happens. Let's say the police catch this rotten son of a bitch, and we get our sweet baby back. Do I get to maim and torture this time, Doc? Do I get to cut his goddamn balls off? Do I get to take a red-hot poker to his eyeballs? Do I get to splash acid down his throat, or maybe into his ear holes? Do I get my just desserts? How about an eye for an eye?"

"I hear you," Dr. Anthony said.

"This time," Seth continued, "there will be no turning the other cheek, because for as long as I live and breathe, I promise you I will get him. Yes, I will get him, and he will be sorry for what he did, and if by some weird or quirky circumstance, I fail, your father and his cronies will."

"Don't worry, Seth," Dr. Anthony said. "This time, I'll help you."

Chapter 70

The clock in the master bedroom was one of the newer digital ones. For Sarah, the green lights were easy to read each of the 100 or so times she looked at them during the night. The last time Sarah checked, it was early Friday morning, at seven-thirty.

The sky had turned from black to gray when she finally fell into a dreamless sleep. Just 45 minutes later, she awoke with a start. Exhausted as she was, it took a couple seconds before her mind cleared and she remembered, with a shudder, all that had happened the day before.

Seth and Anthony had fallen asleep at about three in the morning. Anthony still dozed on a sofa in the living room, and from the aroma, Seth was already up making coffee. Just a few swallows into it, the light indicating that someone was at the door flashed. It was Officer Rodriguez.

"There's still no ransom note," he said.

"Isn't that unusual in cases like this?" Seth asked.

"Yes, by this time, we've usually heard from someone. If nothing happens today, there are a couple of possibilities we'll have to explore. First, it's still possible that Willa wandered away from her school, for whatever reason, and got lost. If that's the case, she may be perfectly fine. Or, she may not be. Naturally, we're concerned about where she was and how she spent the night."

"You said there were two possibilities to explore," Seth said. "What's the second one?"

"There is still a chance, of course, that Willa has been kidnapped. Whoever it was who took her, however, may not be interested in Grandfather's money at all; that's why there hasn't been a ransom note. There are plenty of people out there, usually women who are childless and desperate for a baby, who will steal one and take off. When it happens, the child is usually an infant, but not always."

"What's your best guess?" Seth asked.

"There's no way of knowing yet, but I'm leaning toward her being abducted. I've got to tell you there's a good chance that whoever grabbed your child could be anywhere by now, even thousands of miles away. I'm sorry to be so blunt, but you need to know the truth."

The vigil continued. Dr. Anthony left to attend to some business at his office, and his wife took his place. Sam and Miriam returned, no less agitated than the day before. Seth canceled his class and appointments at the clinic, and Sarah, exhausted as she was, managed to take a hot shower and keep down some toast and coffee.

By this time, the police had arranged to publish Willa's picture in the newspapers. Television stations picked up on the story and ran spots showing Willa's picture. Copies were distributed throughout the city, placed in shop windows, and affixed to light poles.

Neighbors responded by stopping by with food and offers to form a search party. The parish priest came by with comforting words and prayer. Newspaper reporters showed up hoping for interviews, but Seth, rather forcefully, turned them away.

The day dragged on. No ransom note appeared. Seth tried to stay optimistic, even though he knew that as time passed, the chances of Willa being found unharmed diminished. Several times their hopes were buoyed by people who called the police station, certain they had seen Baby Willa. These turned out to be false sightings.

As evening approached, Seth said, to no one in particular, "This is a unique form of torture; we are suffering, especially Sarah, and there isn't one goddamn thing I can do about it. Maybe, I need to start preparing her for the worst. It would be less of a shock if she at least knew some of the truth about kidnapping."

So, off in one corner of the living room, Seth, as gently as he could, described the hard reality for Sarah. It was a particularly difficult presentation.

"No! It's not true! That can't be true! I'm her mother, and I know our daughter is still alive. I would know it if she weren't. How can you say that to me? A mother knows!"

This time, Sam and Miriam brought in dinner, a nice ham and trimmings that nobody ate. At ten, Anthony drove Sam and Miriam home. Weary and discouraged, he went home himself, only because Seth insisted that he not stay over another night. "Please call us, even in the middle of the night, if anything breaks," Anthony said.

Throughout the night, nothing broke. Seth and Sarah tried to sleep, but as exhausted as they were, each managed only about an hour. Sarah dreamed, mostly of Willa's face and chasing her down a street. The rest of the time, they alternated between talking, holding each other, pacing, looking at the green numbers move inexorably toward morning, and watching the sky finally lighten. A little after seven, both showered, dressed, and had coffee. Sam and Miriam showed up just a little later.

When the light above the door lit up once more, Seth scowled and wheeled over to see who it was. "People mean well, I guess, but it would be better if they just stayed away and left us alone."

Anticipating another neighbor or reporter, Seth

was surprised to see one of the policemen who had been on surveillance duty. He had a twisted, silly sort of grin on his face that Seth found irritating. *Why is he smiling? This is no goddamn time to smile.*

The reason soon became clear. A guy with grass stains on his dungarees, dirt stains on his forearms, pieces of red and yellow flowers in his hair, and who was missing one work boot followed the policeman through the door. His name was Mario, and he was holding Baby Willa in his arms.

Perhaps at some time in the history of the world, there has been greater pandemonium and joy. It may be so, but probably not. Sam and Miriam embraced, and both whooped in a manner that would have made Geronimo proud. Together, they jumped up and down across the living room floor, somehow possessed with the energy of teenagers.

Seth pumped his arms and looked heavenward, eyes dripping tears of happiness. *Oh yes. Thank you! Hallelujah! Our horrible nightmare has finally ended, and our baby is back. Our precious child is back!*

Sarah leaned against the living room wall and slowly slid to the floor. There she sat, arms folded across her thighs, emitting enormous sobs. They came from the deepest part of her, the part of a woman where mother's love is born.

Even the policemen, total strangers just 24 hours ago, openly shared their exuberance. "Whew," one of them said, beaming and laughing. "A happy ending for a change. This doesn't happen all that often."

Everyone took turns hugging and kissing Willa until she finally came to her mother. Sarah, empty arms now full again, took her daughter upstairs for a bath and clean set of clothes. To Officer Rodriguez she said, "Willa's wearing a dress I've never seen before."

"Why Mommy crying?" Willa asked. Then, she

promptly fell asleep.

In the living room, Seth introduced Mario to the rest of the family and to the police. "Mario and I have a long history," he said. "I won't go into any of the details now except to say he is our good and dear friend, a true and loyal young man who comes from a fine family. Do you think you could spare a hug, Mario?"

"Hey, man; you bet." Seth, with Miriam standing by, took a minute to tell Mario all that had happened. "I figured somethin' was wrong when I seen the police in front of the house," Mario said. "Jeez, I was hopin' nobody got hurt, or even worst."

Officer Rodriguez took a note pad and pen from his shirt pocket. "I've got to prepare a preliminary report," he said. "Mario, would you tell me everything that happened today, up until the time you found Willa?"

"Sure, but there ain't a whole lot I can tell you. I do landscapin' work for people in this neighborhood. Friday is the day that I usually come to Seth an' Sarah's house, but this week, 'cause of the rain a coupla days ago, we was runnin' a day behind. I spend all afternoon here, 'cause I give their place special treatment, bein' that we're good friends.

"Anyway, I was workin' hard on my mornin' job 'cause I was plannin' to get over here an' start early. That way, I woulda been able to get home earlier than usual, 'cause today is my folks' weddin' anniversary, an' I'm plannin' to take 'em out to a swish place for dinner.

"So anyhow, to get back to what happened, I'm edgin' a lawn, maybe three or four blocks away from here, an' I seen a little girl walkin' all alone by herself on the street. I do one of those, whadya call 'em, double takes, 'cause she looks a little like Willa to me. Then, when I look again, an' she's closer, an' the sun's not in my eyes, I see that it is Willa. Sweet Jesus, I'm thinkin', what the hell is she doin' walkin' down the street all alone. 'Specially the wrong way from her house?

"Then, out of the corner of my eye, I seen this truck, one of those brown United Parcel trucks I think, barrelin' down the street. From the way he's drivin', way too fast, it seems to me that he don't see Willa right there in front of him 'cause she's so small. Without even thinkin' much about it, I run towards Willa fast as I can, an' at the last minute I dive through the air an' knock her out of the way. The truck just misses me, 'cept he clips the bottom of this leg, below my ankle, an' rips my work boot right off. Then the jerk keeps right on barrelin', like nothin' happened.

"'Course, the first thing I do is check up on Willa who's fine 'cept she's cryin' a little from bein' scared. Besides that, all she's got is some scrapes on her knees, some grass in her mouth, an' some dirt on her clothes. As for me, I prolly got a bruise on my foot, but it don't hurt too much.

"Anyway, Willa knows who I am, for sure, so she reaches up with her arms, an' I pick her up. Then, we walked the rest of the way here; I seen the policeman come inside, an' I followed him in. That's what happened."

"Thanks, Mario," Officer Rodriguez said. "We're all very lucky that you were in the right place at the right time. Great meeting you, and I hope to see you again."

"Yeah, thanks, it was great meetin' you too, Officer. Most of the talks I had with policemen in my younger days wasn't so friendly, if you know what I mean. Anyway, I got to get to work on this big old lawn an' garden outside. I'm puttin' in some new hedges, too. The owner's a little fussy sometimes, y'know, like real picky, an' I wanna get things perfect."

Seth stopped him as he was headed out the door.

"Hey, Mario. Can you come by tomorrow? There are a lot of things we have to talk about. Come any time except early in the morning. We'll be home all day, and don't forget to wish Rachel and Angelo a happy anniversary for us."

"Onliest thin' I got goin' is church in the mornin' with my mom an' dad, not that I like to go all that much, but when I do, it makes 'em feel good. How 'bout I swing by 'bout one?"

"That would be perfect, and don't eat lunch. We'll have it here for you, and we'll eat together."

Mario gave the lawn and garden the same diligent treatment he always did. Nothing differed from his usual routine except for a photographer who snapped a couple of shots while Mario was weeding one of the flowerbeds. Seth suspected the guy worked for a newspaper; nevertheless, he let him in for a short interview.

"Just some advice," Officer Rodriguez said, as he prepared to leave. "It would be a good idea to get Willa in for a physical exam as soon as you can. It's my hunch that she hasn't been molested in any way, but you should have your pediatrician check her out, just to be sure. You'll want to put your minds at ease."

"Of course," Sarah said. "I'll take her first thing next week."

"Also, try not to question her too much about what happened after you dropped her off and where she was overnight. If you let her story come out naturally, when she feels like telling you, it's usually better, and frustrating as it might be for all of us, there's a chance we may never learn everything that happened."

That night, dinner, including a bottle of champagne, tasted much better, and the house wasn't ugly anymore. In her usual manner, Willa slept like a baby.

Chapter 71

Everyone awoke happy and clear headed, if still a little tired. Sarah had checked on Willa three times during the night. Seth dropped in on her a couple of times too; in fact, once, like Longfellow's ships, they passed in the night. Both returned to bed content. Willa was sleeping soundly, untroubled, and sucking on her dolly's ear.

At breakfast, no mention was made of events the day before, as if nothing unusual had happened. Sarah remembered that her appointment with the pediatrician was coming up the next afternoon. She also noted that Willa had a play date after her visit to the doctor.

"Should I cancel Willa's date?" she asked.

"Don't you do it, Sarah. We need to go on with things exactly as we were doing before any of this started. I know how you feel; I feel the same way, but we can't start putting her in a bubble to protect her. If you like, I'll take Willa to her friend's house, and you pick her up, but that's it. Would you please pass me the newspaper?"

Seth opened the Sunday paper, and right there, on the first page of the Neighborhood Section was an article entitled: "Local Landscaper Finds Lost Girl." A fine picture of Mario, rake in hand and biceps flexed, accompanied the article.

Later in the day, Mario showed up, precisely on time. Dr. Anthony and his family were already there.

"Hey, Seth," Mario said. "The dude that does your lawn sure does a fine job. Not a weed anywheres,

298

an' wouldja take a look at those new hedges."

"Yeah, he's OK. I'm going to keep him at least the rest of this season, even though I think he's overpaid. How was mass?"

"I got enough trouble with English," Mario said. "So when they get into those Latin parts, y' know, that ominus dominus stuff, I sorta tune out. Didya ever notice how you can look like your payin' attention to someone, but your mind has already drifted way off somewheres else, thinkin' 'bout more interestin' stuff?"

"Yeah, I notice it all the time," Seth said. "Usually in my classes when I'm boring the hell out of my students and there's still a half hour to go."

"Where's Sarah and the baby?"

"They're at the grocery picking up a few more things Sarah needed for lunch. They should be back in about five minutes. Here, have a cup of coffee and make yourself at home."

Everyone barged in at the same time: Sarah, Miriam, and Willa, totally engrossed with picking at the hair on Sam's arms. Mario, the one time social misfit, handled himself well. He poured fresh orange juice for everyone, and the rest of the time he sat on an easy chair with Willa on his lap. With great dexterity, she poked around in his shirt pocket for the chocolate candy he usually had. She found her Snickers bar without a problem.

Miriam kissed Mario on the cheek, and Sam shook his hand heartily. "You took a nice picture, young fellow. Did everyone see Mario's picture in the paper this morning?"

"Are you kidding? Of course we did," Sarah said. "Hey, Mario! You looked like a real stud. Were there lots of pretty girls panting with lust at your door this morning?"

"Nah, only one, an' she was breathin' regular. I

woulda brought her along, but she had her own family party to go to. Hey, whadya think of my new threads? Am I slick lookin', or what? Darn, I left some of my mom's homemade cookies in the car. Lemme step out and get 'em."

Mario returned with a tin of cookies and turned to Seth. "Is that your neighbor's Impala convertible acrost the street? I didn't notice it when I first got here. Fine piece of iron."

"No, I don't think so; they must be having visitors."

Sarah had prepared a fresh salad to be followed by the burgers and chicken breasts Sam was barbecuing on the grill. There were also sweet corn and a huge bowl of fresh fruit. Mario and the rest of the men tossed a few horseshoes while the ladies set the table.

"Dr. Anthony will be calling your mom tomorrow," Sarah said, as everyone filed into the dining room. "We want to arrange for your family to have dinner here sometime within the next two weeks. I hope you'll bring your girlfriend if she'll feel comfortable coming."

"She will, for sure," Mario said. "I think you an' Seth are gonna like her. Her name is Anna Marie, an' she's a quiet, church-going girl, like Dad always says. Never ran with the gangs, neither, an' a good cook, too."

Lunch was delicious and fun. For a change, Sam hadn't burned anything too badly, and the cookies went well with ice cream for dessert. Mario helped clear the table, then had a seat between Seth and Dr. Anthony on the patio.

"So what was it you wanna talk about?" he asked, turning to Seth.

"Actually, it's Sam who wanted to speak with you. Don't move; I'll go and get him."

Sam pulled up a chair and sat next to Mario. "I hope you don't mind, but Seth has told me some of your history. You are a very courageous young man to have endured the beating you took and to have turned your life around and done so well."

"Thank you, sir," Mario said. It's very nice of you to say those things about me, but the changes I made are all 'cause of Seth an' Dr. Anthony."

"When you get older," Sam said, "perhaps you'll be fortunate and have a family like mine—a beautiful wife, two fine children and their mates, and the blessing of grandchildren. Should you indeed be blessed with grandchildren, it is then that you will fully understand how much one human being can love another. You brought baby Willa back to us, and for that we will be forever grateful."

"Thanks for that, too," Mario said, beginning to feel a little uncomfortable, "but I didn't really do nothin' that special, sir. I seen my little friend in trouble, an' I gave her some help is all."

"That help you gave Willa prevented a terrible tragedy, and because of what you did for me and my family, it would make us feel good if you would accept our gift. Actually, I insist that you accept our gift, and please call me Sam."

"You don't have to do that, Sam; nobody does, but if givin' me a present makes you guys feel good, it's OK with me."

"There's a red Impala convertible parked across the street," Sam said. "Here are the keys. It's yours. Drive it carefully and enjoy."

Essentially, Mario regressed to a time somewhere before his fourth birthday, a time when he still couldn't talk. When he got over it, about all he could muster was, "You guys got to be kiddin' me. Oh man, you guys muss be kiddin' me."

Later, when everyone went out to take a look at his new iron, Mario found an envelope taped to the visor above the driver's side window. On the outside it read, "We love you, Mario," and inside, he found three pieces of paper. One was Sam's personal check for fifty thousand dollars. The second was a handwritten note from Sam that read: "See me about investing some of this," and the third was a gift certificate from a shoe store that stocked a large variety of work boots.

Chapter 72

Willa's visit to the pediatrician was routine. She found no evidence of any type of abuse; in fact, Willa was in excellent health. Regarding her weight and height, she was at the 50th percentile in each, and her blood work was normal. On the way out, she grabbed a handful of peanut M and M's sitting in a jar.

The most exciting thing at Willa's play date was watching her friend's younger brother take off his diaper and walk around the family room naked. "How come I don't have a thing that drips pee pee water, too, Mommy?" she asked during the ride home.

Except for Miriam's coming down with a lingering case of shingles, everything quieted down. Seth went to the university; Willa went to the preschool, Sarah did some consulting, Sam invested, and Mario listened to Sam. Soon he had a "portfolio," a word for which he hadn't even known the meaning a year ago.

Though tempted at times, neither Seth nor Sarah questioned Willa. Of course, they hoped to eventually learn more about what had happened, but they followed Officer Rodriguez' advice and didn't push.

"How about a really fun day tomorrow?" Sarah asked at dinner. "We could try one of those new water parks everyone is talking about. My brother and his gang will join us."

The next morning, everyone piled into their cars for the forty-minute ride. About ten minutes out, Willa said, "I like to go for a ride in the car. Once, I went for a ride with Katy."

Seth and Sarah looked at each other with raised eyebrows, hoping she would continue, but Willa busied herself with her stuffed animal instead.

The day at the water park was great fun for everyone, and tiring. No one felt like a big dinner, so on the way home, they stopped for ice cream sodas. While slurping hers, Willa said, "Katy took me for ice cream, and she took me to where she lives, too. Her house has lots of steps, and her bed smelled funny in my nose."

Early the next morning, after dropping Willa at school, Seth and Sarah went directly to Officer Rodriguez' office. "You know where Katy lives," he said, "let's pay her a visit and see what she has to say. Evelyn here will come with us to interpret."

The building manager lived on the premises and let them in. "We're here to see Katy," Officer Rodriguez said.

"I'd like to help you out, Officer, but she's not here. One of the other tenants told me he saw her get into a taxi with some suitcases a couple days ago. She left her apartment in a mess, and she owes rent money, too. From my experience, I'd be willing to bet she isn't coming back."

Outside, Officer Rodriguez said, "I've got a hunch. Let's stop by Willa's preschool and talk to the principal again."

The principal welcomed them into her office. "I'm so happy everything turned out so well for you. Getting your sweet daughter back is the most important thing, but I'd sure like to know who took her from our school and how whoever it was managed to sneak Willa off the grounds."

"Well, we're working on it, and maybe you can help us," Officer Rodriguez said. "Tell me, have any of your staff left since we talked with you last?"

"Funny you should ask," the principal said. "Our

janitor up and left without even a day's notice. He was good enough to stop in and tell me, and when I asked him why he was leaving, he said his father was gravely ill, and he had to go home and help care for him in Europe."

"Thanks. You've been a big help; can we see where the janitor worked before we leave?"

"Of course, if you'll follow me, I'll take you downstairs."

The janitor spent most of his workday in a large area half a story below ground level. It housed the boiler, the electrical systems, a lawn tractor, snow blower, partially filled cans of paint, and various tools and equipment needed to keep the school maintained. Off to one side, there was a small office with a desk, phone, and television set.

On one wall, there was an exterior door opening to a flight of eight steps. The steps led up to a parking lot at the rear of the school where a car could pull to within a couple of feet of the top step.

Back at his office, Officer Rodriguez sat with Seth and Sarah. "Here's what I think happened," he said. "Katy worked for you and loved your daughter, as we all do. She and her boyfriend, the janitor, couldn't have children of their own, so she decided to take Willa. The janitor managed to grab her and take her downstairs without being seen, maybe because Willa was one of the last kids to walk into school that day."

"Please keep going," Sarah said.

"Once downstairs, he called Katy, a person Willa knew and trusted. Katy whipped over in her car and parked it just outside the door facing the parking lot. She went down for Willa and hustled her upstairs. She might have even wrapped her in a blanket making it hard for anyone who might have been in the lot to see what she was carrying. Then, she put Willa into her car and drove off, just like that. I don't know why she and the boyfriend changed their minds, but I'm reasonably certain their original plan was to take Willa with them to Poland."

"What would have happened at the airport?" Seth asked. "Even infants need passports to travel abroad."

"True enough," Officer Rodriguez said, "but Katy had easy access to photographs of Willa at your house, and it wouldn't have been much of a problem to have a phony passport made up for her."

"Like you've said, we may never know all that happened," Sarah said, "but do you have any hunches about why Katy changed her mind?"

"There's no question in my mind that Willa slept at Katy's those two nights, and I think that sooner or later, Willa will tell you about it. I'm not sure, though, and we may never be, as to why Katy and her beau didn't go on to execute the rest of their plan.

"My best guess is that they got frightened after we began questioning the janitor, and they decided to hold off on stealing a child until they got back to Poland. Or, it might be that someone in the neighborhood saw her take Willa inside, and Katy bailed out fearing that person would call us. Of course, it's possible, too, that they simply had a combined attack of conscience and guilt after they snatched Willa.

"Really, there's no way of knowing, unless you'd be willing to travel to Warsaw or Krakow, or wherever the hell they are and track them down, and by the way, I hear the weather in Poland stinks this time of year."

Seth and Sarah were fully satisfied with what they had learned; they were pleased to put everything behind them and watch Willa grow up, and grow she did, outpacing even the most robust weeds. She had her namesake's long legs and posture, her straight black hair with a silver streak on her forelock, her dark complexion, straight nose, green eyes, and the incredible beauty that made strangers stop and stare.

Chapter 73

Mario kept the Impala in showroom shape. He washed it at least once a week and waxed it once every three months, at the same time he changed the oil. He immediately washed off any "insect splat" on the windshield, and he handled bird droppings with similar dispatch.

When he left it at parking lots, he looked for a space at the end of a row to minimize the chance of dings. When he drove, he pampered it as well, never accelerating or braking too abruptly. Cruising along, he often thought back to the silver Buick. As much as his iron had improved, so had he.

Becoming a partner in the business and an investor in the stock market made Mario's financial situation much more complicated. Sam directed him to an associate who was a certified public accountant. He helped Mario set up a financial plan and file his income taxes on time.

"Jeez, Sam, I didn't know nothin' about none of this stuff a coupla years ago, an' I'm not sayin' I'm any kind of expert on high finances now, but I'll tell you what; at leas' I know a whole lot more than I used to, an' it seems like I'm learnin' somethin' new every day. I wish I woulda straightened up and listened to my folks when I was in high school; maybe I never woulda dropped out."

"You know, it's never too late to go back to school," Sam said. "There are lots of places in DC you can go, even in the evening after work, to take courses that count toward a high school diploma. Here's the phone number at my office. I'll have one of my secretaries put together a list of these places for you, and if you're still interested after you sleep on it, give her a call in the afternoon."

It took Mario almost three years, and now he was within a few weeks of getting his GED. He studied hard and late, because to complete his reading and written assignments usually took twice as long as it did for other students. He knew when he needed extra help, and he didn't hesitate to ask for it.

At the end of one of his night classes, Mario walked across the street to the parking lot. Two young guys, dressed in gang colors he remembered very well, were "admiring" his car. One of them held a slotted screwdriver, and the other had a wire stripper. It was obvious that both were high on drugs.

"I guess you guys were plannin' to hot wire my car," Mario said.

"Yeah, that's a fact, Jack, but how didya know?"

"I learned how to hot wire when I was in the same gang you're in. That was back there in the days when I was young, stupid, an' strung out most of the time, juss like you."

"You were in with us, and you dropped the flag?"

"Yeah, best thing I ever quit, too, along with usin'."

"You gonna call the cops?"

"Nah, it wouldn't do no good; juss get your sorry, punk asses away from my car, an' take off, before I get angry."

"We could wreck you, y'know; we got you two to one."

"If you want to try me, take your best shot," Mario said. "You can walk away now, or crawl away later. Either way is fine with me, an' when you're back with the losers you hang with, missing a few of your goddam teeth, say hello to Raphael for me, if he's still bangin' with you. Tell him you ran into his old buddy Mario."

"Are you kiddin; you know Raphael? He's in the joint for pushin' but he's s'posed to get sprung soon."

As the boys turned to walk away, Mario said, "You an' your punk friends don't ever want to be messin' with my iron. If you had any brains, you'd be hittin' the books instead."

"That's for losers," they said, "losers like you."

Mario drove home, thinking things through. *There's gotta be a way to put a stop to these gangs. They're nothin' but trouble for the kids who jump in an' the good people in the neighborhood. Good for nothin' is what they are, plain an' simple. I'm gonna talk to Seth and Dr. Anthony, maybe Sam, too, an' see if we can come up with some ideas. Maybe Officer Rodriguez could help out, too.*

Mario called Dr. Anthony and explained what he had in mind. "I'll get back to you, after I talk with Seth," the good doctor said. "Instead of meeting at Seth and Sarah's, it would be easier and more fun for all of us to go out for dinner, maybe pizza or something. You old enough to legally hoist a few cold ones?"

Over a slice of sausage and onion pizza and a Miller Lite, Mario said, "I came acrost a coupla gangbangers that was gettin' ready to hot wire my car, and after I chased 'em away, I got to thinkin' that maybe it's time to step up and try to get rid of all these gangs, or at leas'…what's that word?…reduce the number of 'em."

"Cutting down on gang activity is a great idea, Mario," Officer Rodriguez said. "On the force, we've been trying for years. Do you have any ideas about how you might go about it?"

"Yeah, there's a coupla ideas I been kickin'

'round in my head. First, kids who wind up jumpin' in start thinkin' about it when they're still young, maybe as young as fourth or fifth grade. I know I did. So…what's that old expression about preventin' a problem bein' easier in the first place than curin' it later on? Whatever, you gotta start early, even before they get to middle school."

"That's correct, for sure," Officer Rodriguez said. "If you wait until senior high school, it's way too late. They think they know everything by then; they've probably had a taste of some cash, so chances are they're not going to listen to anyone."

"There's another thing, too," Mario said. "When I was in grade school, I remember trustin' the other kids more than the teachers, an' I sure didn't trust any policemen, the 'fuzz,' we used to call you guys. What I'm sayin' is if we're talking about goin' into grade schools an' talkin' to the kids, I think someone who used to be a gangbanger an' turned the leaf might be better than sending in a policeman, even a cool dude like Officer Rodriguez."

"Are we talking about you?" Sam asked.

"Sure, I'd give it a shot. I'll tell 'em all about the everyday life of a gangbanger—how you sleep with bedbugs an' roaches after your folks toss you out, what you have to do to survive on the street, how sick you're gonna get of junk food, what it's like to miss holiday dinners—all of that."

"Miriam and I will come; you can count on it," Sam said, "and we'll bring some friends, too. "What else would you do?"

"I know my mom saved a coupla pitchers of my face, all black an' blue an' puffed up, from when I was in the coma at the hospital. I could bring 'em along an' do kind of a 'show an' tell,' sort of like an audiovisual speech. Maybe all that would make 'em at leas' think twice about jumpin' in when they get older."

Everyone liked Mario's ideas and encouraged him to proceed. He finished his final exams two weeks later, and with some help from Seth and Sarah, he put together the outline of a presentation that would last for about an hour. Officer Rodriguez had some connections with the school board and secured time for Mario to make a presentation before them.

"Jeez, I'm nervous as hell," Mario said, as the evening of his scheduled presentation approached. "Here I am gettin' ready to talk to the school board an' some teachers, an' prolly some parents too. Maybe one of my old special education teachers from horror hall will be there. Wouldn't that be somethin'; she'd prolly faint or at leas' be horrified when she sees me."

Chapter 74

On the night of his presentation, Officer Rodriguez drove Mario and his parents to the school district administration building. The parking lot was full, and the boardroom was standing room only. The brochure sent home with the students advertising a presentation by a "Former Youth Gang Member" had piqued the interest of a lot of people in the community.

Mario's presentation was last on the agenda after old business, new business, committee reports, and proposals for new gymnastics equipment and for new instruments for the marching band. Then, three retiring teachers, each with more than thirty years on the job, were recognized for their dedicated service to their schools and the community at large. Each got to make a brief farewell address after which they got plaques engraved with their names.

Sitting through all of this increased Mario's nervousness. Attending to the sign language interpreter helped a little, as did Officer Rodriguez who nudged him and said, "Just be yourself; everyone here will be on your side as soon as you start telling your story and what you'd like to do."

From across the room, Seth, Sarah, Miriam, and Sam gave him thumbs up. Rachel and Angelo, sitting in the row behind him, patted him on the back.

"I was one of 'em," Mario began. "I'm talkin' about the punks you've seen wearin' red an' black clothes, baseball caps turned to the side, bandanas, an' one pants leg rolled up."

From there, he told them about his failure in school, the jumping in ritual, his leaving home, the brutal details of gang fights, his recovery from being beaten, and his stay at the juvenile detention center. Nobody in the audience stirred; in fact, their attention was somewhere between rapt and intense.

"I was lucky," he continued. "I met some people who helped me along the way; I've got a great set of parents, an' I turned my life around. I'm the owner of a landscapin' business now, an' by the way, I brought along a few of my business cards if anyone would like to talk with me about summer specials later on."

After the laughter died, Mario explained his plan. "I'd like to come into each of the grade schools. If I can talk to the kids, tell 'em some of the things about being a gangster that I've tole you, an' show 'em a few pitchers of what guys look like after gang fights, maybe it will get the kids thinkin' 'bout how stupid it is to join a gang."

Mario didn't realize it, but his allotted time had expired thirty minutes before he finished his presentation. He had never received a standing ovation before. Nor, had he ever seen the kind of looks on his parents' faces when people sat down.

"Thank you, Mario. Let the board members think about and discuss your proposal," the chairman said. "We will be in touch with you no later than a week from tonight."

So it was that Mario went back to grade school. For an hour each week, he made his presentations. At every school, he noticed two things. The kids and teachers were fascinated; often they asked him to stay longer and tell them more of his story, and every classroom was quieter than the one he remembered.

It would take a while, and it would be difficult to determine with certainty if Mario made a difference. "Maybe I set at leas' a few of 'em straight," Mario said.

"Even if that's all I done, it would be worth it."

Chapter 75

On his 53rd birthday, Angelo was diagnosed with pancreatic cancer, essentially a death sentence. The doctors were frank in discussing his prognosis, and after thinking about it for about a day, he decided to forego chemotherapy or any other form of treatment.

To his doctor, he said, "I don't think a few more days or even a few more weeks when I'm gonna be terrible sick from the poison you shoot into me is worth it. Juss give me somethin' for the pain, and let me check out like a man."

The disease followed its typical course, and Angelo deteriorated rapidly. Two days before lapsing into a coma, he spoke with Mario at his bedside.

"My son, I have been both happy and sad in my life," he said. "Marryin' your mother, your birth, an' seein' you with your own business made me happy. You droppin' out of school an' joinin' the gang, leavin' our home, an' seein' you beaten so bad you almost died made me sad. There's somethin' I did, though, somethin' I did a long time ago that I never tole you about. It still makes me sad, maybe sadder than anythin' else. Now, I must tell you."

"I'm listenin', Dad. Tell me."

"When you were still a little bambino, an infant maybe a few months old, your mother was terrible sick one night and couldn't take care of you. She was so sick she had to stay in bed, an' it was my job to take over.

"You cried all night long, and no matter what I did you wouldn't stop. Then, when it was almost morning, an' I was so tired I couldn't see straight, I lost my temper, or maybe my mind. I shook you, Mario. I shook you so hard I think your brain got hurt from all that bouncin' back an' forth."

"An' you been keepin' this inside of you all these years?" Mario asked.

"Yeah, I been so ashamed. I know I shoulda tole you, but I guess I never had the guts to stand up an' admit what I did."

"That don't make sense to me, Dad. Look at me. I'm fine in every way. This has been eatin' at you for all these years, an' fact is, there's no way you can be sure that what you done hurt me. For all you know, for all any of us know, I came into the world a little off the old rocker to begin with. Remember you used to tell me how hyper I was, like even from the first day?

"Anyway, the best thing I ever done was make you and Mom proud of me. I seen it all over your faces that night of my speech at the school board meeting. Forget what you think you might of done all those years ago, Dad. I love you more than anythin', an' here's somethin' that's gonna make you happy an' help you forget."

"What is it, Mario? What is it that will make me happy?"

"You remember Anna Marie; you met her a few times when I brought her over to the house?"

"I do remember; she's a fine girl. You tole me she goes to church and makes a fine lasagna."

"That's the one, Dad, an' I got an engagement ring in my pocket I'm gonna give her real soon."

"I'm happy, Mario. You an' Anna Marie get goin' an' make a nice family for yourselves. I'm goin' to sleep now, Son. Maybe you could come back later with your Mom."

Mario did come back with Rachel that evening,

and he came back with Rachel the next day, too, when Angelo died.

Rachel was ready. She covered him with a blanket, made the sign of the cross, and said, "Goodbye, my sweetheart. You left me too soon, and I will remember you always, a fine man and a dear husband. At our wedding you said, 'We love each other a ton,' and we did."

Six months later, Mario asked Anna Marie to marry him. With one knee on the floor of the Three Brothers Italian Restaurant, and six tables of raucous paisanos cheering him on, he said, "I would be a very happy man if you would be my wife. I will be a good husband an' make a good life for us, an', maybe, we could have a coupla kids. I got a nice house picked out for us, so whadya say, Anna Marie? Here's a ring I been carryin' around, too. So, whadya say?"

"What took you so long?" Anna Marie asked. "Of course, I'll marry you, but let me look at the house first before you put anything down on it. The ring is beautiful, and as far as having a couple of children, we're already having one."

"For real?" Mario said.

"For real." Seven months later, Angelo Jr. was born. No birthmarks, just one black eye and a mild case of jaundice. Seth and Sarah were his Godparents.

Five Years Later

Chapter 76

The President of Gallaudet University retired, and the Board of Trustees conducted a search for his replacement. Turmoil was the result; in fact, what transpired was more like a flat out revolution.

The university, established at the time of the Civil War, had been headed by a series of six presidents from that time to the present. None of them was deaf. This time, from a group of three finalists, two of whom were deaf, the sitting board, like those before them, chose the single candidate who wasn't.

In announcing their decision, the Chairman of the Board, a hearing man, actually said, "The deaf are not yet ready to function in the hearing world."

Had he sat up all night to think of the most egregious insult imaginable, he couldn't have been more effective. Such ignorance was roughly analogous to saying, at a meeting of the American Association for the Blind and Visually Impaired, that blind people are only capable of selling pencils on street corners.

The students and a group of faculty members, including Seth, were incensed by the fact that a Deaf person wasn't chosen for president. So were many alumni who joined students and faculty in expressing their anger.

Students invited the newly appointed president to meet with them to discuss their grievances. She refused, saying: "It is the solely the role of the Board of Trustees to choose a new president." Such an attitude, anything but inclusive, only served to increase the students' outrage.

Students and faculty protested. They shut down the university by placing heavy gauge locks on campus gates and further barricading them with school busses. Once the busses were in place, they deflated the tires, making it almost impossible to remove them. To further emphasize their dissatisfaction, they burned board members in effigy and gave interviews to the press.

Over a period of a few days, the students were active in publicizing their demands. More than 2,500 marched on Capitol Hill. Network news channels aired interviews with protest leaders. Rallies were held on campus, day and night.

The students sought three outcomes. First, the new hearing president would resign immediately, and a Deaf president would be installed in her place. Second, everyone sitting on the existing Board of Directors (seventeen hearing members and four deaf) would resign and be replaced by a new board whose membership would be at least fifty-one percent Deaf. Third, no reprisals against students, faculty, or staff who had participated in the protests would be imposed.

Ultimately, all of the protesters' demands were met. It was a great day, a tremendous victory for the students at Gallaudet and for the Deaf population at large.

Seth had some personal victories at the university as well. In a faculty evaluation study, students majoring in psychology named him the "Most Effective Faculty Member." He was promoted to full professor and granted tenure at the same time.

"I can't get fired, and there are no more promotions available, so I guess I don't have to suck up to anyone anymore," he said to Sarah.

"And when did you ever suck up to anyone, Doctor?" Sarah asked.

He winked but resisted the temptation to talk dirty. Apart from Seth's success in academia, he had become a wealthy man. "I'd like to know more about our finances," Sarah said. "I know we're holding pretty heavy, but specifically, what do we have?"

"Yeah, we're doing nicely," Seth said. "We own three condominiums, a couple of apartment buildings, and two strip mall shopping centers."

"We have stocks, too, right?" Sarah asked.

"You bet we do. There's been a little slump lately, but the dividend checks keep coming."

"How much help has my dad been?"

"Are you kidding? Everything he touches turns to gold. We bought 5,000 acres of barren land in Clarke County, and two months later, the state announced plans to build a superhighway right through it. We made more than a tidy profit."

With all their wealth, Seth and Sarah lived conservatively; their only extravagances were new cars every couple of years, skydiving, and travel. They were particularly fond of Paris and visited twice a year, usually accompanied by Willa, now ten years old and a student at the Maryland School for the Deaf.

A budding thespian, Willa was an enthusiastic member of the school's drama club. Small parts in her initial efforts grew into larger parts until she was usually first or second lead. Like her mother, she enjoyed wearing make up and dressing in outlandish costumes, but she didn't need either to draw attention, beautiful as she was. Along with her acting skill, she was talented at ballet. In a few years, she would audition for the American Theater for the Deaf.

Willa's interest in the theater included attempts at play writing. One of her earlier efforts, a one act play, was about a young child who got lost. The lead character was a little girl taken from her school by her nanny.

She brought the plot outline home and showed it to Sarah, "Nanny takes her for ice cream and buys her a new dress. She sleeps at Nanny's house for two nights and eats strange tasting food. Nanny packs suitcases, because they are going on a trip. The little girl begins to cry and says she doesn't want to go, because she misses her Mom and Dad and they might worry about her. Nanny drops her off on a street corner not far from where she lives. She tells the little girl to go straight home and never tell anyone where she had been. On the way home, the little girl gets lost. She almost gets hurt when a big truck comes by that would have run her over, except for her friend who pushes her out of the way at the last second."

"Officer Rodriguez got it exactly right," Sarah said, after reading the outline to Seth later on. "Of course, we still don't know why Katy changed her mind."

"That's only because Willa doesn't know either," Seth said. "It's good she's telling us through her play, though. It's been up there, kicking around in her mind for a long time; now, maybe she'll forget it."

Like many young children, Willa was interested in her family, including the people who came before her. "Pappa Sam and Nana Miriam have been close by my whole life, so I know a lot about them," she said, "but I never even met Pappa Robert and Nana Willa. Here I am named after her; I know I look like her from pictures I've seen, but I don't know anything else about her. Same thing with Pappa Robert. All I know are a few stories you've told me."

With Sarah at his side, Seth told their daughter about her paternal grandparents. He told her how they met when they were children; he told her about their school and their work, and he told her about how they cared for him when he was injured. But most of all, he told Willa about their magnificent love affair. "Your grandmother and grandfather were very devoted to each other; besides being husband and wife, they were best friends."

"Didn't they die at almost the same time?" Willa asked.

"Yes, when Nana Willa got sick with cancer, Pappa took care of her. He kept her clean; he dressed and fed her, and he sat with her on the porch for long talks. When Nana couldn't walk anymore, he carried her through the woods, one of her favorite places. He loved her so much that when she died, so did he. It took eighteen days, but he started to die the moment she did. Sometimes gentle people like Pappa die from a broken heart."

Seth brought out some pictures of their house Willa had never seen. "This is the garage where my father taught me to box and wrestle; this is the back yard where he taught me to curse, and this is the kitchen where my mother made the most delicious breakfasts."

"Here's a picture of Uncle Jacob," Willa said. "He looks so young."

"Yes, one summer Pappa Robert got us jobs building garages, and Jacob stayed with us almost three months. He was my best friend at school, and he still is. When you're older, I'll tell you about a statue he made one time."

"It's way past your bed time," Sarah said. "Tomorrow night we can have another talk. Maybe Daddy will tell you how he convinced me to be his girlfriend."

Chapter 77

Sarah had just about given up on having another child. After a second miscarriage two years earlier, neither she nor Seth felt like dealing with the stress of another pregnancy, even were she able to conceive. They remained very active sexually, however, always exploring novel approaches. One night, while resting after a particularly creative session, Sarah said, "Hey, it's only kinky the first time."

With Willa away at school, Sarah found time to flex her professional muscles. She made presentations at meetings of various organizations concerned with rehabilitation services for the deaf. She wrote and published several articles that appeared in scholarly journals. She organized a group of women faculty and staff and raised funds to provide scholarships for future teachers of the deaf and for rehabilitation specialists.

The dean and other higher ups at the university, quite aware of her contributions, not to mention Sam's, responded favorably to her application to work as an instructor. Along with her work at the clinic, she began teaching an undergraduate course in rehabilitation therapy. Soon, she was promoted to assistant professor.

"Do you suppose two professors in the same family are one too many?" Seth asked.

"Probably," Sarah said. "When does the good doctor plan to submit his resignation?" Sarah's outgoing personality was perfectly suited for the college classroom. Students were drawn to her, and the fact that she filled her lectures with anecdotes about real people, some of whom she had seen as recently as ten minutes before class, provided a welcome respite from discussions of dated and arcane theory so many students found pointless. At campus watering holes and other places where students gathered to partake of juice from the college grapevine, she and Seth were known as the "Dynamic Duo."

Jacob's firm was opening an office in DC, and he was promoted to managing partner. He came to visit the Monday before Thanksgiving to scout out office space and find a place to live. Of course, he feasted with the family on Thursday night.

Jacob had not yet married but still wanted to. "My mother says I'm too picky, and maybe she's right. Ever since Carla dumped me, I haven't met anyone I'd like to spend Labor Day with, let alone the rest of my life. You guys are really lucky."

"Yes they are," Miriam said, "and you might be, too, Jacob. One of my lady friends has a niece who graduated from Gallaudet some time back. I've heard she has a great personality. If you'd like to meet her, I happen to have her number. Perhaps she's available Saturday night."

"Thanks, Miriam, but no. I've had a few too many blind dates, and I've learned that 'great personalities' are very often a red flag. Honestly, I don't mean to be snooty, but the first time Seth and I saw Sarah, it was assets that had nothing to do with her personality that we noticed first.

"So, if you have a lady friend who has a niece like Sarah, someone with the 'total package,' someone who is bright and beautiful and has a great personality to boot, put me at the top of the list when you're passing out her phone number."

"That's a tough assignment," Miriam said. "Sarah has always been quite unique."

"I know it, and Seth knows it too. He adores her, you know."

"Yes, when it comes to being crazy about their wives, Seth is very much like Sam."

"Yes, dear," Sam said.

Chapter 78

Sam and Miriam aged gracefully. Whatever the reason—wintering in South Florida, access to excellent medical care, working hard to remain physically fit, being rich, or maybe just being lucky enough to inherit longevity genes—they both looked and conducted themselves like much younger people.

An article appeared in Forbes Magazine listing the wealthiest 100 people in the country. Sam made the list with an estimated net worth of 800 million dollars. He was amused when he saw the article. "I hate it when people underestimate my wealth," he said.

Sam played doubles a couple of times a week with three of his pals, all of whom were about his age. When he won, he claimed that it was solely due to his skill, but when he lost, he said: "You guys were lucky; my partner and me got some bad bounces."

Miriam enjoyed tennis too. She took endless lessons until she was officially ranked as an "advanced beginner," a rather glaring oxymoron. Nevertheless, she liked the game almost as much as her new outfits, frilly things in which she and her lady friends flitted about, giving their ample cellulite an airing.

Tennis, an occasional round of golf, theater, working out, trips to museums, bridge games, and dinners with friends were pleasant pastimes but left them feeling somewhat unfulfilled. These kinds of activities, as much fun as they were, simply weren't personally gratifying enough to satisfy either of them.

"Let's do something that's good for other

people," Sam said, while they were lounging by the pool.

"And what might that be?" Miriam asked.

"How about I check at the school district office to see if they need volunteers? They must have a few classes for deaf kids where we could help out."

"I think I might like that," Miriam said, "especially if we could do it together."

The next morning Sam stopped by the school district's central administrative office. A receptionist, tending toward frumpy, asked how she might help him.

"My wife and I are retired, and both of us would like to do volunteer work in your schools. We're both proficient in American Sign Language and the finger spelling alphabet, so we could either tutor or interpret for your deaf kids."

"Have you worked with children before?" she asked.

"Our two children and three grandchildren."

"How much time would you be able to give us each week?"

"We could make it three mornings a week, say between 8:30 and lunchtime, at least until the middle of April when we go north for the summer."

Miriam and Sam spent a day in training with the "Volunteer Grandparents" program. Then, they went to work. Both were assigned to schools where deaf children were in attendance. The kids had been placed in regular classes, that is, classes with children who weren't deaf. Without exception, the children they worked with were the only deaf children in their classes.

While their teachers were talking, the deaf students relied exclusively on Sam and Miriam, trying their best to understand the point of the lesson. When they didn't, which was quite often, Sam and Miriam switched from interpreting to tutoring.

Sam, the softie, couldn't help but bring his work home with him. He talked about "his kids" to anyone willing to listen, and he began documenting his work in a diary. "Y'know, Miriam," he said one day at lunch. "I love what we're doing, but I'm not sure how much were helping the kids."

"What do you think the problem is?" Miriam asked.

"Well, I know the teachers mean well and are trying their best, but the arrangement, this mainstreaming thing, just doesn't work for me. The kids are isolated. Nobody speaks their language, and if it weren't for us, they would be totally lost. The kids have to keep their eyes glued on us, and when they do, they miss everything else that's going on in class. If they're in any stream at all, it's more like a creek, and they don't have any paddles."

"I've had the same feeling myself," Miriam said. "The other kids, the hearing kids, don't really interact with them, and our guys are the only deaf kids in their classes. So, they have no hearing friends, and they have no deaf friends. They never see a deaf adult; they have no advocates, and everyone around them thinks they're handicapped, instead of just different."

"My thoughts exactly," Sam said.

"And, I see some other problems, too," Miriam said. "As good as we may be at signing, there is always a delay between the teacher's words and ours, and something gets lost in the translation. Our kids don't seem to know their teachers very well, either. Where is the personal relationship, the interaction between student and teacher we all had?"

"Yes, and being the only deaf kids around," Sam said, "no time in class is devoted to discussions of Deaf history or Deaf culture. No one knows their language, and no one knows their customs."

"So, what are you proposing?" Miriam asked.

"Let's build a new place for deaf kids, a place for them to go to school and to live," Sam said. "We'll make it a model school with the best of everything. That way we'll attract deaf kids and deaf teachers, not only from Florida but from across the whole country."

"One thing about you, my dear husband. You never think small."

First thing in the morning, Sam called Jacob. "Miriam and I want to build a school, a residential school for deaf kids. We want your firm to handle it, and we want you to head up the project."

"Wow, this is no small undertaking," Jacob said. "You'll have to find land; you'll have to recruit teachers and administrators; you'll have to clear the local zoning commission, and you'll need money, lots of money, Sam."

"Don't give it a thought. I'll take care of all of that. You know the money is no problem; I've had a plot of land in mind I was going to develop for residential housing and a shopping mall. I play tennis and golf with the chairman of the zoning board, and there are some very capable people in my family, close friends of yours, who know everything there is to know about educating deaf kids. Are you in?"

"Yeah, I'm in, Sam, but first I've got to clear it with the big boss in Manhattan. For starters, he's going to ask how many students you're planning to accommodate and what you're willing to spend."

"Tell him we're thinking about approximately 200 to 250 students, and, including the cost of the land, I think we're looking at about 30 to 35 million. Seth and Sarah will be working on an estimated annual budget, but I don't have it yet."

"OK, Sam, I'll be back to you in a couple days."

"Get on it, and let me know if the boss gives you

any problems."

Indeed, planning and building the school turned out to be a family project. Sam bought a beautiful parcel of land, 100 rolling acres, with a small lake and lots of trees. Seth and Sarah consulted with Jacob, almost on a daily basis. Together they came up with an architectural style for student living and learning not available at any other residential school.

Instead of rooms in dormitories, they envisioned student suites. Two students would have their own living room and bedroom on either side of a bathroom Thus, only four students, in place of the usual horde, would have access to their own tub, shower, and toilet, and with living rooms separate from bedrooms, they would have more space to move around.

Another innovation, heretofore unheard of, was coeducational living. "Let's join the 20th century," Sarah said. "If we give our young people an opportunity to live in proximity to each other, I'm sure they'll be better at it when they get older."

Miriam, still hesitant about such radical thinking said, "But being so close together, won't they engage in; y'know 'hanky panky' in their suites. Won't we be encouraging a sinful life style?"

"Mom, they're going to be having sex anyway," Sarah said. "Would you rather they go at it in a car or in some deserted storage shed or in their own rooms?"

The classroom buildings, physical fitness facility, library, student living quarters, student health clinic, and administration building were set up in a typical college quadrangle arrangement. No building looked like any other; some were contemporary, some were prairie style, and some were traditional. All were equipped with modifications to accommodate non-ambulatory students and those with other kinds of physical differences that affected their ability to move around independently.

They hired Mario to design the landscape. Walkways would crisscross the quad, and mature trees, shrubbery, and flowerbeds would enhance the entire area. Fishponds and small waterfalls would be featured, too. "First school I ever done," Mario said. "I could get used to this. I'm gonna offer my services to office buildings an' hospitals, too."

Seth and Sarah were in charge of program development. Most often, residential schools for the deaf provided services for children and adolescents between three and eighteen years old. Sam's school, however, would be available from birth through death. "Womb to tomb," he liked to say.

Planning meetings were held, one morning every week, without exception. When it was time to discuss plans for program development, Sarah took over. "Our deaf infants will be visited at home no less than once each week. We'll provide lessons in ASL for parents, older siblings, and other family members who need them. For anyone who needs information or any kind of support, we'll have a parents' group with regularly scheduled meetings, audiological testing, as well as other support services, including occupational therapy and physical therapy will be available."

"All that sounds great," Sam said. "What else?"

"Residence at the school will begin at age three for children whose parents want to enroll them that early," Sarah continued. "From then on, children will be grouped into preschool, elementary, and high school levels. A lead teacher who is Deaf will administer each level. They, in turn, will be supervised by the principal, also Deaf."

"How many kids in a class?" Jacob asked.

"No more than eight," Sarah said, "and, as much as possible, they will be taught by teachers who are deaf. If we must hire hearing teachers, a criterion for employment will be proficiency in American Sign Language. Classrooms will be furnished with state of the art equipment, and all students will have regular access to computers. These newfangled gadgets are making a tremendous impact on student learning, and from what I've seen, technology in the classroom is like a revolution waiting to happen."

"What about when they leave us? Will we stay in touch?" Sam asked.

"Seth and I estimate that about forty percent of our students will go on to colleges, almost exclusively Gallaudet or the National Training Institute in Rochester, New York. Another forty percent will enroll in some type of vocational training school, and the remainder will attempt to enter the work force immediately after they graduate."

"What are we going to do for those who don't go to college?" Miriam asked.

"With a majority of our students not seeking higher education, that is, an undergraduate or graduate degree, we will be offering courses and experiences preparing graduates to assume gainful employment and to live independently in the community," Sarah said. "So, our curriculum includes a vocational assessment program, occupational skills training, job placement services, resume preparation and interview skills, onsite job supervision and follow up, and courses focusing upon independent living skills."

"Tell everyone about what we're planning for our alums, even the older ones," Seth said.

"No student who graduates from Sam's school will ever disappear from the rolls," Sarah said. "Alumni follow up studies will be done every two years, and services—vocational adjustment, medical, mental health, and financial planning—will be available through old age."

Sam's school was indeed a model school. One of it's important objectives was to do research to compare the success of alumni to graduates of mainstreamed programs offered in the public schools, too many of whom, despite their diplomas, remained functionally illiterate and unemployable. Should such research yield significantly favorable results for "Sam's Kids," perhaps the trend toward closing residential schools would stop.

Sam and Miriam devoted many of their years as senior citizens to the school. On "opening day," an aura of excitement prevailed as children, adolescents, and their teachers began their new adventure. Sam stood in front of the administration building with Miriam, Seth, Sarah, Mario, Anna Marie, Rachel, and Jacob. "Now it finally begins. We have done a good thing," he said.

Chapter 79

Anna Marie had made a late afternoon appointment for Angelo Jr. at the pediatrician, so Mario was in no hurry to get home after work. He decided to drive through the old neighborhood to kill some time. It had been years, and the dry cleaners, the place where he once committed "catslaughter" to demonstrate his worthiness to the gang, had been replaced by a liquor store. Many of the other stores were gone, too, and a large number of apartment buildings had been torn down.

He drove through the streets slowly, checking out old haunts and the ubiquitous graffiti. First in line at a stoplight, he thought he recognized a stoop-shouldered man crossing in front of him. The man's face was in profile, making him difficult to see; however, his gait and pony tail seemed familiar. When he turned to admire Mario's car, there was no question that it was Raphael.

The light changed to green. Mario pulled through the intersection, parked at the first available space, and walked across the street. By this time, Raphael had turned his back and was looking at the window display of an army surplus store. Mario approached and tapped him on the shoulder.

"Hey, Raphael; you remember me?"

Raphael turned and stared a few seconds before showing any sign of recognition. His eyes were rheumy, his beard was scraggly, and he smelled stale. "Yeah, it's my old buddy Mario. I'll be damned if it ain't my old buddy Mario. I hear you made it big, even got a wife and kid."

"Yeah, I'm doin' good, much better than I ever thought I would in the old days. You still bangin', Raphael?"

"Not much else I can do," Raphael said. "I was in the joint for a while, and no one will hire me now, even if I had the skills for a real job."

"You ratted on me, didn't you, Raphael?"

"Yeah, I did. I admit it. I tole the police where you lived, 'cause I was pissed at you and your old man. You lookin' to even the score?"

"Y'know, Raphael, I could take you apart any time I want. You look weak an' sick to me, like one good push an' you'd fall over, but fact is, you did me a big favor. Goin' to Juvy was one of the best things that ever happened to me. I got my mind straight while I was in, an' when I came out, I had the skills I needed to get a good job."

"You won't believe me, but I'm happy for you," Raphael said.

"Yeah, look at me, Raphael. I got my own business; I got it made, an' you're a sick, tired gangbanger, a pusher an' a junkie, a real loser prolly gettin' high on crystal or booze every day, 'cause you can't stand your life."

"I can't say you're wrong 'bout any of that," Raphael said. "My family don't want no part of me; most times I'm on the street, and truth is, I can't tell you one goddamn person who gives a crap if I live or die. I mean, I scrounge enough money to eat, but I gotta tell you that most of the time, I don't feel like it. I don't even care what I look like anymore, if I'm clean or what I'm wearin'. Seems like the world's turned to shit and the hogs ate it."

"You 'bout ready to turn the leaf?" Mario asked.

"Yeah, but how am I gonna do that? I got no job and no place to stay except that filthy gang house. You tell me how I'm gonna turn the leaf."

"OK, between now an' tomorrow morning at eight you clean yourself up. Take a bath, shave, put on a clean pair of jeans an' a shirt, and have a decent breakfast. Here's my card with my address. Be there on time."

"What am I gonna do when I get there?" Raphael asked.

"You're gonna go to work as a lawn maintenance man," Mario said. "Take it or leave it, an' you gotta decide right now."

Raphael cleaned himself up, and he made it to Mario's office on time. He worked that day mowing and edging lawns. It was unskilled labor that Raphael barely had the skill or strength to do, but he improved day by day for two weeks until he showed up stoned.

"I gotta let you go, man. I gave you a shot, but you blew it," Mario said.

"You did, Mario, You gave me a shot, an' I thank you for that. Problem is, I been bangin' so long, and with bein' on the street and in the joint, I just don't know how to live like a normal dude any more."

"How 'bout I find you a place for rehab? You could go away for a few months, get off the street, get yourself clean, an' try again."

"I don't think so," Raphael said. "I'm too tired. I'm juss not up for it now."

The next day Raphael went down to the basement at the gang house. He stuck a gun in his mouth and splattered his brains all over the roaches.

Raphael's mother and Mario were the only two people at the funeral.

Chapter 80

Mario expanded his business to include commercial properties in addition to private residences. He had a fleet of five trucks, each fully equipped to provide total landscaping service. He actually had to turn down a few new customers; however, busy as he was, Seth and Sarah continued to get the highest priority treatment.

Except for diabetes, Rachel was healthy. "You're gonna have to cut down on the pasta and bread, Ma," Mario said.

"Yes, I know, but the doctor said I can cheat once in a while if I exercise and take my insulin every time I'm supposed to."

"I can put you to work on one of my crews, if you want exercise."

"I don't think so, son; not that I wouldn't be your best worker, but I'm allergic to grass." With the proceeds of Angelo's life insurance policy and the money she made from an occasional catering job, Rachel was able to get by. She grew very close to Anna Marie, her parents, and certainly to little Angelo. She couldn't help but compare him to what his father had been like at the same age.

"You mean he sleeps through the night, and he never wakes up screaming? He pays attention when you read him a story, and you can take him to a friend's house and not worry that he's going to scratch the coffee table or kill her pet? You don't know how lucky you are, Anna Marie. I'm still not sure Mario can go into a supermarket without licking the apples."

The Holy Family Children's Home had been converted to an apartment building that offered government subsidized, low rent housing for senior citizens with limited incomes. "How strange it would be if I wound up living back there," Rachel said. "It would be like bookends for my life."

"Don't worry, Ma," Mario said. "We ain't gonna let that happen; you could always come an' live with us; we'll give you your own room, an' you can bet that we won't charge you nothin' for rent."

In fact, Rachel did go to work for her son, and she managed quite nicely. With the expansion of Mario's business, she took over as bookkeeper. She handled billing, accounts receivable, payroll, and all correspondence. Soon, she had a nice surplus in her savings account.

"Wancha take a vacation, Ma?" Mario asked. "Do a little travelin' for a coupla, three weeks."

"You know, I've always wanted to go to Europe. Maybe I could find some kind of tour and see the Eiffel Tower, Big Ben, and the Prada Art Museum. Maybe I could visit more capitol cities, too."

She didn't cover them all, but she did see Paris, London, Madrid, Rome, and Berlin. "All that on Monday," she said when she returned home, "and I met a very dignified, elderly gentleman on the tour. He lives in Arlington, and he insisted I give him my telephone number. He's already called and asked me to dinner and a movie. He's nice enough, never married, rather set in his ways and a little portly, but certainly nice enough."

When Angelo Jr. started school, it was a nervous couple of months for Mario. He remembered what a disastrous time in his own life his school years had been. Each night, at dinner, he asked his son how his day went and if he had any homework to do. "Always do what your teacher says, and don't talk back. Zip up your lip and don't talk back, and if you need any help with anythin', you should ask Mom right away."

"You need to stop worrying so much and relax," Anna Marie said. "Angelo Jr. is doing fine; I stay in touch with his teacher, and she says he's one of her best kids. He's smart and he's already learning to read and do numbers, and she told me he likes to play the piano in class. He played a tune he only heard her play one time. She thinks he may have a special talent for the piano and says we should try to get him some lessons."

When the little guy brought home his progress reports, Mario finally eased up. "Sweet Jesus, looks like we got ourselves a winner, an honor roll kid. I'll be darned if Mario, me, the dropout, don't have an honor roll kid. Jeez, I'm gonna have a kid that goes to college, maybe even one of those Ivory League schools."

"Do you think I might have had just a little something to do with it?" Anna Marie asked.

"Are you kiddin'? For sure you did. I never understood how those...whatya call 'em...genes work, but little Angelo musta got all your good ones an' none of my bad ones."

Anna Marie and Mario remained close to Seth and Sam and their families. They shared birthday parties and holidays, and all sorts of family gatherings. Sam didn't discriminate. Everyone was family, blood relative or not, and Miriam proved she was an "equal opportunity shopper" when it came to buying clothes, toys, and books for Willa and a grand piano for little Angelo.

Chapter 81

"You've got a special child," the piano teacher said. "Angelo Jr. has perfect pitch and an unusual memory. He hears a song once; he remembers it and picks out the right notes on the keyboard. Honestly, I'm not sure how he does it, but he even finds the right chords with his left hand. These are things I never taught him; they just seem to flow out of him naturally."

"What should we do?" Mario asked.

"Keep bringing him here; I'd say at least twice a week if you can. The truth is that I've never had a student like your son, and it would be my pleasure to bring him as far along as I can. Don't worry about the price of private lessons either; I'm so thrilled to work with him, I'll charge you the group rate. Sometimes, I'll forget to charge you at all."

Angelo Jr., unlike almost every other child taking piano lessons, actually enjoyed practicing. Neither Anna Marie nor Mario had to remind him to practice; if anything, they had to remind him to stop. He did it first thing in the morning and last thing before bed. In total, he spent three to four hours a day at the keyboard.

At first, he didn't like learning to read notes; instead, he preferred playing what was in his head. Soon, he was composing songs of his own, much to the amazement of his parents and everyone else. One of his tunes was a beautiful, soft song he played for Anna Marie on Mothers' Day. "How does he do that?" Mario asked. "Where does it come from?"

"All I can think of is that he was born that way.

His brain must be different," Anna Marie said. "Even doctors, neurologists, don't know everything about our brains yet. Look at you, dear husband. You're pretty much of a mystery, too. You were supposed to have all kinds of trouble after your injury, but somehow none of it happened and you turned out better than you were before."

Little Angelo wasn't shy about performing. His teacher arranged recitals, and there were always opportunities to play for Seth, Sarah, Sam, and Miriam, all of whom were in awe, especially Sam. "He's still a couple of years away from being able to reach the pedals," Sam said, "and he's already playing Bach and Beethoven. I think maybe we have a child prodigy here."

It turned out that Sam was correct. As Angelo grew older, he reached a level of virtuosity on the piano that none of his family had ever witnessed or thought possible. He entered and won competitions, and soon, his room was filled with plaques and certificates of merit.

"I can't take him any further," his teacher said. "He needs someone better than I am, someone to challenge him further and bring him to his highest level of play, and, by the way, I'm positive that level is still a long way off."

"Can you point us in the right direction?" Anna Marie asked.

"I do know of a school, and I've already talked to them about scheduling an audition for Angelo Jr. If he wants to go, and he passes the audition, I think I can get him a partial scholarship, at least."

"Don't worry," Mario said, "nothin' is too good for our son. If you can't get us no help with a scholarship, I'll scrape together the tuition, even if it means takin' out a loan. This is the son of Mario and the grandson of Angelo we're talkin' about here."

Willa was a bit of a superstar, too. She had leading roles in all of the plays at her high school, and she was in rehearsal for her debut performance in the National Theater for the Deaf, an organization, which more than any other, has shown the world the extraordinary talents of Deaf actors. More than fifty touring seasons and over 6,000 performances have resulted in a much greater acceptance and appreciation of signed language.

Theater was something Willa loved, but ballet was her real passion. Like all people who are deaf, she relied on her sense of vision to learn about her world. Thus, she was unusually aware of body movements and naturally drawn to dance as a form of creative expression. What helped her, as well, was the small amount of residual hearing she had for low-pitched sounds. This ability, in combination with attending to sound vibrations, gave her some awareness of the timing and rhythm of a piece.

Also, her dance instructors, being well versed in ASL, were able to rely upon signing during their instruction. They counted visually to establish the basic rhythmic pattern, just as instructors of hearing students count out loud. All of this, plus countless hours of practice, was what it took for Willa to excel.

Seth reveled in Willa's ballet. She always looked like her grandmother, but when she danced, the resemblance was uncanny. Her shape, her posture, her grace and suppleness, how she held her arms and hands, the curve of her neck—all of it came together into a package of elegance that never failed to moisten his eyes.

I wish they were here to see their granddaughter.

Chapter 82

It was the first week in April, and the cherry blossoms were in full bloom. Three thousand trees had been planted in 1912, a gift from the mayor of Tokyo to signify friendship between his country and the United States. Most of the trees stood around the tidal basin and the Washington Monument.

To avoid the crowds, often overwhelming on weekends, everyone packed a picnic dinner and went on a Wednesday, in the middle of the afternoon. Seth, Sarah and Willa, Dr. Anthony and his family, Sam and Miriam, Mario, Anna Marie and Angelo Jr., Rachel and her portly friend, and Jacob and his date—all came for the festivities.

Sarah and Seth organized a softball game, relay races, croquet, and what turned out to be a raucous volleyball game. Anna Marie and Rachel planned the menu, a veritable feast that could have fed twice as many as those present. Mario and Jacob brought the liquid refreshment, ice, and coolers.

Sam and Miriam organized "rest and relaxation" with blankets for the young folks to sit on and picnic chairs for the older crowd. Dr. Anthony and his crew brought trays and organized the clean up detail.

Over his third piece of fried chicken and second beer, Sam grew reflective. "What a wonderful day this is. It's an absolute joy to see everyone together having such a good time. All of us, family and friends, should be very grateful."

"You're not going to get emotional are you?"

Miriam asked.

"No, but think about it. Here we are, as diverse a group as you could possibly find. We have deaf people, a paraplegic person, a person who has recovered from traumatic brain injury, an orphan who never knew her parents, a university professor, an architect, a physician, a landscape designer, a precocious pianist, and a stunning ballet dancer. Then, too, there's you, my dear wife, my chief executive officer and speaker of the house. I am so pleased to be with you, and I love you very much."

"You forgot to mention someone," Seth said.

"Who's that?"

"You, Sam. Our families have dipped into each other's lives and bonded as one. Much of it is because of you; you have always been there for us, not just with material things, but also with wisdom and good counsel. We're all very grateful to you and your speaker of the house."

"Hey, enough of this" Sarah said. "Who wants to play another game of volleyball?"

"Juss onc morc thing," Mario said. "I still ain't so good at public speakin', but sometimes a man's gotta do what a man's gotta do. Not long ago I was a gangster, gettin' wasted every day, an' headin' for prison. Without Seth an' Dr. Anthony I'd prolly still be there, or I'd be dead. Now, here I am with my family, my wife an' son, an' my mom. If I haven't tole you in a while, there's no place in the world I'd rather be than with you guys.

"I see my son an' he's everythin' I wasn't. Honest, I don't know how it happened, but he does good in school, he's a good ballplayer, an' his piano teacher says he's got a rare talent. Me, Mario, I got a son with a rare talent; can you believe it? I wish his Poppy was here to see it.

"So what I'm sayin' is that maybe I only got a wife and two others here with my blood, but I'm tellin' you flat out, the rest of you are my family too. An' fact is, I'm damn proud of it. Now I'm ready to kick some butt in volleyball."

It was dark by the time everyone headed home. Willa and Angelo Jr. had fallen asleep on their blankets, as had Sam in his chair. When Miriam woke him, he said, "Of course I wasn't snoring; it had to be Seth."

There would be more picnics, more concerts, more ball games, and more dance and piano recitals. There would be celebrations on holidays, weddings, and great grandchildren, and there would be deaths.

Chapter 83

It wasn't a specific disease as much as the overall ravages of old age that caused Sam to fail. Determined as he was, he stayed home until Miriam and the nurses couldn't provide the intensive care he needed. Crotchety, tired, and never particularly fond of hospitals, he said, "They're bad places to be with all those sick people and their germs floating all over the place. Even Dr. Anthony will tell you that."

Finally, Seth, Sarah, and Miriam drove him, all spit and vinegar, to the hospital where Dr. Anthony was waiting. "I've reserved a special room for you," he said. "It's spacious and it has a pleasant view of the park."

"Don't tell anyone I've got some clout here," Sam said.

"The news is already out, and nobody minds," Dr. Anthony replied.

"Lots of old people here," Sam said, "and why do these joints all smell the same?

"Miriam, we need to build a new one that doesn't smell so bad. We'll do it near the coast and pump in some of that good ocean air. Maybe get a restaurant chef, too. Last time I ate hospital food, I got sick as a dog. Do you remember, Miriam? I was so sick I was afraid I wasn't going to die."

She'd heard his joke at least fifty times, but she smiled and said, "Yes, dear."

At first, Sam had a steady stream of visitors. Miriam saw to it that his cronies and business associates got ten minutes, but family stayed as long as they liked.

All of them, even the young ones, came.

Day by day, he declined until everyone knew, including Sam, that he wasn't going home. "Guess I won't be walking out of here sporting a new pair of tennis shoes," he said.

"Don't talk like that," Miriam said, wiping away a tear.

"Stop being so glum, dear wife. I've had a terrific ride, a little too short maybe, but a terrific ride."

He had left strict instructions not to use heroic measures to prolong his life, so when he stopped eating, Miriam didn't allow intravenous feeding. Nor would she allow him to be hooked up to a respirator.

For the last few days of his life, Sam slept long hours at a stretch, and when he slept, he dreamed.

He dreamed of a family picnic among the cherry blossoms.

What a wonderful day this is. It's an absolute joy to see everyone together having such a good time. All of us, family and friends, should be very grateful.

He dreamed about the wealth he had accumulated, and it comforted him to know that no one in his family or the generations to follow would ever be in need.

You don't have to be a genius. All you have to do is buy low and sell high.

He dreamed about talking with Mario, a young man not of his blood whom he came to love like a son.

Should you indeed be blessed with grandchildren, it is then that you will fully understand how much one human being can love another.

He dreamed about the school he had built, a place for deaf children to live and learn about their language and culture, a place that prepared them to be teachers and doctors and lawyers and skilled workers of all types.

Now it finally begins. We have done a good thing.

He dreamed of the little girl who left them for a while but came home to dance like an angel.

Let me hold her; her skin is so soft, like velvet, and I can't get enough of her smell in my nose.

Of course, Sam dreamed of Miriam, his chief executive officer and speaker of the house. A devoted mother and grandmother, and a strong, determined, sometimes difficult woman, she was exactly what was needed to keep him in line. He loved her like crazy.

Sam stopped dreaming early the next morning when he died. His knees were drawn to his chest, and his hollow cheeks were streaked with dried tears. Miriam was at his bedside. She kissed him and pulled a blanket over his head.

The family continued to prosper and grow in stature. Seth was promoted to Dean of the College of Liberal Arts at Gallaudet and elected President of the National Association for the Deaf, an advocacy group strong in its support for Deaf Culture and American Sign Language.

Sarah was promoted to associate professor, the highest rank attainable without a doctorate. Her active participation in creating a labor union for faculty and staff got her interviews on national television networks. She continued to teach and publish in professional journals; and she devoted much of her time to managing Willa's career. Aggressive as Sarah was, she got right up to the edge of "stage mother," but never crossed the line.

Willa performed with The National Theater for the Deaf and traveled to large cities in the United States, Europe, and Asia. In addition, she was a lead performer with the Washington Ballet, a group recognized throughout the world for its classical ballet training and for presenting superior classical and contemporary ballet programs in the DC area. She had a ton of suitors, too, none of whom she allowed her mother to manage.

Anna Marie and Mario had another child, a daughter they named Abriana Rachel after both grandmothers. Abby did well in school and liked music, too. At an outdoor big band performance, Mario asked her to pick out any instrument under the band shell, and he would see to it that she got lessons. When she picked the tuba, he said, "Pick somethin' else."

As for Angelo Jr., he won The New York Grand Prix International Piano Competition when he was eleven years old. The competition was between young pianists between the ages of nine and twenty-one from all countries, and an international panel of world-class musicians judged it. Finalists were offered a chance to perform at Carnegie Hall where they competed for cash prizes. Somehow, Sam had known it from the first.

Dr. Anthony continued his private practice, and he headed a research team that designed and tested new prosthetic devices. His work was funded by the National Institute of Health, and the product made it easier for thousands of amputees to move about independently, in comfort, and to lead more productive lives. One of his patients, a leg amputee, was an Olympic track and field competitor in the hundred-meter dash.

His older daughter married a patent attorney in a DC law firm. Their child, Isabella, was Sam and Miriam's great grandchild, the first child of the fourth generation. The younger daughter, a natural athlete like her father, ran marathon races and finished an Ironman competition in Hawaii. A very large offensive lineman who started for the Redskins was courting her.

Miriam outlived Sam by five years. She was healthy and vigorous until a few months before she died. She volunteered at Dr. Anthony's hospital, and she attended as many of Willa and Angelo's performances as she could. She never missed a family gathering, nor did she ever forget anyone's birthday or anniversary. The family learned not to forget hers either.

Toward the end of her life, she began donating her shoes to charitable organizations. Somewhere, there were hundreds of poor women wearing designer shoes.

At last, there was Jacob, now a full partner in his architecture firm. He married a Deaf girl he met at a Gallaudet homecoming event. Seth was best man at the wedding, and he was relieved when Jacob showed up on time wearing freshly polished shoes, both of which were black. So were his socks.

A year later, Jacob and his wife were parents of twins, identical in every way including their deafness. Jacob and his wife bought a house not far from Seth and Sarah, and they were together a lot. Often the four of them joined Mario and Anna Marie for a night of bowling. Mario still wasn't very good, but, at the concession stand, the hot dogs, cheeseburgers, and sausage pizza were still pretty decent.

Epilogue

The clock on my nightstand glows a soft green and reads 4:18. I'm flat on my back in bed, and except for night-lights in the bathroom and hall, it's dark in the house. Passing cars cast shadows on the bedroom ceiling and walls, and I feel a slight rush of warm air every time the furnace kicks in. In a few hours, the sun will rise, and, happily, so will I.

It's going to be a great day. I'm presenting a paper at the annual convention of the American Association for the Deaf. I've presented at professional meetings many times in the past, but I'm a little nervous this time, because my wife and daughter will be in the audience. I think a little nervousness is probably a good thing; it keeps me on my toes.

My wife sleeps next to me. Except for nights when I'm away at conferences or consulting, she's always there. She sleeps quietly, on her side, hair strewn atop her pillow. A few times during the night, she moves her hands and arms. She signs because she's dreaming, and she tells me I do it as well. Fact is, there are no secrets among the deaf, even when we are asleep.

Sarah and I have grown up together. She was a campus activist, a creative, incredibly bright free spirit with funny colored hair, and I was a new crip bent upon revenge and ashamed of my perceived inadequacies. That she didn't run the other way amazes me to this day. Fact is, her choosing to stick with me changed my life.

Along the way, we were blessed with a beautiful

and talented daughter who, with each year that passes, resembles my mother more and more. Her willowy physique, her manner of moving, her wide-set green eyes, her smooth, dark skin, the white streak on her forelock—all are there to remind me of a woman, a courageous woman filled with love, who died way too soon. Less than a month later, my dear father joined her. His passing, sad as it was, was a good thing, for he truly couldn't live without her.

There were times when I lay in darkness hating the prospect of another sunrise, nights when I was right on the edge, thinking about overdosing on medication and ending my life. When I think back to those nights, I'm not ashamed; rather, I'm thankful that, with help, I was able to overcome what is nothing less than a dread disease. Indeed, depression is like a malignant tumor, a cancer that eats at your body and soul and cannot be willed away. What a good life I would have missed, as would our daughter and all those who will come after her.

As for the future, Sarah and I are beginning to plan our retirement. Our pensions from the university along with her father's wise investment counsel will make it possible for us to do so before we get too far into senior citizenry. We have a lake house picked out in New Hampshire where we will spend our summers and autumns, and we hope to see as much of the world as we can during the rest of the year. It is our hope that Jacob, Mario, and their families will be with us as often as they are able. I will see to it that they are able.

"The ears of the deaf shall be unstopped." Though it says so in the Holy Book (Isaiah 35:5), it has not happened. Not yet. Until such an event occurs, let us be. Let our children communicate as they wish. Do not force them to speak. Do not submit them to surgery. Instead, choose to learn our beautiful language and speak with us. Let us know each other and celebrate our differences.

About the Author

Alan Balter was born in Chicago and attended the Chicago Public Schools. He entered the University of Illinois in Urbana in 1956 where he earned a Bachelor of Science degree in Psychology in 1960 and a Master's degree in Special Education in 1962. Subsequently, he taught adolescents with developmental delays at the Niles West High School in Skokie, Illinois. He returned to the University of Illinois and earned a Doctor of Philosophy in Special Education in 1967.

After working as the Director of the Niles Township High Schools Department of Special Education, he took a position with Chicago State University in 1969 where he prepared teachers for children and adolescents with developmental delays, learning disabilities, and emotional disorders. After 32 years at the university, he retired in 2000.

He and his wife Barbara, also a retired teacher, enjoy extensive travel and fourteen grandchildren.

Made in the USA
Middletown, DE
30 January 2017